Stage
Presents

Book Five in the Serendipity Series

Brieanna Robertson

Whimsical Publications, LLC

Florida

Stage Presents is a work of fiction. Names, characters, and incidents are the products of the author's imagination and are either fictitious or are used fictitiously. Any resemblance to actual events or persons, living or dead, is entirely coincidental.

If you purchased this book without a cover, you should be aware that this book may have been stolen property and reported as "unsold and destroyed" to the publisher. In such case, neither the publisher nor the author has received payment for this "stripped book."

Published in the United States by
Whimsical Publications, LLC
Florida

www.whimsicalpublications.com

Cover art by Traci Markou
Editing by Janet Durbin

ISBN-13: 978-1-936167-14-2

Printed in the United States of America

For the rest of the night, Nasarra waited in anticipation for any scene that man was in.

She had given up searching for her purse and had finally managed to find it at intermission lodged in the next person's seat. After making the mad race to the bathroom, she looked in her program to see who that magnificent actor was. He stared up at her in beautiful black and white, beside his character's name, Raoul Vicomte deChagny. He wore a mischievous smile and the lighting used in the photo highlighted his finely sculpted facial features. She glanced down at the name. Caleb Makepeace. She frowned. Even his name sounded familiar!

Act II seemed to fly by, and when the last song was sung, Nasarra was extremely disappointed. She had waited to see this musical for so long, and now, all too soon, it was over like some fantastic fantasy. When the performers came out to take their bows, she stood up and was quite certain that she clapped the loudest. Especially for that magnificent performer, Caleb Makepeace.

When the curtain closed and people started to file out of the theatre, Nasarra walked as slow as possible, trying to take in all of the sights and lock them away in her memory. There was no telling when she would be in a theatre like The Curran again.

It was pelting rain when she finally managed to wander her way to the door. It cloaked everything in mist and the steam from the manhole coverings on the street wisped and weaved in a slow, beguiling dance of mystery. She smiled. She had found the rain annoying the other day, but now she found it magical. It seemed to make the night complete.

She stepped outside and turned the collar of her jacket up to protect her neck from the dampness. Pivoting on her heel, she started up the street, but rammed into a person who was walking in the opposite direction with such a force that it knocked the air from her. She staggered back, trying to regain her senses, and looked up at the poor person she had just run over. Her eyes nearly bulged clear out of her skull. She had just mowed over the handsome actor with the beautiful voice! She squeezed her eyes shut in humiliation. This was great. Just great.

"Excuse me," she whispered. She stepped aside to let

him by and averted her eyes to the pavement. He did the same, in the same direction, and they were right back to where they had started. She swallowed, feeling really dumb. Things just kept getting better and better. She stepped to her left; he stepped to his right. She stifled a groan. She stepped to her right; he stepped to his left.

A beautifully rich and masculine chuckle escaped the man's throat and he stepped back. "Did you want to dance?" he teased. "Is that what you're going for? You want to dance a minuet?"

Nasarra blushed. "I'm sorry," she murmured.

He flashed her a dazzling smile. "That's all right," he assured. He frowned slightly, looking her over, and some small bit of recognition came to life in his eyes. He pointed to the program she clutched to her chest. "You were at the show tonight?"

Nasarra nodded, attempting to swallow the lump in her throat.

"You were in the front row, weren't you?"

She stole a glance at him and nodded again.

He grinned. "I thought so. I always look out into the audience when I'm on stage, and I happened to glance over at you. I saw your fiery red hair and thought to myself, 'that can't be the woman I ran down in the street the other day.'"

She gave a nervous laugh. "Yeah, that was a crazy day."

His grin broadened. "My name's Caleb," he said, extending his hand.

Nasarra stared at him. This was incredible. She held her hand out numbly and shook his, amazed by the power of his grip. "Nasarra." Her voice came out like the croak of a dying frog and she cleared her throat. "Nasarra," she stated.

His eyes swept over her again. "Nasarra. That's a very pretty name."

She smiled shyly. "Thank you." She braved a glance up at him and couldn't help but feel heat course through her body at his stunning smile. It was mischievous, playful, and the small dimple it created in his cheek made her heart falter.

"So, I guess we're even," he said.

She frowned.

"I ran you over. You repaid me in like kind." He folded his arms and raised an eyebrow. "Where should we go from here?"

ACKNOWLEDGEMENTS

"Life is like a book—write each chapter as it comes."
-Kristen Norris

This one has always been for you, K-10.
I miss you every day. You inspire me still.

Prologue

The phone sounded like it was coming from a far off location. It roused Maxim from his sleep and he desperately tried to avoid it by groaning and rolling over onto his side.

"Max," his wife Alyx muttered, nudging him in the back with her elbow. "Your phone."

He grumbled something incoherent and tried to ignore both wife and cell phone. The cell phone was adamant. So was his wife.

"Max!" Alyx shouted, flinging her hand over and smacking him on the shoulder. "Pick up your phone!"

He groaned again and blindly fumbled for his black-framed glasses on the nightstand. "Hold on, I have to find my glasses," he muttered.

Alyx expelled a huge sigh and flopped over onto her other side. "You need your glasses to hear the other person on the phone?" she grumbled.

"I can't see without my glasses," he insisted.

"You need to see to talk? You're beyond silly."

He chuckled, located his glasses, shoved them on, then reached for his blaring cell. "What?" he muttered into the phone, not even bothering to check who it was before answering.

"Oh, well good morning to you too, Mr. Sunshine," the person on the other end greeted.

Maxim blinked several times and sat up, adjusting his glasses. He was surprised that the person calling him so early was his editor. But, then again, she lived in New York and was three hours ahead of him. "Susan," he said, "what a surprise." He glanced back at Alyx, who shoved her pillow down onto her head. He smiled, reached out to touch her shoulder affectionately, then swung his legs out of bed and made his way to the kitchen for a much needed cup of coffee.

"Yes, I'm sure it is," Susan's sarcastic voice continued. "Although, it shouldn't be. You do know you have a deadline to meet, right? You promised us a second novel three years after the publication of your first one. Guess what? Time is running out. When can we expect your next best seller?"

He winced. What was he supposed to say? *Sorry, Susan, but I don't have squat? I set three years as a deadline because it seemed like a long time? My muse took a vacation?* He settled for, "Oh, it's coming along. I should have it to you in a few months." What was he saying? The only way he was going to be turning a manuscript into them was if divine inspiration struck and blessed him with the temporary capacity to not eat, not sleep, and write 24-7 for about two straight months. His muse would have to come back from the Bahamas, then move in, which he was sure his wife might have a bit of a problem with. Alyx was very supportive of Maxim's work, but he was pretty sure that having a husband on autopilot with his butt glued to an office chair was a little too much for even her to handle.

It was all right because Susan wasn't buying it anyway. "Mmmhmm," she said, sounding about as believing as a mother talking to her rebellious teen. "Maxim, don't make me have to hassle you. I guarantee you won't like it."

"I won't!" he cried, dumping grounds into the coffee maker. "I'm telling you, I'll have a manuscript soon." The call waiting beeped and he frowned. "Hold on a sec." He clicked over. "Hello?"

"Hey, Max," his brother Jeff's voice came, followed by a huge yawn. "What are you up to this morning?"

Maxim rolled his eyes and finished with the coffee pot. "Well, I was attempting to sleep in, but that's apparently not allowed." He opened up a cupboard and pulled out a bowl. "So, now I'm listening to my editor harp on me and I'm going to make breakfast for Alyx." He opened up the fridge and pulled out some eggs and milk.

"How come your editor is bothering you?"

"Oh, because I'm supposed to turn in a manuscript that I haven't even started yet."

Jeff sucked in his breath. "Ouch."

"Yeah. Lemme call you back when I get her off the phone."

"'Kay."

Maxim clicked back over. "You still there?"

"Sure am," she drawled. "So, tell me, what is this masterpiece of yours about?"

He grimaced. She was toying with him. Great. "Uh...it's about..." He almost screamed in jubilation when his call waiting beeped again. "Hey, hold on. I have another call again."

"Convenient," she muttered right before he switched lines.

"Hello?" he answered. He cracked a few eggs and began to beat them in the bowl with a whisk, cradling the phone against his shoulder.

"Hey, Maxim! How are you?"

Maxim blinked in surprise at hearing the voice of his friend who lived in San Francisco. "Torrey," he replied. "I'm fine. How are you and Taegen?"

"Good. Do you have a second? I wanted to ask you a favor."

"Uhh...I have a second, but not much more than that. My editor is hanging on the other line."

"Oh! Okay, I'll be fast. Look, do you remember my friend Nasarra? The one who runs The Amazing Psychotic restaurant with her husband?"

"Yeah." He added some milk to his eggs, then dropped in some cinnamon.

"Well, it's coming up on their anniversary and she wanted to do something really special for Caleb. She mentioned that she wants to turn the story of how they met into a play and then perform it at the little theatre she and Caleb teach at."

Maxim raised an eyebrow. "That's a cool idea."

"Yeah, the only problem is, she doesn't think she can write the script well and no one else will help her. So...I was wondering if maybe you could come down here for a few weeks, talk to Nasarra, and maybe write the script?"

Maxim halted all activity for a minute while his brain started to spin. His friend wanted him to go to San Francisco and help *write* a love story? It was too perfect. He got his best inspiration from true events anyway. "Torrey, you just saved my life," he stated.

"How so?"

"Hold on just a second." He clicked back to his editor. "Susan, I need to take this call, but let's just say I have a story for you, okay? It's about an actress. I really have to go. It's like Grand Central Station over here."

She sighed. "You'd better not be lying to me."

He rolled his eyes in irritation. "It'll be done, all right? Go nag one of your other authors." He switched back over to Torrey without even saying goodbye. That woman drove him insane. He was grateful that being married to Alyx had turned him into a more assertive person. Otherwise Susan would walk all over him, in really tall stiletto heels.

He huffed and continued to beat his French toast mixture. "Thank you, Torrey," he said. "You just effectively got my editor off my back."

"How did I manage this?" he queried.

"I might use Nasarra's story as inspiration for my next novel."

"You'll do it, then?"

"Sure, I could use a vacation. My writer's block is terrible." A knock sounded on the door and Maxim turned his head toward it, accidentally upsetting the position of his phone against his shoulder. The cell tumbled down and landed in the bowl of French toast mix. Maxim blinked and stared at it for a second, then peered closer to the bowl. "Torrey?" he questioned. "Can you still hear me?"

The person at the door knocked again.

Maxim grabbed the bowl and headed toward the door. He opened it to see his good friend, Javan, on the other side.

Javan arched an eyebrow and glanced down into the bowl. "What are you doing?" he questioned.

"Talking to Torrey," Maxim replied dryly.

Javan looked back up at him and frowned. "Did you decide to try and send him breakfast through the phone?"

Maxim rolled his eyes, shook his head, and stepped out of the way so Javan could come in. "This morning has been insane. What are you doing here so early?" He went back into the kitchen, fished his phone out of the egg mix, then turned to face his friend.

"I slept like crap and I was sick of tossing and turning. Thought I'd come harass you guys for awhile."

Maxim frowned and folded his arms across his chest while Javan rifled through the fridge. "Why didn't you go harass your girlfriend?"

Javan heaved a sigh and let out a frustrated groan. "Oh, she friggin' dumped me last night."

Maxim's eyes widened. "Oh...that sucks. I'm sorry, man. What happened?"

He shut the refrigerator door and turned back to Maxim. "I dunno, dude. She just up and told me we weren't going to work. Just my luck, I guess." He snorted. "I'm never going to find myself a girl."

"Sounds like you could use some time off. Got any vacation time at the theatre?"

"A little. Why?"

He shrugged. "Torrey's friend Nasarra wants me to write a play for her anniversary. I have to talk to Alyx about it first, but I'm pretty sure I'm gonna go do it. I could use some company if you want to come hang out for a week or so."

"Sounds good. Just keep me posted."

"I'll give you the details after I get everything sorted out." He yawned and stretched. "I'm gonna go get in the shower. Help yourself to whatever." He made his way back to his bedroom to get some clothing, his mind turning the idea of going to San Francisco over and over. Torrey's request had come at just the right time. His first best seller had been based off of true events that had happened on a road trip he'd taken with his friends. If Nasarra's story was good, odds were he would have enough material to write something else. Basically, that meant Susan wouldn't drag him out and beat him.

He passed by Alyx, who was dozing again, and pressed a gentle kiss to her cheek while he smoothed her raven hair. He then headed into the bathroom. Susan not beating him black and blue was a good thing, and the outcome he much preferred. He was anxious to get started on the project as soon as possible.

Chapter One

Nasarra was the same as Maxim remembered—vibrant, full of life. She was all smiles as she came to sit down at the table across from him after closing at The Amazing Psychotic. She let out a huff and shoved a hand through her thick, curling, red hair. "Man, today was insane." She flashed a stunning grin. "I'm so glad Torrey talked you into doing this for me. I don't know what I'd do otherwise. None of my friends have any writing talent whatsoever."

He chuckled and took a sip of the coffee she had brought him upon his arrival. He was happy to be in San Francisco doing this project. Especially since he'd had a royal blowout with his wife before he'd left. He still couldn't wrap his mind around it. Alyx was usually so easy-going, but she'd flipped her lid when Maxim had told her about his plans to come do this project. He was not a confrontational person by nature and he'd tried everything to defuse her wrath, but she had been intent on ripping him another one because he was going to be gone for almost a month, and would be missing the opening night of one of her plays. He'd told her he'd already seen a hundred of her plays, but that had obviously been the wrong thing to say. So, he'd told her he would back out and not do the project so that she wouldn't be upset. For some reason, this had angered her even more and she'd flung a shoe at him and told him not to patronize her.

He loved his wife with everything he had, and he missed being with her, but he couldn't deny that it was nice to be spending some time with Torrey and Taegen instead of being yelled at. She'd been yelling a lot lately. It was strange. Several weeks ago, she'd thrown a regular temper tantrum because he'd left refried beans in the sink. It had been so bad he was actually considering never eating beans again. He wished he knew what was bothering her, but every time he asked, she just grumbled that she was fine and that he was the one being a jerk. For the first time in his marriage, he felt completely lost.

"I have a copy of your book, you know," Nasarra said suddenly.

He arched an eyebrow and came back to the business at hand. "Oh yeah?"

She smiled. "Of course! When it came out Torrey was in here hocking it out to every customer that walked in. He was very proud."

Maxim felt his cheeks burn and he rolled his eyes, trying to shrug it off like the praise didn't matter to him, even though it did very much. "Well, did you like it?"

She frowned. "Like it? Maxim, please. Would I have you writing my husband's anniversary gift if I didn't think you were anything less than amazing?"

His cheeks burned even worse and he let out a self-conscious chuckle. "So Caleb doesn't know anything about this?"

She shook her head. "He's gone for about two months teaching a children's theatre master class in New York for a friend of ours." She wrinkled her nose. "He was really out of sorts when he left. For some reason he got it into his head that I had sacrificed all of my dreams for him, and he'd really managed to depress himself. It didn't matter what I said. He was hell bent on thinking that he'd ruined my life or something." She rolled her eyes. "Men... Anyway, I wanted to do something really special to show him how much I love him and how the past several years have been everything I could have ever hoped for and more. That's where you come in."

He smiled and took another sip of his coffee. "Right. So, you just want me to write your story in script form?"

"Yeah, and when you're finished, I'm going to give it to the company at Lazy Little Theatre and we're going to perform it for him when he comes home."

He pulled out a tape recorder, readying it. "I have to say, that is one of the cooler anniversary gift ideas I've ever heard of. So all you need is my writing skills? You don't need me to do anything else?"

She shook her head. "Just write our story; I'll take care

of the rest." She gave him a thoughtful look. "Torrey told me that you were thinking of using our story as inspiration for your next novel?"

He gave her a pained expression. "I hope so. Otherwise I'm going to be executed."

She giggled and sat back in her chair. "Well, use whatever you like. You have my permission."

"Thanks," he said with a grin. "So, do you want to start telling me a little bit of your story? We can do some tonight and then pick up tomorrow if you get tired. I need a lot of detail, though, if you don't mind."

"Not a problem. Let's see... I guess I'll just start at the beginning then, huh?"

"That's usually the best place to start a story," he teased. He pressed the record button on the tape player and sat back as she began to speak...

San Francisco, 1997

Nasarra drummed her fingers against the counter in complete and utter boredom. Another sodden customer wandered by and she sighed. Of course it would have to rain like mad on the day she only had a half an hour to get to her other job. She grimaced, not looking forward to another six hours of work. All she really wanted to do was go home.

Home. Right. What did that mean? If it meant going to a half-dilapidated duplex where she roomed with a frightening exhibitionist artist who spent his off time tap dancing on Market Street for a few extra dollars, then she was right on the money. However, if it meant what it did to most people, a sanctuary and refuge away from a chaotic world where one could relax and unwind, she was way off the mark. Relax? What did that mean? That word was as foreign to her vocabulary as "home" was. She didn't relax. She worked. Constantly.

"Nasarra."

Nasarra turned her gaze up to her friend Amanda, who was smiling.

"Your prison sentence is over for the day," she teased.

Nasarra glanced at her watch and rolled her eyes. "And the other one is just beginning," she muttered. She grabbed her purse and coat from under the cash wrap then turned to her friend. "Will you punch out for me?" she asked. "I'm only going to get to my job if I sprout wings."

"Fly then," Amanda assured. "I've got you covered."

"Thanks." Nasarra strode to the escalator and ran down the steps, trying to ignore the headache that had nagged her all day. On Mondays, Wednesdays, Thursday nights and Fridays, she worked in the women's clothing department at Macy's. It sat right above the cosmetics department and fragrances constantly wafted up the escalator, blending together in a concoction that made Nasarra's head want to split in half. She hated it. It was routine and boring. Full of "here's your change" and "have a nice day." Not to mention all of the stupid credit cards she was supposed to try and sell. She swore she could recite that speech in her sleep.

She made it to the front door and pushed it open, putting her purse on top of her head in an attempt to shield herself from the downpour. The fog was worse than usual, but she tried to ignore it as she jaunted up the street. She only had about twenty minutes now to get to her second job at Max's Opera Café, which she worked on Tuesdays, Wednesday nights, Thursdays, Friday nights and Sundays. At least she could say that she enjoyed this job. The staff was full of out of work actors and actresses that were always entertaining. Working with a bunch of eccentrics was a good way to feel like you weren't working at all.

The restaurant had a piano player at night and, sometimes, some of the employees would sing. Nasarra made sure that she did so whenever she got the chance. She loved to sing and it made her feel, for just a brief moment, that her lifelong dream of being on Broadway wasn't such an impossibility.

She smiled and thought about the event that had planted the love of acting in her. When she'd been little, her mother had taken her and her sister to see a touring production of the play *Oliver*. Nasarra had been completely captivated by the entire thing. The lights, the props, but most of all, by the performers' ability to become their characters so fully. She had been mesmerized by the way they could fill the entire theatre with their powerful voices, and evoke such emotion from the audience.

The boy playing Oliver had especially caught her attention. He hadn't been much older than her, and he'd marched across the stage like he'd grown up on it. Nasarra had never had an abundance of self confidence and seeing that little boy walk like he owned the world had made her ache to know his secret. She gave credit to that boy for locking in her the desire to become a performer. From that moment on, all she wanted to do was move and inspire people the way he had inspired her.

Nasarra dodged a spray of water sent her direction as a car sped down the street, and she continued to run. She felt as if she would be running for the rest of her natural existence. A hamster in a wheel she could never get out of. It had been that way ever since she'd moved to the city, with stars in her eyes and a naïve girl's dreams of velvet curtains and applauding crowds.

Upon her arrival into San Francisco, she had checked into a sleazy motel where the cockroaches reigned and she was afraid to walk around barefoot because of the mysterious stains on the carpet. She'd remained there until finding her duplex, which she quickly realized she was not going to be able to pay for by herself, even with working two jobs. She had eked out a few months living on only beans and weenies until she had found Rafe. Now...she had Rafe and she was living on Geary Street, far, far away from her original dreams of New York, Julliard and Broadway theatres. She had become a statistic. She had gone from a once-upon-a-time theatre diva in training to just another shmoe trying to make a living. It was enough to make her sick.

Nasarra came to a screeching halt suddenly as she ran past The Curran Theatre. She stopped and stared longingly of the posters from *The Phantom of the Opera.* She walked past them every day and always stopped to gaze. She sighed as the rain rolled down her back and shoulders. She would give anything to see it, but she had to spend her money on more practical things. Like food.

She started to walk away, but cast a regretful look back at the posters. Something stirred inside of her and her sister's voice, Nasarra's voice of reason, instantly invaded her thought process. *You can't afford to be frivolous with your money, Nasarra. I'm not going to bail you out if you bankrupt yourself.*

Nasarra bristled as she remembered her sister saying those words to her the last time they had spoken. If she remembered correctly, their parents had gone bankrupt *because* of putting Shawna through law school. Nasarra would be in New York right now if it hadn't been for her. While her selfish sister had continued to bleed her parents dry to pursue her own ambitions, Nasarra had forgone her own education in order to help her parents pay the mortgage. She didn't see how Shawna had a right to say anything, but her words still lurked inside of Nasarra's mind, forcing her to think rationally when she would rather do otherwise.

It didn't help that Shawna had done so well for herself after law school. She now worked at a prestigious law firm and had married a very wealthy defense attorney. They were in Beverly Hills living something that resembled *The Lifestyles of the Rich and Famous*. She had a good career, a husband, and owned her own magnificent home. All Nasarra had was an eccentric roommate.

It disgusted her to think that, even after all her success and riches, Shawna had never given an ounce of money back to their parents. Family didn't matter to her. Nasarra didn't matter. Just so long as she got what she wanted out of life. People were pawns to her, puppets to manipulate. Shawna Williams lived in Shawna Williams Land and no one else was able to get into that exclusive club. She was one of the most self-centered people Nasarra had ever known, and yet, everyone catered to her and always had. They bent over backwards to give her the world at her feet. Nasarra spent most of her time trying to make *everyone else happy* and she was lucky if she even got a good tip. It had never made sense to her. More than likely, it never would

Nasarra sighed deeply and turned away from the theatre. Shawna was right. She did need to save her money. She began to wander up the street, but stopped and glanced back at the theatre for a third time. She groaned. All right, she had a credit card. What good were credit cards for but for charging things that weren't supposed to be charged? Wasn't that the whole point? Why should she miss out on an awesome play just because she had insecurities about her sister? She bit her bottom lip, a nervous habit she'd had forever... She shouldn't. She had bills to pay.

But wouldn't it be heavenly just for one night to feel like she was a real theatre person? That she could go to a play dressed classy and hobnob with other theatre lovers and feel all that closer to her dream?

She glanced at her watch and rolled her eyes. Man, she was going to be killed. *You need to budget better, Nasarra...* She scowled as if Shawna was standing right there in front of her, threw her shoulders back and strode defiantly to the theatre. She went purposefully through the door and over to the ticket booth, whipping out her Visa before she had time to talk herself out of it. "Give me a ticket to Saturday's show, please," she said. "And I'd like seats front and center, as close to the orchestra pit as possible." If she was going to splurge, she may as well go for the glory.

The woman at the booth plunked away on her keyboard as Nasarra tapped her fingers impatiently against her elbow. Her boss was going to draw and quarter her. When the woman handed her the ticket and her card, she snatched them both and shoved them in her purse, fleeing out the door and back into the torrential rain.

Nasarra grinned as she ran up the street, feeling joy bubble up inside of her. She knew deep in her heart that she was never going to make it to New York so why not just indulge in something she would enjoy? She had nothing to lose. If she started running low on money, she would just make Rafe tap dance harder.

"Hey, buddy!" an angry driver shouted suddenly. "Watch where you're going!"

Without warning, Nasarra plowed right into a man who was running backwards, shouting an apology to the driver. The collision caused her to drop her purse, which expelled most of its contents on impact with the ground.

"I'm so sorry!" the man exclaimed. He bent to pick up her purse at the same time she did and they cracked heads.

"Ow," Nasarra groaned, rubbing her forehead and wincing.

"Man, I'm batting a thousand today, aren't I?" the man laughed. "I'm so sorry about that."

She threw a pained smile up at him as she bent to pick up her lipstick, which was rolling toward the nearest sewer grate, and her wallet. Thank goodness her ticket had remained safely inside the bag. She shoved her stuff back into the purse and stood up. "It's fine," she said, her voice breathy from the rushed mode she was still in. Her heart lurched just a little because she realized for the first time just how amazingly attractive he was.

"Are you all right?" he asked her. "I didn't hurt you too badly, did I? No concussion?" He grinned.

She let her eyes roam appreciatively over him for a moment. He had sunset-colored hair pulled back at the nape of his neck in a short ponytail, and his green-gold eyes were light and sparkling. He was tall, taller than her, which was always a plus since she was an Amazonian nightmare compared to everyone else in her family. He looked absolutely spectacular in the black leather jacket and khaki pants he was wearing. Broad shoulders, strong jaw, slight cleft in the chin...yeah, she could forgive being run over by this hottie any day.

"No, I'm fine," she said with a smile. "No biggee." She put her purse back over her head and waved as she continued to dash up the street. She was slightly puzzled by the fact that he had seemed familiar to her in some way. Maybe the confidence she saw resonating off of his frame, or the sparkle in his unusual eyes. She was sure she'd seen him somewhere before, but she couldn't place him.

She shook her head and hailed a cab. She'd probably just seen him walking up the street one day. If he lived in the area, it was quite possible. Although, she thought sure she would remember such a good-looking man. She didn't have a love life, or even much of a social life, so if she'd seen him before, odds were she would have followed him for a ways and drooled until her heart's content.

She opened up the cab door and got inside, shaking the water off the arms of her coat. Opening up her purse and glancing over her ticket again, she grinned. She had a seat in the very front row. How cool was that? She giggled like an excited little girl. This was the best decision she had made in awhile, no matter how frivolous it was.

Chapter Two

"So, when are you going to the play again?" Amanda asked as she and Nasarra enjoyed their lunch in a nearby park.

"Saturday," Nasarra replied, pulling out her squashed tuna sandwich. A piece of paper fell out and she bent to pick it up. She unfolded it and frowned. It was a huge smiley face and had *Keep smilin' Red!* scrawled on it. Nasarra rolled her eyes and placed it back into her bag with a smirk and a shake of her head.

"Who was that from?" Amanda asked.

"Rafe," Nasarra said. "He's insane."

"He writes you notes in your lunch?"

"Like I said, he's insane." She smiled and watched a speckled pigeon guard a French fry that was too big for him as she bit into her sandwich. She made a face. She hated putting her lunch in the mini-fridge in the break room. It always made her food have that classic, soggy-bread, sixth grade cafeteria taste.

"So...what are you wearing to the play?" Amanda continued.

Nasarra shrugged. "I haven't decided yet. I thought I'd look for something on Friday during break."

"Do you have to work at Max's tonight?"

She shook her head. "No, and Rafe is making Poor Man's Goulash tonight."

"What in the heck is that?"

"Rice-a-roni, chicken, corn and provolone cheese all mixed together in this gooey pot of heaven."

Amanda made a face. "That's kind of sick, Nasarra."

She shook her head emphatically. "No, it's really good!

Do you want to come over?"

"And ruin you and Rafe's romantic dinner of paste? I wouldn't dream of it." Amanda raised an eyebrow.

"Okay, first off, Rafe is never romantic, and second, it's not paste."

Amanda snorted. "Whatever. It's a step above ramen and a step below a good, frozen ninety-nine cent pizza. Why don't we look for a dress for you after our shift? Since all you have to go home to is poor tap dancer Rafe and his famous Poor Man's Goulash, why don't you just look tonight?"

Nasarra smiled and nodded, but briefly thought that she shouldn't have to be dress shopping for a play at all. She should be *in* a play, getting dressed in a costume. She should be going into the backstage door of a long-running Broadway play in about ten minutes. What she *shouldn't* be doing is giving change for hundred dollar bills and bagging people's clothing and saying "apply for the Macy's card and receive ten percent off your purchase" until she had nightmares about it. She had been the lead in seven out of twelve high school plays and she'd had minor parts in the others. She'd been lead soprano in her high school elite choir. Everyone she had known had told her she was going to be someone big. Her drama teacher had told her she was going to be the next Sarah Brightman.

Shawna had told her she should go to a respectable college and worry about theatre later, but Nasarra just wanted to act. *She was going to be the next Sarah Brightman.* Now, she was here. In Macy's. Bagging clothing. It wasn't right.

"Ready to go back to work?" Amanda asked suddenly.

Nasarra groaned. "No." She stuffed her trash into her bag and flung it into a nearby can. The last thing she wanted to do was go back into that place. She hated Macy's. If she didn't get an employee discount, she would never shop there. She didn't see why she had to work there. She heaved a sigh and stood. Her life had fallen into a very dull and monotonous routine. A routine she would give anything to change, but had no way of doing so.

* * *

"Hey, Caleb!"

Caleb waved to one of his fellow cast members as he

pushed open the backstage door of The Curran and strode through the corridor toward the dressing room.

"You ever get here on time?" the cast member asked with a grin.

Caleb smirked. "I try. It just never works in my favor." Most of the time it was due to the fact that he had to park his bike on the North 40 and hike in like a tourist. It sucked. Then, yesterday, with the downpour, almost getting killed by that car, and completely running over that beautiful woman... He shook his head. He didn't believe in The Fates, but if he did, he knew they would be laughing at him.

He shoved the dressing room door open and flopped his duffel into the nearest chair.

"Hey, Caleb!" his friend exclaimed.

Caleb slid his gaze to Craig and rolled his eyes. The man looked entirely too pleased with himself and he knew exactly why. He pulled a chair out and took a seat, facing the mirror and tugging his duffel over so he could start emptying the contents.

"Soooo?" Craig sidled up behind Caleb and grinned at him in the mirror. "How was your date last night?" He waggled his eyebrows.

Caleb sighed. "Well, she tried to give me a palm reading and ended up licking me."

Ricky, one of the other cast members, frowned. "She licked you?"

"Yeah. I felt like I was in that horrible *Saturday Night Live* skit with Christopher Walken. You know, *The Continental?* One minute she's looking at my palm, and the next she's telling me I have a very promising love line. Then she licked me. I swear, it was right out of the skit!" He shot a dirty look up at Craig. "Then, if that wasn't bad enough, she asked me if I would take her home."

Ricky raised an eyebrow. "That's bad?"

"In order to take her home, she had to ride on the back of my bike. In order for her not to fall off, she had to have her arms around me. I swear on my life, she almost twisted my nipples off." Caleb shuddered.

Ricky guffawed and Craig smothered a laugh of his own.

Caleb glowered. "I'm not even kidding. I'm chafed as we speak. Anyway, we get back to her apartment and she invites me in. I'm trying to figure out how to decline nicely when she saunters up and whispers in my ear that she's just re-cellophaned the bed, has a brand new bottle of baby oil, and is itching to try out her new handcuffs and cat-o-nine tails."

Ricky laughed so hard he almost turned purple. "You have *got* to stop letting Craig set you up on blind dates, man."

"Tell me about it," he grumbled.

"Hey, she seemed nice to me," Craig protested.

Caleb gave him a level glare in the mirror. "She was a dominatrix."

Craig shrugged. "Some guys like that kind of thing. Besides, not *all* of the dates I set you up on are bad. What about that Cindy girl? She was nice."

"Her armpits and legs were hairier than mine! She looked like a gorilla!"

"Okay, okay, what about that Amy chick? She was a dancer!"

Caleb's eyes bulged. "An *exotic* dancer!"

"All right, what about Debbie?"

"Need I remind you that Debbie was, in fact, a *man*?"

Ricky fell out of his chair, wheezing.

Caleb slashed the air with his hands. "No more! I am done with your frightening freak dates, Craig! My love life doesn't need your help!"

Craig shrugged. "Fine, dude. I was only trying to help. When was the last time you went out with a girl?"

"You mean a normal girl? I don't know. You've set me up with so many circus clowns I'm not sure I remember what a normal girl is."

"Well excuse me for caring. I thought maybe if you found yourself as hottie you'd loosen up a little. All you ever do is work. You perform here every night almost and when you're not performing here you're working at that local theatre."

"Lazy Little Theatre is where I first started acting. That place is like home to me."

"That's fine. I don't have a problem with it. All I'm saying is that you could use a little time to yourself. You need a vacation. You know, relax..."

Caleb frowned and turned in his chair to look Craig straight in the eye. "Are you trying to tell me you think I'm uptight?"

Craig raised his hands. "Not at all, man, but when *was* the last time you took a vacation?"

Caleb snorted and turned back toward the mirror, dismissing Craig. "Would someone please pick Ricky up off the floor before he laughs himself into a coma?" he grumbled. He savagely opened his makeup tote and started to rummage through it with next to no purpose. Nice, his friend thought he was uptight. He wasn't uptight. He loved acting. So what? He performed all the time. Who cared? At least he was doing what he loved. He liked to help out at the little theatre. It made him feel like he mattered, like he was making a difference.

It was all he had left.

* * *

Nasarra heaved a sigh as she tried to untangle her bracelet from the fabric of the dress she had tried on. She resisted the urge to just tear it off, and patiently unhooked it. She then smoothed the dress and looked at her bracelet to make sure it wasn't damaged. A friend of hers in high school had given it to her and it was very special. It symbolized her dreams and she'd always felt like if she broke it, her dreams would be shattered. She knew it was silly. Maybe she had just been living with an eccentric artist for too long. It didn't matter. She just knew she didn't want anything to happen to it.

Turning her attention away from her bracelet, she looked in the mirror and made a face. This one made her look like a hooker. She wasn't even going to bother showing it to Amanda. She had tried on practically every dress in the store and everything was either too short, the wrong color, or didn't fit right. So far, she had looked like an oompa loompa, an Amish woman, and now, a prostitute. Not to mention a whole slew of other scary combinations. It was useless. She would just have to resign herself to the fact that she would be going to the play looking horrid.

Suddenly, the door to the dressing room burst open and Amanda hurled a long, black dress at Nasarra. "Try this one," she commanded. "I found it hiding on the wrong rack."

Nasarra frowned, but obeyed. She pulled off the nasty dress she was wearing and slipped the black one on. She prepared herself for the worst as she looked in the mirror, but no scream of terror escaped her lips. It was beautiful. It was long and black with tiny gold sparkles hidden within the fabric. The back was cut low and it complemented her curves nicely, making her look elegant and regal, which was a first.

She'd always felt out of place in her family looks wise. Shawna was gorgeous. She was petite and wore a size two. She had luxurious blonde hair that waved just enough to make it absolutely divine. Her eyes were a soul-probing blue and her skin was fair and creamy.

Nasarra looked like a frightening freak next to her sister. Their father was part Puerto Rican and she had received his olive complexion, which contrasted greatly with her fiery, curling red hair. She had no idea where her hair had come from. No one in her family had red hair. Must have been some rogue DNA from the 1800's. Her eyes were an emerald color and she was slender, but taller than average for a woman. She looked absolutely nothing like her sister. When she'd been little, she had sometimes wondered if she was adopted.

She smiled and opened the door to promenade in front of Amanda.

"Woo hoo! Lookin' hot baby!" Amanda exclaimed, standing up from where she had been lounging in boredom.

"I think I found my dress," Nasarra said with a satisfied grin.

"I'd say so. Now take it off and give it to me. You've been here for an hour. Your darling Rafe will be worried."

Nasarra frowned. "What is it with you? You think Rafe and I have a thing going on or something? The guy's neurotic."

"Please, he's an artist and he's French. What more could you want?"

"You haven't met him. He's a very cool guy, but you try living with him and then we'll talk."

Amanda smiled. "Hurry and change. I want to go home. *Buffy's* coming on tonight."

Nasarra giggled and returned to the cubicle. She changed back into her regular clothes and exited the dressing room. Amanda took the dress from Nasarra upon her exit and almost fled with it to a cash register.

"What are you doing?" Nasarra called after her in bewilderment.

"Being nice," she stated. "So shut up and accept it." She handed the cashier her credit card before Nasarra could stop her, and grinned up at her. "Don't say I never did anything for you."

Nasarra sighed, feeling guilty. Her friends shouldn't have to be buying her things just because she was practically dirt poor. It wasn't fair. She was just a mooch, a leech on society. She would never amount to anything, just like Shawna had always said...

* * *

Nasarra opened the door to her apartment and breathed in the heavenly aroma of dinner. She smiled. "Rafe!" she called. "I'm hoping that's my goulash I smell!" She closed the door and walked into the front room. Her eyes widened and she let out a shout as she walked in on Rafe standing before a half painted canvas, completely and totally naked. "Rafe!" she shouted, turning her back.

Rafe spun. "Oh, I'm sorry, Red!" he exclaimed in his slight French accent. He sought refuge behind the sofa and began searching for his boxer shorts.

Nasarra sighed. "How many times do I have to come home to you in your birthday suit?" she cried.

"I am sorry!" he apologized again, walking back out in his underwear. "I find that I create better in the nude."

She rolled her eyes and turned back to face him. She folded her arms. "Well, do you think maybe you could foresee when I'll be coming home so I don't have to keep looking at your...creative process?"

He flashed her a beautiful smile that made his light blue eyes sparkle. "Of course."

She shook her head. "Where's my dinner?"

"On the stove. I just finished it." He ran his hand through his dirty blonde waves and followed her into the kitchen. "How was work?"

Nasarra pulled a plate out of the cabinet. She began dishing herself some food. "Uneventful. How about you?"

"About the same. What did you buy? I saw you come in with a bag." He hopped up onto a barstool and leaned against the kitchen counter.

She nodded. "I got a dress for the play on Saturday."

"You're looking forward to that?"

"Um, yeah. I've only wanted to see it for my whole life." She got a drink out of the refrigerator and took her dinner to the sofa. Rafe followed shortly and sat down next to her with his own dish. "Anything good on TV tonight?" she asked.

He shrugged.

Nasarra reached across Rafe for the remote and glanced down at his bare chest. She frowned. "You been working out?"

He grinned. "You can tell?"

Her eyes widened. "Slightly. Dang, when did you get all buff?"

A faint blush touched Rafe's handsome face and he smiled down at his plate.

Nasarra grinned and turned on the television. Such was her life. Every night she sat on the sofa and ate dinner with Rafe, who usually had some part of his body bare. Every night she watched television or movies while he worked on his paintings, then she went to bed. It was always the same. No changes. No deviation. Her life was in a predictable rut that she could do nothing about. A wave of grief suddenly washed over her and she sighed sadly, wishing, once again, that things had turned out differently.

Chapter Three

Nasarra scrutinized herself in front of the mirror. She tucked back a flyaway curl and adjusted her dress so that it looked right. She smiled. She had managed to come out looking rather elegant, or so she thought. If she imagined hard enough, she could almost pretend that there was some handsome man waiting downstairs to escort her to the limo they would be taking to the Tony Awards. She giggled at her fantasy, knowing full well that the only person waiting for her outside was Rafe. Somehow, though, even that didn't bother her. She was so happy to be going to the play that nothing else mattered.

She left her bedroom and went out into the living room to fetch her purse and jacket. Rafe was sitting on the sofa, shirtless again, with a pair of sweats rolled up to reveal one tap shoe on and the other off. Nasarra frowned. "Why are you only wearing one shoe?" she questioned.

Rafe glanced back at her over his shoulder. "I was too tired to take off the other one."

She smiled. "Hard day on Market Street?"

He nodded. "I just about danced myself to death. Plus, it was raining, which really sucked. I had a good audience today, though. They seemed to like the fact that I was dancing shirtless in the rain."

She laughed. "Well, of course! Any woman with half a sex drive would be going crazy to see a guy with your physique all shiny and dripping."

Rafe blushed a deep shade of crimson and frowned at her. "I think you just like to embarrass me."

Nasarra grinned devilishly.

"You look lovely."

"Thanks. Is it still raining?"

He shook his head. "I don't think so, but it's foggy and damp so wear your jacket."

"Yes, Mother."

He grinned. "Have a good time."

"See you later." Leaving the building, she stepped out into the brisk evening air. She found the mistiness refreshing and it made her feel alive, so she merely draped her jacket over her shoulder, not wanting to relinquish the delicious chill. She looked up at the many sparkling lights of the city as she walked, and sighed in contentment. No matter how many disappointments she had suffered, she did not regret coming to live in this city. It was beautiful and she could not imagine living anywhere else. Except maybe New York.

Nasarra arrived at the theatre just as the doors opened and she proudly displayed her ticket to the doorman. She marched into the house, taking her seat in the front row after buying a program from the woman in the lobby. She looked around the theatre in amazement. It had three balconies and each side had opera boxes. Everything was gilded and ornate, just like something out of one of her dreams. She was sitting right in front of the orchestra pit and could see the musicians inside tuning up. Her eyes drifted to the stage and her heart almost ceased beating. It was huge, seemed to go on forever. She sighed. Oh, to be up on that stage...

She fell back into her chair with a smile of satisfaction on her lips. For once, she was one of those envied people in the first row. She was one of those women people like her looked at and whispered jealous things about. She was a wealthy theatre patron, if only for one night. Suddenly, the lights dimmed and she bit her bottom lip in excitement. The theatre grew quiet and Nasarra sat upright in her seat. Her attention riveted on the stage, waiting.

The opening of the show was powerful and explosive, making her afraid to breathe for fear she would shatter the excitement of it all. Her eyes never left the stage as the performers weaved their magical spell over her. The characters came to life as she watched, and she found herself reacting along with them, as if she was there too.

During Act I, Scene III, she became a bit preoccupied with trying to locate her purse, which had managed to disappear under her seat, but she forgot her search when she heard the most beautiful voice in the known world. She slowly turned her eyes back up to the stage and her heart did something of a flip when she spotted the man who owned it. He looked so passionate, so in tune with his character. She longed to be where he was.

She frowned. He looked slightly familiar... *Yes! Holy cow!* It was the hottie who had run into her on the street earlier that week! But, that wasn't all. Something else called to Nasarra. Something deeper. Where else had she seen him before? He mesmerized her. She couldn't tear her gaze from him. It was like he was hypnotizing her with his unusual green-gold eyes and his wonderful voice. Suddenly, he stopped singing and Nasarra blinked. Two other people replaced him on the stage and she shook her head. Okay, that had been bizarre. She shook her head again and resumed her search for her purse.

For the rest of the night, Nasarra waited in anticipation for any scene that man was in. She had given up searching for her purse and had finally managed to find it at intermission lodged in the next person's seat. After making the mad race to the bathroom, she looked in her program to see who that magnificent actor was. He stared up at her in beautiful black and white, beside his character's name, Raoul Vicomte deChagny. He wore a mischievous smile and the lighting used in the photo highlighted his finely sculpted facial features. She glanced down at the name. Caleb Makepeace. She frowned. Even his name sounded familiar!

Act II seemed to fly by, and when the last song was sung, Nasarra was extremely disappointed. She had waited to see this musical for so long, and now, all too soon, it was over like some fantastic fantasy. When the performers came out to take their bows, she stood up and was quite certain that she clapped the loudest. Especially for that magnificent performer, Caleb Makepeace.

When the curtain closed and people started to file out of the theatre, Nasarra walked as slow as possible, trying to take in all of the sights and lock them away in her memory. There was no telling when she would be in a theatre like The Curran again.

It was pelting rain when she finally managed to wander her way to the door. It cloaked everything in mist and the steam from the manhole coverings on the street wisped and weaved in a slow, beguiling dance of mystery. She smiled.

She had found the rain annoying the other day, but now she found it magical. It seemed to make the night complete.

She stepped outside and turned the collar of her jacket up to protect her neck from the dampness. Pivoting on her heel, she started up the street, but rammed into a person who was walking in the opposite direction with such a force that it knocked the air from her. She staggered back, trying to regain her senses, and looked up at the poor person she had just run over. Her eyes nearly bulged clear out of her skull. She had just mowed over the handsome actor with the beautiful voice! She squeezed her eyes shut in humiliation. This was great. Just great.

"Excuse me," she whispered. She stepped aside to let him by and averted her eyes to the pavement. He did the same, in the same direction, and they were right back to where they had started. She swallowed, feeling really dumb. Things just kept getting better and better. She stepped to her left; he stepped to his right. She stifled a groan. She stepped to her right; he stepped to his left.

A beautifully rich and masculine chuckle escaped the man's throat and he stepped back. "Did you want to dance?" he teased. "Is that what you're going for? You want to dance a minuet?"

Nasarra blushed. "I'm sorry," she murmured.

He flashed her a dazzling smile. "That's all right," he assured. He frowned slightly, looking her over, and some small bit of recognition came to life in his eyes. He pointed to the program she clutched to her chest. "You were at the show tonight?"

Nasarra nodded, attempting to swallow the lump in her throat.

"You were in the front row, weren't you?"

She stole a glance at him and nodded again.

He grinned. "I thought so. I always look out into the audience when I'm on stage, and I happened to glance over at you. I saw your fiery red hair and thought to myself, 'that can't be the woman I ran down in the street the other day.'"

She gave a nervous laugh. "Yeah, that was a crazy day."

His grin broadened. "My name's Caleb," he said, extending his hand.

Nasarra stared at him. This was incredible. She held her hand out numbly and shook his, amazed by the power of his grip. "Nasarra." Her voice came out like the croak of a dying frog and she cleared her throat. "Nasarra," she stated.

His eyes swept over her again. "Nasarra. That's a very pretty name."

She smiled shyly. "Thank you." She braved a glance up at him and couldn't help but feel heat course through her body at his stunning smile. It was mischievous, playful, and the small dimple it created in his cheek made her heart falter.

"So, I guess we're even," he said.

She frowned.

"I ran you over. You repaid me in like kind." He folded his arms and raised an eyebrow. "Where should we go from here?"

She fought for words, but of course, nothing would come to mind. She would have loved to sound witty and intriguing, but instead, she just stared like a deer in the headlights.

He gave another soft chuckle. "Listen," he said slowly, "this might sound kind of sudden...and unusual, but I was heading over to The Grand Café. I'm starving. Would you like to join me? It's just up the road."

Nasarra saw spots. She was going to pass out. That would be really embarrassing. She shook herself mentally and silenced her scrambled thoughts. She shrugged and tried to look casual when, in truth, she felt as if her heart was going to pound right out of her chest. "Sure," she said.

His grin remained ever-present and was growing more desirable as the seconds ticked by. "Excellent." He turned and offered his arm. "I would hate to think that it might take another collision to convince you."

She gave a breathy laugh that embarrassed her right into the ground and she took his arm, happy to have him turn her up the street so she didn't have to look into his eyes anymore. She was vaguely aware of the fact that she was getting soaked. Somewhere in the back of her mind she knew that her carefully styled hair was getting stringy, her makeup was smeared, and she would have to dry clean her brand new dress, but none of that really mattered to her. Hello, she was walking down the street to The Grand Café with a very good-looking man who had the most beautiful voice in the world! Everything else came second.

"Did you enjoy the show?" Caleb asked suddenly.

Nasarra blinked. "Huh?" She looked up at him, and he met her eyes in question. She shook her head. What was the matter with her? She was acting like a total idiot. "The show," she repeated. "Yes, I liked it very much. I've wanted to see it forever."

"Really?"

She nodded.

"I've been in it for awhile now. I love it. I never get tired of portraying my character." He took another glance down at her and smiled.

"You perform very well," Nasarra said shyly.

"Well, that's a relief. A man always likes to hear that his performance was good." Caleb laughed.

Her eyes widened as she caught his joke. She looked up at him and felt herself blush. He looked even more handsome when he laughed. He had smile lines around his eyes that lit up his entire face and made him seem warm and engaging.

She felt awkward as she walked with him and all conversation skills she may have had seemed to vanish. She really needed to get out more. This was just sad.

The Grand Café didn't offer much to eat. There remained only some leftover desserts that looked about a month old. Nasarra got a piece of chocolate cake and Caleb got some sort of dry-looking, flaky pastry thing. There was an abundance of liquor at their disposal, but Nasarra got a simple coffee. Like she needed to get tipsy and make an even bigger idiot out of herself. Caleb ordered coffee, as well, probably just to make her feel comfortable, and chose a table in the far corner of the dimly lit room.

"So, tell me," Nasarra said as they sat down, "why exactly did you invite me to come with you?" *Talk about cutting right to the chase. Good job, Nasarra. Ten points for creativity.* She rolled her eyes.

Caleb met her gaze and took a swallow of coffee. "Because you're beautiful, and I wanted someone to talk to," he stated.

She smiled down at the table. *Ten points to him for blunt honesty.*

He grinned. "So, you like plays?"

"Yes, I love plays!" Her eyes snapped to his in enthusiasm. "I used to dream of being on Broadway."

"You don't anymore?" he asked with a frown.

She shrugged as sorrow washed over her. "Dreams are dreams. They aren't anything more than that." She swirled her coffee around in her cup.

"Why do you say that?"

"Because life gets in the way. Life crushes dreams." She speared her chocolate cake as if to drive her point home.

He raised an eyebrow, and when she didn't elaborate, he said, "Explain?"

She met his eyes and debated with herself. The man probably didn't want to hear a sob story. She shook her head. "It's not really that important."

"You just said 'life crushes dreams' while very vehemently stabbing your cake. I would say that's probably a little important, at least to you." His eyes were full of warmth and sincerity even in his teasing. He folded his arms on the table. "Come on, comfort of strangers and all that."

She let out a sigh and shrugged self-consciously. "I've loved theatre since I was a little girl. I was always driving my family crazy blaring the soundtrack to *Cats* or *Evita*." She smiled at the happy memories. "I loved to watch the classic musicals like *Oklahoma!* and *South Pacific*, and my mom enrolled me in a theatre youth class during the summers. When I got to middle school, I took drama and choir, and I started taking after school dance classes as well. Jazz, tap, ballet, all the essentials. I loved it all. I wanted to go to Julliard, you see."

She glanced up at him from where she had been staring at the wood grain of the table. It was difficult for her to talk about this part of her life because it made her so sad. It was even more difficult to talk about it to a complete stranger who was really handsome.

"Sounds like you had a good start," he said. "And a supportive family, so that's nice."

She nodded and averted her gaze again. "Yeah, my parents have always been as supportive as they could be. They encouraged me to go after my dreams, and I probably should have been smarter about the whole thing. I could have easily applied for scholarships, or could have spent my summers working to save for college. I just blindly assumed that my family was going to take care of it because they were paying for my sister to go to law school. When you're a kid, sometimes you don't realize that there are bigger things going on than you and your dreams."

He frowned thoughtfully and rested his chin in one hand. "What happened?"

She should have found his interest and the intent way he was looking at her unnerving, but it was quite the opposite. For whatever reason, now that she was spilling her guts, she found him remarkably easy to talk to. "My parents fell into financial distress because of my sister's education. She didn't care, and they felt obligated to continue supporting her, mainly because she is really good at guilting everyone in to doing what she wants. I didn't want my family losing everything they had worked for, so my senior year, I got a job after school to help them, and I've just been working ever since. Moving to San Francisco is the only thing I've been able to manage, and just barely, but at least I got to have my own life finally."

He opened his mouth to say something, but she found herself not wanting to hear anything that might sound like sympathy or pity. This was not supposed to be a therapy session. "Anyway,"—she waved her bite of cake with her fork airily—"that's my story. What about you? Have you always been an actor?"

He cleared his throat discreetly and sat back in his chair. "Um, yeah. I mean, I've always done acting in some form. I went to college at NYU and graduated with a double major in performing arts and teaching."

Her eyes went wide. *Ten more points for amazing ambition.*

"Yeah, I taught theatre at a community college for awhile. Then I decided I wanted to give Broadway a try."

She knew she was quickly taking on the starry-eyed gaze of a groupie. "How long did it take you to get the part you have now?" she asked. "I mean, was it as difficult as everyone makes it out to be? Hundreds of auditions and rejections? Or were you just so brilliant that they gave you a part right away?" She clamped her mouth shut. *Yeah, that just flew right on out there... Great...*

He blinked in surprise, then chuckled. "It really all depends on the casting director. Each director has his own idea of how he wants a part to be played. Some want you to be a carbon copy of another performer they've had in the past. You may as well just forget it in auditions like that. You'll never be good enough in that setting. Other directors are just looking for new talent. Every audition is a gamble, a chance. I've just gotten lucky sometimes."

"What else have you played in?" she asked. She saw

amusement reflected in his eyes. Probably due to the fact that her unbridled enthusiasm about his craft was bubbling forward like an overflowing pot of boiling water.

"Let's see, I have been Joseph in *Joseph and the Amazing Technicolor Dreamcoat,* Rum Tum Tugger in *Cats,* several other off-Broadway plays and now Raoul in *Phantom.*"

"Good lord." Nasarra stared at him. "That's impressive. Have you ever been rejected?"

He chuckled. "Of course! There's no word an actor understands better than 'rejection.'"

She heaved a sigh and shook her head. "If you've been rejected then I wouldn't stand a chance ever," she muttered. She was talking to herself more than him, thinking out loud.

Caleb frowned. "Okay, there's one thing in this world I can't stand, and that's listening to people get down on themselves."

She met his gaze and pain stabbed at her heart. The pain of regret and longing that she was so familiar with. "I wanted Broadway more than anything," she admitted quietly. "I was so set on going there, had it all planned out. Then, in the blink of an eye, it was gone and it all fell apart. Now, I'm stuck here with the ghost of a dream that will never be." She bit her bottom lip and tried to keep from embarrassing herself by crying. She'd already embarrassed herself enough.

Caleb reached out and placed his hand over hers in an effort to comfort her. "I'm sorry," he murmured.

She seriously did not want him to say he was sorry for her. That was exactly what she had been trying to avoid. She tried to shrug it off like it didn't matter. What good did it do to dwell on things that only hurt? She glanced up just enough to look at his hand on hers. His touch was gentle, reassuring. It gave her strength and made her smile just a bit. "So," she sniffed, trying to change the subject away from her shattered hopes...again, "when did you decide you wanted to be in the theatre?"

Caleb must have gotten the point that she didn't want to pursue the Broadway topic so he let it drop. "When I was a kid," he replied. "I auditioned for a play when I was little and I was hooked. The first professional musical I ever performed in was *Oliver.*"

Nasarra's head jerked up and she stared at him. "*Oliver?*"

He nodded.

"How old were you then?" She leaned forward in her seat and halfway across the table.

He raised an eyebrow and looked almost frightened for a moment. "Ten," he answered slowly.

She gasped and fell back into her chair. "That's who you are!" she exclaimed. "You're Caleb Makepeace!"

A few people in the restaurant gave Nasarra a perplexed look, but she paid them no heed.

"Yes, I know I'm Caleb Makepeace," he said. He glanced around in a pained fashion, then met her eyes and winced. "You're...not gonna...lick me now, are you?" He shifted uncomfortably in his chair.

Nasarra blinked rapidly and frowned. "What?" She shook her head. "No, listen. When I was eight my mom took my sister and me to see that play. Were you part of the touring cast that performed in San Diego?"

He nodded, his concern melting into a look of intrigue.

She grinned and pointed at him. "I saw you. I saw you in that play. That's why you seem so familiar to me. I've been trying to figure it out all night. Even the other day when you ran into me, I thought you seemed familiar. You were that adorable little boy marching across the stage! You were the boy that inspired me!"

Caleb's eyes widened in surprise. "I-I inspired you?"

She nodded. "I went home that night and decided that you were doing what I wanted to do. Something in the way you carried yourself across the stage with such confidence called out to my soul. You awoke a passion in me that has never been quenched."

He stared at her for a minute, then let out a breathy laugh that much resembled the one she had given him earlier. "Wow, those are words you don't hear every day." He gave her a playful frown. "You hand out your best lines on all your first dates?"

She felt her cheeks grow hot. Date... That word had been all but eradicated from her vocabulary. He considered this happenstance a date? Well, she definitely wasn't going to complain. "Ever since I saw that play, I have wanted to do what you do," she continued. "I felt the same when I watched you tonight." She shook her head in wonderment. "You are amazing. You have such a wonderful gift."

Caleb gave a bashful smile and his cheeks turned a slight

shade of pink. "Thank you." He fell silent, as if not knowing how to follow that compliment. Instead, he took a bite of his pastry. He made a face. "It's a bit dry," he said, coughing. He made another face. "Okay, actually, it tastes like it was dehydrated and then run over."

She laughed.

He took a gulp of coffee and returned to the conversation. "So, you used to live in San Diego?"

She nodded. "I moved here a few years ago. Where are you from?"

"Here, actually," he said. "I was born here. I obviously lived in New York for awhile, but I came back here when I got cast in *Phantom*. My mother and father retired shortly after and moved to Point Reyes. They gave me their home in Sausalito."

She smiled at him. "You know," she said whimsically, "I've never met you before, but I feel like I've known you forever. You have been with me my whole life, inspiring me, keeping me going. Whenever I felt discouraged, I thought of you. You are a stranger, and yet, not."

Caleb gazed at her for a long moment then sat back in his chair with a heavy sigh. "You have to stop saying stuff like that to me," he said. "I'm going to blush my head right off." He glanced at his hand, which was still over Nasarra's. He squeezed it a little with a smile then tackled his pastry again. He made another face, which caused her to giggle. "This thing is awful," he said.

"Mine sucks too," she laughed.

He smiled and looked at his watch with a sigh. "I have an appointment with an old director friend of mine tomorrow," he said. "At, like, six a.m. So, unfortunately, I have to be heading home."

She was disappointed that he had to go home so soon, but she nodded. Getting to spend some time with him was better than none at all. It was like looking up to a rock star or a sports hero for your entire life and then, miraculously, getting to chat with them for awhile. Caleb, even though he had been a little boy at the time, had always been her role model. The fact that she had been able to converse with him was so far beyond any of her wildest dreams. The fact that he was beautiful was just an extreme bonus.

"Let me walk you to your car?" he asked.

"Oh, I don't have a car. I only live down the street from the theatre."

"Let me walk you home, then?"

She grinned and nodded happily.

Caleb paid for their dessert and they stepped outside into the pouring rain. He scowled up at the sky and turned Nasarra toward the inside of the sidewalk. "Walk under the awnings," he said. "I don't want you to have to get any more wet and cold than you already have."

She smiled up at him. *Ten more points for chivalry.* If this man got any better, she was pretty sure he would start to radiate light.

Nasarra groaned when she reached her apartment, searched through her purse, and realized that she had forgotten her key. She let out a large sigh. It would take the entire Marine Corps marching through the living room to wake up Rafe. She turned to Caleb and gave a sweet smile. "Just a sec." She turned back to her door and bludgeoned it as if she intended to knock it down. "Rafe!" she bellowed.

Caleb chuckled softly.

"Rafe!" she shouted again. "Open the door!"

There was some shuffling inside and the door finally cracked open, revealing Rafe, whose hair was sticking up in all directions and who was clad only in a pair of blue bikini briefs.

Nasarra shielded her eyes and groaned. "Rafe, *why* do you come to the door like that? Why are you even wearing that? You're not in Europe anymore."

Rafe frowned and shrugged. "All of my boxers are dirty," he replied. "Besides,"—he pointed to Caleb—"it's nothing he hasn't seen before." He met Nasarra's eyes and winked. "Or you either."

"Don't remind me! Go back to bed!" She shooed him away and then turned to Caleb, who was grinning. "That's my roommate," she explained. "He's...French."

Caleb chuckled and reached his hand out to gently wipe underneath her eye. "Your mascara is running," he murmured.

She felt like butterflies had attacked her stomach. "I had a nice time," she whispered, looking down in a shy gesture.

"Me too," he agreed. "I'm glad you came with me. I took a chance in asking you."

"I took a chance in accepting," she said, "but I'm glad I did."

"So am I, sweetie." He took his hand away, which until this point, had still been caressing her cheek. He sighed. "Maybe I'll see you again?"

She smiled. "Maybe. I just hope it's sooner than twelve years this time."

He grinned. "Me too. Have a good night."

Nasarra nodded and expected him to just go. It surprised her when, instead of taking a step backward, he walked up the last stair and stood directly in front of her.

"You going to give me your phone number?"

His voice was a sensual purr and it made her knees wobble in a threatening manner. "Um...sure." She fumbled to open her purse again and look for some sort of writing utensil, but she dropped it. All of the contents purged again. She let out a frustrated huff. "Great," she muttered. She bent to pick it up, but his hands on her shoulders stopped her.

"Here, let me get it. Don't move. I don't want to bash your noggin again." He chuckled and picked up her things, handing her bag back to her with a sexy, lopsided smile.

"Thanks," she whispered. "I, um—" She looked over her shoulder back into the apartment.

"Where do you work?" he asked.

She glanced back up at him. "Um, Macy's and Max's Opera Café."

"Perfect. I love Max's. How about this, don't worry about the phone number. I'll just come find you sometime, okay?" He reached out and tucked back a stray curl.

She nodded, her throat constricting.

"All right then. You have a good night, Nasarra."

"You too." She bit her bottom lip.

He gave her a warm smile and leaned forward to press a soft kiss to her cheek, then he turned and she watched him walk away with that confident swagger. She touched where the impression of his lips still burned on her cheek.

She didn't go inside until she could no longer see his retreating form. That was the second time Caleb Makepeace had come into her life, and he'd left her with the same feeling now as he had after she'd seen *Oliver*. Like she could fly. Like the world was not a sadistic place... Like she could do anything.

Chapter Four

"Nasarra, would you please tell me what happened on Saturday night?" Amanda begged. "You've been grinning like an idiot all day. Was the musical really *that* fabulous?"

"The musical was wonderful," Nasarra said, folding a shirt that someone had returned. "I enjoyed it very much."

Amanda raised an eyebrow. "But that's not why you've become a grinning fool, is it? What did you do *after* the musical?" She leaned against the counter with one hand on her hip, as if waiting for an explanation.

Nasarra shot Amanda a sly look. "I went to The Grand Café," she replied coyly.

Amanda's eyes narrowed. "Alone?"

"Not...exactly." She glanced at her friend again.

Amanda's face lit up. "You met a guy!" she shouted. "I knew it! Did you sit next to him at the play?"

Nasarra giggled and shook her head.

"Did you run into him while hurrying to the bathroom? Because, as well all know, you can't sit for too long without running to the bathroom."

Nasarra laughed harder. "No, I didn't run into him while dashing to the bathroom, and leave my tiny bladder out of this."

"You're killing me!" Amanda cried. "Tell me!" She made a strangling gesture, sending the bracelets at her wrist jangling.

"He's a performer," she replied.

"Oooh. What's his name?"

"Caleb Makepeace."

Amanda made a face and giggled. "Who's he making peace with?"

Nasarra shot Amanda a contemptuous look.

She waved her hand as if to erase the statement. "Sorry. Anyway, where did you meet him?" She gestured for Nasarra to keep it coming.

"I ran into him after the show." She rolled her eyes. "It was really stupid. I wasn't paying attention, as usual, and I plowed right into the guy. It was embarrassing, but he was very nice. Then..." She shrugged. "He just kinda asked me out."

"Just like that?"

She nodded. "He told me he was going to The Grand Café and asked if I wanted to go. We had coffee, talked about the theatre, and I found out that he's the same little boy I saw in *Oliver* way back in the day. All in all, it was a very nice evening." She glanced at her friend and saw that she was standing with her arms folded, wearing a silly grin. Nasarra groaned inwardly. She knew what that look meant.

Amanda pushed a strand of light brown hair off of her forehead. "You love him, don't you?"

"Amanda! I can't love him. I don't even know him!"

"Are you going to see him again?"

"I'd like to see him again, but I don't know. He asked for my phone number, but I couldn't find anything to write on and only succeeded in looking like a flustered imbecile. I told him where I work. It's up to him to make the next move."

"I bet he loves you."

Amanda's brown eyes danced with amusement and it made Nasarra laugh. "Amanda, I only had coffee with him. It was one of those spur of the moment things that are really nice when they happen, but never happen twice. I'll probably never see him again." She flung another article of clothing down and sighed. Although, it would be nice if he showed up one day, brought her flowers maybe...

She rolled her eyes. She needed to get her head out of the clouds. That was how she'd ended up where she was. Life was not a fairy tale. She knew that better than anybody. All fantasizing would get her was disappointment. Caleb had been an amazing night. More than likely, that was all he would ever be.

* * *

Caleb heaved a sigh as he fiddled with the stirring straw for his coffee. Six a.m. Yeah, right. It was just like Nathan to leave him hanging. The guy existed in his own time zone. First, he'd canceled their original appointment and moved it to Monday because he'd had something last minute pop up. Now, thanks to his current tardiness, Caleb had wandered Ghirardelli Square for an hour, and had been sitting in the chocolate store for another.

He looked down at his second cup of coffee and smiled to himself as he thought of the awful dessert he'd eaten at The Grand Café. That woman... He could still smell her. She'd smelled like coconut and passion. If passion had a smell, this woman had owned it. The fire burning in her eyes when she'd spoken about the theatre had been a huge turn on. The fact that she hadn't tried to lick him, whip him, or rip his nipples off hadn't hurt either.

He hadn't been able to stop thinking of her. Sure, it was all fun and humiliating when Craig set him up on his horrid dates, but meeting a genuinely interesting woman who was beautiful and had a ton in common with him was a different matter. Knowing how attracted he was to her made him defensive. Knowing how much he had thought of her since he'd left her doorstep was downright alarming. It was territory he would rather leave alone.

"Caleb Makepeace."

Caleb slid his gaze up to the tall figure that came to stand in front of his table. Red hair, cocky grin, could have been Conan O'Brien's brother. Yup, it was Nathan all right. Even though he hadn't seen him in years, there was no mistaking his old friend.

Caleb sighed and looked at his watch. "Nice of you to grace me with your presence, Nate," he grumbled.

Nathan grinned and took a seat across from him. "So, that's how it's gonna be, hmm?" He shrugged. "Fine, I'll just cut to the chase then. You owe me a favor and I'm collecting."

Caleb arched an eyebrow. "Come again?"

Nathan's smile was positively demonic. "I'm producing this new play."

Caleb gestured for him to continue.

"Last year I was in Nevada taking care of some business and I happened to stumble across this performance in remembrance of this young girl. Apparently, she had been very involved in the arts and had died unexpectedly due to an allergic reaction."

Caleb's eyes widened. "That's awful."

Nathan nodded. "Yes, it is very tragic, but there was something about the story that touched my heart. This girl had been an organ donor and, as a result, had saved the lives of several people. Everyone I talked to about her said she had been so full of life, and had been inspiring to so many." He leaned forward and put his elbows on the table. "Caleb, the more I learned about this girl, the more intrigued I became. Most of us spend the entirety of our adult lives trying to find our place in the world, trying to matter. This thirteen-year-old child touched so many hearts in her short life, and her story is touching lives still. It got to me."

"So, you wrote a play about it?"

"Yes. It's an artistic approach at telling her story. I wanted to do it like a remembrance, a tribute of sorts. I've already found my leading lady. She's an amazingly talented girl, and I'm pretty sure I can take care of the other young cast members in the play, but I wanted to tell the story from the characters' adult perspective. Like, years later, all of her old friends had gotten together again to reminisce. I wanted to show how their lives had been affected or changed because of their friend."

"Sounds like a good idea."

"The only problem is, I don't want just any old actors to play these parts. They need to be special."

Caleb frowned. "Special as in...?"

"I'm not sure," he huffed. "That's just it. I'm no good at looking at a person and seeing that little spark of genius. That was always your forte."

Caleb raised a wary eyebrow. "What are you getting at, Nate?"

"I spoke to Carolyn at Lazy Little Theatre because I know that place has turned out some of the Bay Area's best talent. I don't want to cast this play with seasoned actors who go all diva on me. I want a group of people who have a measure of innocence about them, that special drive and hunger. You know what I mean?"

He nodded. Like Nasarra...

"I'm, of course, having an open call audition in several months, but I wanted there to be some new talent in the mix. New talent with potential. Therefore, I've rented out the YMCA at Point Bonita for a month and a half. Carolyn is going to host a theatre camp for three months."

"Theatre camp?"

"An intensive crash course in the theatre. Acting, dancing, singing, the whole nine yards. The really good ones will be cast in the musical *Seven Brides for Seven Brothers,* to be performed at Lazy Little Theatre at the end of the course. Out of that cast, I want you to pick the people you think are the most promising, and send them to my open audition in New York."

Caleb blinked. "So, that's the favor you're calling in? You want me to watch a play?" Nathan's smirk made him uneasy. He hated when his friend smiled like that. It meant trouble was right around the corner.

"No, no, no, my friend. That's not all. I told you, I need you to find me people with that little extra something. You can't do that by watching a play alone. No, Caleb, I want you teaching the advanced acting portion of the theatre camp."

Caleb's stomach dropped and he felt the color drain out of his face. "No," he said immediately. "I can't. I have to perform at The Curran. I—"

"Relax," Nathan interrupted. "You can still perform on the days you have a show to do, but most of your performances are at night and you will be teaching during the day." He shrugged. "You spend all of your free time at the little theatre anyway. This shouldn't be that different."

Caleb shook his head adamantly. "My answer is no, Nathan. I don't want to teach again."

Nathan snorted. "You're acting like I'm giving you a choice."

Caleb gave him a pained look. "You don't understand. I can't—"

"You can and you will. You owe me. I set you up with your audition for *Phantom.* I'm calling in my favor for this. You don't have an option."

Caleb felt sick, and his heart was doing somersaults in his chest. He hated Nathan in that moment. He knew what he was asking and he didn't care. He knew Caleb wouldn't back out because he was honorable.

He let out a shaky breath and ran a hand through his hair. Nathan sat back in his chair with a victorious smile, and Caleb wanted to throw up. The last thing he wanted to do was teach anything ever again. His friend was twisted, and he really, really loathed him right then.

Chapter Five

Several days later found Caleb parked out in front of Nasarra's duplex, his motorcycle idling as he wondered just what on earth he thought he was doing. He'd been out of sorts since grudgingly accepting to teach at the theatre camp, and aside from performing at night, had been next to useless. All of his friends at *Phantom* were getting sick of his moping and brooding moodiness. He didn't blame them. They had no idea what kind of turmoil was going on inside of his head. All they knew was that he was being temperamental and pissy.

A friend of his was starring in a production of *Arsenic and Old Lace* at one of the local theatres in town, and he'd planned to go see it alone, but for some reason, he found himself sitting outside of Nasarra's place. He knew she'd probably love to go, and although he didn't know why, he felt like her company might soothe some of his chaotic feelings. He'd thoroughly enjoyed spending time with her that night at The Grand Café, and he had no doubt that she could turn an otherwise ordinary night into something amazing.

So... Why was he just idling?

He felt anxious as he sat there, not to mention a little more than stupid. Why was he just sitting there like a terrified teenager? He was wasting all of his gas. If he was going to sit there he may as well at least turn off his engine. He turned the ignition and let out a heavy sigh, sitting back against the seat. This was ridiculous on so many levels. He felt stupid for sitting out there, trying to get up the nerve to go inside. It was only a play, for crying out loud. It wasn't like he was taking her to the Eiffel Tower to propose. It wasn't even technically a date. But he was viewing it as such despite what he tried to tell himself.

He felt stupid for wanting to consider it a date when he knew he shouldn't. He had made himself a promise years ago not to ever get involved with another actress, but he felt stupid for even sticking to that rule. What kind of person made rules for their life like some kind of instruction manual? Like anybody could really control what happened in their life. In the grand scheme of things, no one really had control over much.

Most of all, he felt stupid for sitting out there on his motorcycle like a stalker, contemplating why he felt stupid when there was, hopefully, a gorgeous redhead inside who could make him forget his problems for awhile.

Using this as a deciding factor, he slung his leg over his bike, forcing himself to try and look calm as he approached her door. He took a deep breath and knocked, wondering just what it was about this woman that made him feel so flustered.

Rafe answered the door, but at least he wasn't in his skivvies. That image would haunt him for the rest of his life. He was holding a bowl of something that looked like cold macaroni and cheese.

"Hey," Caleb greeted with a smile.

Rafe frowned thoughtfully. "Do I know you?"

"You met me once, but you were kind of asleep at the time."

Rafe grinned. "Oh yeah! That night after the play. You were with Red. Come on in." He held the bowl out to him. "Want some?"

Caleb cringed. "Uh...no, thanks." He stuffed his hands into his pockets and took a quick look around the place. It was pieced together with nothing that matched and everything seemed, not messy, but in slight disarray. He smiled. It looked exactly like his apartment in New York had looked. He noticed that creative people tended to be more than a little disheveled. They had so much going on in their head, they didn't have time to do mundane things like organize their paperwork or put the laundry away.

"So, what was your name again?" Rafe asked.

Caleb turned his gaze back to the Frenchman. "Caleb," he answered. "Is Nasarra home, by chance?"

With a great clatter, Nasarra suddenly came flying out

from her room and crashed into the storage closet directly across from it. Her shoulder slammed into the door and Rafe turned toward the racket with a frown.

"Sonofa!" She righted herself and scowled at the object that had apparently tripped her. She pushed back her fly-away hair and muttered something under her breath about Rafe leaving his weights in the doorway to her bedroom.

Rafe stifled a laugh and turned back to the television.

Caleb smiled at her, thinking it was adorable that she was flushed. "Hey there," he greeted. "You're home."

She gave a nervous laugh. "Yeah." She attempted to smooth her hair again and frowned. "What are you doing here?"

He shrugged. "I was in the neighborhood." At her skeptically raised eyebrow, he chuckled. "No, actually, a friend of mine is in a production of *Arsenic and Old Lace.* I was going to see it tonight and I thought maybe you'd like to go with me." His did his best to give her an engaging smile.

She stared at him then started to chew on her bottom lip. "Um..." She threw a glance over at Rafe.

"Go, Red," he said without bothering to look away from whatever it was he was watching.

She grinned and looked back at Caleb. "Well, I have to work kind of early tomorrow and—"

"Go, Red," Rafe repeated.

Caleb chuckled. "I think he wants you to go."

She scrunched up her face. "I'm getting that feeling too." She put one hand on her hip and frowned. "You're very spontaneous, aren't you?"

"I can be."

"Ok, let me grab my purse and a jacket." She disappeared into her room for a few more seconds, then returned and threw a goodbye to Rafe as they walked out.

"I only have my Harley," Caleb said as they approached his bike. "I hope you don't mind."

She snorted and gave him a look that screamed, *Gimme a break, dummy.* "Yeah right," she said. "I'm *really* going to mind riding through the city on the back of a motorcycle."

He grinned. "All right then." He handed her a spare helmet. "Let's get going." He climbed on and started it up, liking how her arms snaked around his waist to hold on. It was a much better sensation than the grip of that last woman who had been behind him. "Ready?" he called back to her.

"Yeah, let's go!"

He chuckled. Her enthusiasm was sexy, and contagious. The part of him that had been dark and sullen lifted as he sped off down the street, and he knew he'd made the right decision in asking her out.

* * *

The theatre Caleb took them to was not a grandiose, elegant theatre like The Curran had been. It was good sized and nice, perfect for a large local production, or maybe for a touring ballet. Nasarra studied the layout, remembering high school, and smiled.

"What are you thinking about?" Caleb asked, catching her look of joy.

She turned her head to meet his eyes as they waited for the play to begin. She was still having a hard time getting her heart to beat normally. She'd almost gone into cardiac arrest when she'd heard him talking to Rafe. When he hadn't come looking for her at work, she'd figured she would never see him again. It had been more than a shock to see him in her living room. "Oh, I was just remembering the plays I did in high school. Even though our high school theatre was much smaller than this, the way it's set up kind of reminds me of it."

He smiled. "Were you in all the plays?"

She grinned devilishly and nodded. "And don't forget after school theatre and dance. I even helped the director of my acting workshop with some of the younger kid classes and with stage work. He used me as a techie several times and even taught me how to run the lights and sound."

"It's refreshing to listen to you talk, Nasarra," he said.

She frowned. "Oh yeah? How so?"

"Your love of the theatre makes me remember how I felt when I first started acting. The passion, the fire. You hold all of that inside you and I see it shine in your eyes when you speak." He touched one of her wayward curls. "It's sexy."

Her face turned hot and she looked down, giving another one of those breathy laughs she hated herself for. "Never thought an obsession could be sexy."

His smile was dark and enigmatic. He leaned toward her

so his mouth was close to her ear. "Some obsessions are," he whispered. "Dangerously so."

She swallowed hard and was grateful that the lights in the house suddenly dimmed, indicating the start of the show. Caleb pulled away with a soft chuckle, and she exhaled a long, slow breath. The man sitting next to her was wicked. Wicked and delightful.

Her attention was suddenly wrenched from the stage as she felt a touch against her hand. She looked down to see Caleb caress her fingers with his tentatively, as if asking her permission. She smiled and a delicious shock went through her body. She touched her fingers with his in like kind. At this, he slipped his whole hand over hers and she turned hers to fit with his. She smiled shyly, still staring at the stage, feeling very girlish and giddy. His hand was warm, strong, masculine. How long had it been since she had been close to a man other than Rafe? High school? Geez...she really was a loser.

After the play, Caleb and Nasarra waited for the other audience members to clear out, talking about what they had enjoyed in the production. When most everyone had left, Caleb turned to her with a grin. "Would you like to go back-stage?"

Her eyebrows shot up in the air. "Yes!" she shouted.

He chuckled and stood, offering his hand again. He led her up the stairs onto the stage and around the curtain to the wings. Techies were busy putting away props and gave Caleb confused glances as he nonchalantly made his way to the back door. He pushed it open and Nasarra glanced around her in wonder as she followed him down the hall toward the dressing rooms. All of the walls were painted beige and the floor was plain white tile. The building looked old, and she wondered how many productions it had seen. How many dancers and actors had walked across the very floor she was walking across?

As if in answer to her question, the wall at the far end of the hallway was, more or less, a gigantic mural painted with the logos of the different productions that had passed through. Signatures of the cast members circled them and she walked toward it as if in a mesmerized trance. "Caleb, look," she breathed, touching the one of the ballet *Giselle*. "Look at all these productions."

He smiled. "That's not even half of them," he said. "This theatre has been around for quite some time. Only the larger productions sign the wall."

She looked up at him. "Have you ever signed it?"

"No. I have never performed in this theatre."

She turned back to the wall and studied it in awe. All of these people. They were all doing what she wanted to do. They were all living their dream. They had left their mark. They were not just one of the masses... Not like her.

"Caleb Makepeace, is that you?" a boisterous voice called.

Nasarra and Caleb both turned to see a blond man of about Caleb's age coming toward them. He had a very square face and his eyes were pale blue and friendly. Nasarra recognized him as Mortimer Brewster from the play.

Caleb grinned. "Connor Douglas," he said. "You look just as ugly as ever."

Connor let out a loud peal of laughter and the two shared a brotherly embrace. "I should have known it was you wandering around back here. One of the techies just came running in here saying that a strange man and woman came backstage. You're the only one I know with that much audacity. Mr. I've Been To Broadway. Think you own all the theatres now, huh?"

Caleb laughed and gave a playful shrug.

Connor chuckled. "How have you been, buddy? I haven't seen you in ages!"

"I'm good," Caleb replied. "I'm back home now, actually. Performing at The Curran."

Connor raised an eyebrow. "You're in *Phantom?*" He shook his head. "Man, Caleb, you get around. The last time I talked to you, you were somewhere in, what was it, Oklahoma touring with *Cats,* and before that you were rivaling Donny Osmond in *Joseph,* weren't you?"

Caleb laughed again. "I wouldn't go quite that far. I was only in that play for six months. Donny Osmond made the role his."

Connor smiled then glanced at Nasarra, catching and holding her eye. "So, are you going to tell me who this beautiful woman is, or can I make a move on her?"

Nasarra blushed and looked down bashfully.

Caleb shook his head. "What is wrong with me? I'm

sorry. Connor, this is Nasarra. Nasarra, this is Connor, the friend I came to see tonight."

She extended her hand and Connor pumped it with enthusiasm. "Nice to meet you."

"Connor used to manage a small local theatre company here in the city. It's called Lazy Little Theatre. Have you heard of it?"

Nasarra shook her head.

Connor smiled. "I miss it there. Carolyn's doing an awesome job, though."

"I'm at Lazy a lot. I help out," Caleb added.

"Yeah, Carolyn contacted me and asked if I would help her with this drama camp thing going on up at Point Bonita." He held his hands out to the sides. "I have no idea what it is. I'm supposed to talk to her about it tomorrow."

Caleb gave Connor a meager smile.

"Well, I need to get out of this makeup before it glues permanently to my face," Connor said, "but why don't we go out and get some coffee when I'm done? I'd like to catch up."

"Sure, we'll go wait out on the stage. That way I don't frighten any more members of your stage crew."

Connor laughed. "All right. I'll see you in ten minutes or so."

Caleb nodded and began to lead Nasarra back toward the front of the theatre. Most of the techies had vacated and Nasarra stopped to stare out across the empty stage. The set was still up, but the curtain had been drawn down in front of it, leaving just the lip open and bare. She bit her bottom lip and a great joy welled up inside of her like a geyser ready to blow. She grinned and, without warning, ran out across it and did a leap, followed by two *pique* turns and then some *foites*.

Caleb stood back and folded his arms, watching her with a smile on his lips. She did an attitude turn and stopped with a giggle, turning to face the empty audience.

Years of experience flooded back to Nasarra as she stared out at the vacant seats. She grinned, feeling like she had come home. The stage was where she was meant to be. It had always been so. She held her arms up in the air and words she had forgotten she even knew flew out of her mouth. "You do me mischief! Fie, Demetrius! Your wrongs to set a scandal on my sex: we cannot fight for love as men may do: We should be woo'd and were not made to woo. I'll follow thee, and make a heaven of hell, to die upon the hand I love so well."

Caleb grinned broadly and applauded, walking across the stage to meet her.

Nasarra blushed and looked down, realizing how silly she must look.

"*A Midsummer Night's Dream,*" he said. "So, you're a Shakespeare girl, are you?"

She nodded enthusiastically. "Of course! What actor isn't? He's, like, the founding father of the craft!" She sat down on the edge of the stage and sighed. "We did *A Midsummer Night's Dream* when I was a senior. We always did at least one Shakespeare play a year." She looked up at him as he came to sit beside her. "And every year we had actors come to our school who belonged to the Oregon Shakespeare Company in Ashland, Oregon. They would do workshops for my drama class."

He smiled. "Ashland has a wonderful Shakespeare Festival."

"My drama class took a trip to Ashland every year to see the plays. It took forever to get there, but it was always so much fun. Just a bunch of theatre geeks wandering around Ashland like we owned it, feeling invincible." She laughed. "Sneaking out of our hotel rooms when the chaperones went to sleep and having sordid adventures involving boys and alcohol."

Caleb raised an eyebrow. "You snuck out to drink and make out on your theatre trip?"

She giggled and shook her head. "Not me. I was always too scared. I knew I'd be the one to end up getting caught and then I'd never be able to go again. It was too important to me. Besides, I wanted to get a good night's sleep so I could give the actors the attention they deserved when I watched the plays. I didn't want to be nodding off and hungover."

He grinned and reached out to tuck back one of her ever-unruly curls. Her stomach clenched. She loved when he did that. The simplest gesture, yet it was so divine.

Her smile fell and she looked down. "I can't stand it sometimes," she said suddenly. "I mean, I don't regret sacrificing my goals to help my family, but there are times... Like now, here I am on this stage and I feel like it's where I belong. I feel more at home here than I do at my own place. It's like I'm meant to be here."

Caleb sighed and rubbed his hand across her shoulders in a gesture of comfort. "Nasarra, you *are* meant to be here," he said. "If you feel it still, it's still the case. You just lost your way. All you need is to get back on the right path."

She felt tears prick at her eyes again, but she forced them away. She wished she could believe his kind words, but life wasn't that simple. "How did you end up getting such an early start at your career?" she asked. "I mean, you were in a touring production when you were ten."

"That was luck," he stated. He chuckled. "When I was a little kid I was always very dramatic. Ask my mother. Half the time she would find me standing on the kitchen table with a spatula in my hand and a mixing bowl on my head, singing."

Nasarra laughed. "A mixing bowl?"

"I have no idea why. I guess I thought it was hip or something." He shook his head and laughed. "And I would always sneak into my mom's sewing room and steal her supplies. When she would come into my room, all of my solider dolls were clad in frightening, haphazard sequined numbers."

She laughed so hard her stomach began to hurt.

"I'm sure she was seriously concerned about my sexual orientation for awhile."

Nasarra wiped at the tears that were coming out her eyes at the picture he painted. "I would have been concerned too!"

"So, she finally decided to enroll me in this theatre class for kids. She was hoping it would help contain all my creative energy, I think. It all went from there. I loved it. It was my niche and my calling. I was there almost as much as I was at school. I was always involved in the student plays. The director was the one who told my mom about the *Oliver* audition. I begged her for two whole weeks to let me try out. She finally gave in, and the rest is history. I toured with the musical for a year and went into home schooling, but afterwards, my parents told me that there would be no more show business until I had a diploma. They wanted me to have a proper education in a public school. So, I just continued to do what you did. Drama in high school, acting and dance on the side, choir."

She kicked her feet absently over the side of the stage and smiled. "And do you still make pretty costumes for your army men?" she teased.

He rolled his eyes. "No, I grew out of that around my junior year. It was hurting my reputation with the ladies."

She laughed, loving how easy he was to talk to, how comfortable she felt around him. She had been in awe of Caleb for years, even more so since she'd met him in person, but some of the worship she had viewed him with was beginning to dissipate as he became more three-dimensional, more of a real person and not just an icon. She genuinely enjoyed his company and was beginning to think that she would rather banish her childhood fantasy of him altogether if she could just continue to get to know the real man.

"Okay, you guys, ready to go?"

Connor came striding across the stage, and Caleb and Nasarra stood up and followed him out of the theatre. Caleb and Connor lapsed into reminiscent conversation. Nasarra just listened, understanding that they hadn't seen one another in a long time. She smiled and her heart felt warm as Caleb reached out to take her hand in his as they walked. It made her feel like she was part of the group, like he *wanted* her to be part of the group, and that was a feeling she wanted to hold onto forever.

Chapter Six

Max's was getting slammed. She hadn't seen so many people at dinner since she'd started working there. "Table five is irate!" she shouted to one of the cooks as she retrieved an order. "The guy says he's been waiting for a half an hour for his food!" She didn't give the cook a chance to respond. She just grabbed her plates and whirled back out of the kitchen.

She hadn't heard from Caleb at all since he'd taken her to the play, and that had been well over a week ago. It bummed her out. She'd really started to like him and she'd entertained herself with the idea that he might like her also. But apparently, he had just found some other pretty girl that was more interesting than her. The possibility saddened her, for Caleb had made her feel strong and powerful and capable of moving mountains to get where she wanted to go. He'd actually made her think for a split second that she might be able to resurrect her dreams. His words had made her believe in herself once again, but now she was no longer the famous Broadway star she had allowed herself to picture a week ago as she'd sat with Caleb and Connor. She was back to being plain, boring Nasarra Williams, salesperson and waitress. That was all she was and all she would ever be. It hurt.

She probably shouldn't have done all of those crazy dance steps across the stage and started spouting Shakespeare. She'd probably made herself look like a fool.

A dull ache had settled into Nasarra's heart and she knew of only one thing that would make it lessen. It was the only thing that ever made her feel any better. Being on stage. She glanced around the restaurant and let her eyes linger on the piano and microphone where the employees would sing.

It was busy, but she could afford to take a fifteen-minute to entertain the customers.

She looked over to the entrance as the door opened and grinned as she saw Rafe walk in. She waved, her mood brightening momentarily.

Rafe smiled and went over to her. "Hey, Red," he greeted. "I was bored and we have no food so I thought I'd come by and say hello...and get something to eat."

She grabbed his arm and pulled him toward the piano area. "Come on," she said. "Sing a duet with me."

His eyes bulged. "I beg your pardon?"

"You're just in time," she continued. "I was going to sing. Now you can sing with me."

"Are you insane? I can't sing!" he cried.

"Sure you can," she assured.

He shook his head frantically as she continued to drag him along. "I can't! I-I'm French! I don't know much English!"

Nasarra frowned at him. "Give me a break. You speak better English than I do." She reached the piano and left Rafe standing petrified behind her. She told the man at the piano that she wanted to sing "A Little Fall of Rain" from *Les Miserables*.

Rafe started to shake his head even more emphatically. "I don't even know that song!"

Nasarra barely glanced at him. "Read the words on the sheet music," she instructed. "I've heard you sing at home. You have a good ear and you're always improvising with my showtunes. Come on, I can't waste a lot of time waiting for you to grow some balls. I'm not supposed to be doing this as it is." She picked up the microphone and began to sing her part. She knew that Rafe wouldn't chicken out and leave her there to look like a fool. He was an exhibitionist. He tap danced on Market Street and painted in the buff. He was as much of a performer as she was.

When it came time for Rafe's part and she turned to where he had been standing, her eyes widened and her heart felt as if it had plummeted into her feet. Rafe was off to the side, looking very much relieved, and approaching her was... She swallowed hard. It was Caleb. She stared at him and felt the color drain from her face.

He grinned and began to sing.

Nasarra's eyes focused on him and she sang the song mechanically. Her mouth moved, but she was no longer aware of any sound coming out. The enormous echo of her heart drowned out any other audible noise. As the song ended, she felt the need to do something to prove herself because she was sure that her voice had come out forced and squeaky.

Caleb put his microphone back into the stand and took his place at a nearby table while Nasarra told the man at the piano that she wanted to sing "With One Look" from *Sunset Boulevard*. She turned back to the audience with trembling hands and sang to the best of her ability.

When she had finished, everyone applauded loudly and she bowed, flushed and somewhat embarrassed. She pushed her hair and glanced at Rafe. He grinned and winked at her. She let out a shaky breath then held her finger up to Caleb, indicating she would be with him in just a minute. He nodded and she bolted.

The man was insane. That was all there was to it. She ran to the kitchen, retrieved the food she'd had back up while she was singing, and rushed it to her waiting tables. When all of her customers were satisfied, she made her way back to Caleb, who was talking to Rafe.

"Nasarra!" Caleb exclaimed with a grin as he saw her approach.

She cut him off. "You pop up in the strangest places!" she cried. "And always when I least expect it! You scared me half to death!"

His eyes softened. "I'm sorry, I didn't mean to scare you. I just wanted to surprise you."

"Well, mission accomplished."

He chuckled. "All things aside, do you have any idea how well you sing? You have the most beautiful voice I have ever heard!"

"Oh get out," she spat.

He shook his head. "I'm serious! Your voice is so powerful! You could fill the entire Curran Theatre without a microphone!"

She stared at him. She'd been doing a lot of that lately. Staring... "You really think so?"

He nodded. "Look, I wanted to talk to you about something. When do you get off?"

She looked down at her watch. "Ten minutes."

"Nasarra, go," one of her co-workers called. "I've got you covered."

Nasarra looked back at her and grinned. "Oh my gosh, Jackie, you're the best! Thank you!"

Jackie grinned and waved her away.

Caleb smiled at her. "Excellent. Will you walk with me?"

She nodded and turned to follow Caleb out the door, waving at Rafe as she did so. They were instantly blasted with the lights from the plaza around which Max's was situated and the crisp night air attacked her bare arms. She shivered, wishing she had remembered to bring her jacket. She crossed her arms in a futile attempt to keep warm and walked slowly next to Caleb. "Where in the world did you come from?" she asked, shaking her head. "I didn't even see you come in."

"I came in when you were getting ready to sing. I saw Rafe standing up there looking ill and I thought that I would relieve him. I didn't even get to wave hello before he shoved the microphone into my hand and ran behind me like I was a shield." He laughed. "You should have seen the look on your face, Nasarra! You looked like someone had shot you."

"Well what did you expect?" she cried. "I haven't seen or heard from you in a week and, all of a sudden, you appear out of nowhere to sing *Les Mis* tunes with me?"

"I always loved that play," he mused.

She frowned. "Caleb, you're missing the point here."

He grinned down at her.

"Weren't you supposed to be performing tonight?"

"The play ends at nine-thirty. I..." He sighed and held his arms out helplessly. "Well, let's face it, Nasarra. I couldn't get you out of my head. I just blazed out of there and got here as fast as I could."

Nasarra said nothing. He couldn't get her out of his head? Well, he hadn't missed her enough to think of her up until now. She rubbed her arms again and shivered. Warm, black leather suddenly encompassed her shoulders and the smell of cinnamon invaded her nostrils. She breathed it in and closed her eyes. "Thank you," she murmured, "but I don't want you to freeze."

Caleb shook his head. "I'll be fine. Cold air does me good." He glanced down at her again with that devilish smile playing on his lips. "Especially when I'm walking next to such a beautiful woman."

She blushed furiously. "How come I haven't heard from you until now?" she blurted. Maybe if she pretended to be annoyed she wouldn't focus on how arousing he was.

"Things have been insane lately. That's part of what I want to talk to you about. Nasarra..." He stopped walking and took her by the shoulders, turning her to face him. "I have a feeling about you."

She arched an eyebrow. "A feeling?"

He nodded. "How serious are you about attaining that goal of yours?"

"What are you talking about?"

"Granted, I haven't really seen you act, but I have seen you recite a Shakespearean monologue with an awful lot of passion, and I know you dance well enough to hold your own. Not to mention, you have a phenomenal voice."

She crossed her arms. "Caleb, what are you getting at?"

He took a breath. "Lazy Little Theatre is hosting a grueling three month long theatre camp. Master classes on acting, singing and dancing will take place every day for about a month and a half up at Point Bonita. At the end of that month and a half, there will be an audition for the musical *Seven Brides for Seven Brothers.* Only the best will make it in. Out of that cast, several actors will be chosen to go to an open call audition in New York for a new play."

Nasarra stared—again—and a tingling sensation washed over her in a wave. "New York?" she whispered.

He nodded. "I want you to go to the theatre camp. I think you have a shot."

Her awestruck look morphed into a frown. "I can't spend all my time up at Point Bonita, Caleb. I have to work! Besides, you really don't even know how well I'd do. You're just going off of a hunch."

He shook his head and put his hands on her shoulders. "Nasarra, listen to me. I don't know you that well, and you're right, I've never seen you in action, but I know one thing. You speak about theatre with such passion. That doesn't come from nowhere. That comes from someone who has stood on the stage, who has heard the applause, who has tasted the personal glory that can only come with a curtain call. You did improvised dance steps across a random stage, for crying out loud!"

She felt her cheeks flush with color. She still couldn't believe she had just let loose like that.

"Nasarra, if you have a dream, follow it. Perhaps you have had some setback, some bumps in your road to success, but that doesn't mean you have to brush your dream aside like a meaningless thought. If all you hear is music, play it. If all you see is stars, be an astronomer. If you love toilets, be a plumber."

Nasarra laughed in spite of herself.

Caleb chuckled and continued. "And if you love to sing and act,"—he took her face in his hands gently and stared into her eyes as if to make sure she understood what he was saying—"be on Broadway."

She sighed. "You make it sound very romantic, Caleb, and I'm sure that would be wonderful in a paperback novel, but it doesn't make sense in my life anymore. I don't have room for it."

He shook his head. "I refuse to hear you say that. Nasarra, I have known actors with so much skill that they could have been one of the greats, but they could never do it. You know why? Because they lacked something. They lacked passion. The passion *you* have. The passion I see radiating from your eyes whenever you mention the theatre. It would be such a terrible waste to see that passion die. I imagine you would be spectacular to see."

She couldn't even formulate words. How could a person she barely knew have so much faith in her? It was overwhelming. She frowned in thought as she let herself consider his proposition for just a second, then she shook her head. "Okay, how much does this camp thing cost?"

He waved it away. "That doesn't matter."

She raised her eyebrows. "Doesn't matter? Oh, so a bunch of actors are going to master classes for free?"

He sighed. "No. A lot of people are being bussed in and are staying at the dorms while the camp is going on because they are not local. It's just like a summer camp, only for adults."

Her eyes narrowed. "So, only the local actors are free?"

He heaved another sigh and rolled his eyes. "No—"

"Then tell me how much it is, Caleb!"

"Nasarra!" He slashed the air with his hands. "Look, it

doesn't matter, okay? I have the ability to get you in without any kind of fee so just do it, would you?"

She snorted. "It's not possible. I work almost every single day, sometimes double shifts! If I don't work, Rafe and I don't eat. I can't let him just fend for himself. He's my roommate and my friend. It's not an option." Even as she said the words, her heart ached in her chest. Here was someone handing her a chance at what she'd always wanted, and she was flinging it aside to be responsible. Life sucked.

Caleb let out a ragged breath and scowled at her. "You're trying my patience," he grumbled.

She folded her arms and knew all too well that her facial expression was all attitude. "Poor baby."

He stared at her for a second, then gave a soft chuckle and shook his head. "You're a little infuriating, aren't you?"

She gave a nonchalant shrug. "I'm a redhead *and* I'm part Puerto Rican."

He nodded and raised his eyebrows. "That would do it."

She giggled and some of her stubborn bravado melted away.

"Look..." He took her face in his hands and stepped closer, gazing down into her eyes. "I'm not good at a whole lot of things, but I *am* good at recognizing talent when I see it. I would absolutely hate to see yours go to waste when I know in my heart that you could be something spectacular." She opened her mouth to speak, but he shook his head and shushed her. "Just think about it."

She bit her bottom lip and drew in a shaky breath. He was so close...

He smiled and placed one arm around her waist to pull her closer. He took a flyaway curl and wrapped it around his finger. "I love your hair," he murmured. "It's beautiful."

His nearness made her aware of the intense warmth that coursed through her body. "You like it even though it makes me infuriating?"

He grinned. "Especially because it makes you infuriating." He rested his forehead against hers and sighed.

She closed her eyes and tried to rein in her wild heartbeat. She hadn't been this close to a man in ages. Since high school, relationships were something she never had time for. Romance was something she never had time for. If anyone had ever wanted to date her, she had been unaware of it.

Her mind had been too busy with other things. She was glad it had silenced its troubled thoughts now. She liked being this close to someone.

Without thinking, she placed her hands on his chest and ran them slowly up to his shoulders, feeling the texture of his body beneath his shirt.

Caleb drew his breath in sharply and closed his eyes for a moment. When he opened them again, his gaze met hers with burning intensity, and he pressed her against him so that the length of her body was aligned with his. "You're bewitching me," he whispered. He tilted her head and cradled her cheek in his palm while he pressed a slow, unhurried kiss to the line of her jaw.

Nasarra closed her eyes and sighed in bliss.

"Promise me you'll think about it."

She giggled. "You're relentless."

He raised his head and smiled at her. "Absolutely." He tangled his fingers in her hair again. "Promise."

She sighed in surrender and nodded, her eyes focusing on his beautifully sculpted lips. "I'll think about it."

"Good." He brought his face close to hers. He lingered there for a moment, caressing her skin with his thumb and igniting her entire body with his taunting hints at an impending kiss. Slowly, he lowered his lips to hers.

Something like an electrical current shot through Nasarra and she twined her arms around his neck. His kiss was full of gentle, tender passion. In a world where she had only known failure and coldness, Caleb's warmth and compassion was like a soothing balm to her broken spirit. She kissed him back with equal feeling, loving the enchanting velvet sensation of his lips and his touch. She wondered for a moment how she could have gone most of her life without having this. She had been cheating herself.

She made a happy noise in her throat as he moved his lips over hers and trailed his hands down her back to press her even closer. Shockwaves coursed throughout her body at the contact. What she knew of Caleb thus far had been playful and gentle, but she got the impression that there was a strong undercurrent of dark passion and strength. It was arousing on the highest level.

He pulled his lips off of hers with a sigh and placed his forehead back against hers. His shoulders drooped and he closed his eyes as if he felt ashamed.

Nasarra frowned. "Are you all right?"

He shook his head and looked up at her. "Forgive me, Nasarra," he murmured. "I shouldn't have done that."

Whoa there! Stop the truck! Back up! She was really confused. Had she or had she not just shared in a really hot kiss with the man in front of her? Why was he apologizing? "Why not?"

His eyes reflected so much emotion that she couldn't decipher, but she could detect sadness in the midst of the turmoil. "I like you," he said. "I really do...and I care about you."

She really didn't understand. "I like you too, Caleb..." She shook her head. "Listen, I'm really kind of lost here..."

"I don't want to hurt you," he said. "I *won't* hurt you."

"You aren't making any sense." This was aggravating. *Ten points for awesome kiss. Minus ten for completely messing with my head.*

"I know, Nasarra." He averted his eyes for a moment and looked like he was waging some kind of war with himself. "I'm not very good at this. All I know is that I like you, I *really* liked kissing you, and that terrifies me."

She blinked. *Minus ten more points for obvious emotional baggage.* Dang it, the pluses and the minuses were starting to equal out.

He let out a frustrated growling noise. "I'm really sorry. I blew it on more than one level. I should have just kept my mouth shut."

She waved it away. "Oh come on, Caleb. Don't beat yourself up. We all have issues." She smiled, hoping to make him feel better. "For what it's worth, I enjoyed the kiss." Even though the romanticism had been completely obliterated.

He gave a forced chuckle. "That's what I was afraid of." She frowned, but he shook his head. "Don't worry about it. It's my problem, not yours. Let me walk you home?"

He held his hand out to her and she took it, deciding to let the kissing subject drop. She had freakish insecurity issues about her sister. Obviously, Caleb had some issues with something in his past. That was okay. So long as they weren't all-consuming, issues were livable. She wouldn't write him off just yet. She'd be the world's biggest imbecile if she did. He would tell her when he was ready. In all reality, she didn't know him that well, regardless of how comfortable she felt with him.

As they walked, she let her mind hash over his offer to join the theatre camp. She ached to be able to do it, but she really couldn't figure out how it was possible. As much as she would love to not care about finances and rent, they were necessities. She really didn't see how she could get around them...

Chapter Seven

"You need to do it, Red."

Nasarra rolled her eyes as she tried in vain to pick up some of the junk strewn across the living room. "We've been over this, Rafe. You pounding your opinion into my head is not going to change the fact that I work too much to have time to go to this theatre camp."

He snorted and folded his arms. "Well, you'll just have to quit one of your jobs."

She made a slow turn and stared at him. "Yeah, and I don't really fancy the thought of being homeless, thanks." She pitched a pillow onto the couch in irritation.

He sighed. "You're not going to be homeless... Would you stop?"

She ignored him and bent down to pick up some candy wrappers off the floor.

"Nasarra!"

That got her attention. She stood straight and spun to face him. He *never* called her by her name. It was always Red.

"Stop," he commanded. "Listen to me. You can quit your job at Macy's. I know how much you hate working there. Change your shift at Max's to work only at night. Then you can go to the theatre camp."

"But—"

He held his hand up. "You have worked your butt off to keep a roof over our heads so that I only have to work part time. You've given me the opportunity to pursue my passion of being an artist. You've taken care of me since I met you. You're always taking care of people, always doing things for anyone but yourself. For once, let me take care of you."

She frowned in confusion.

"The other night when I was at Max's, I spoke to the manager about a job. I haven't said anything because I didn't know if they'd hire me, but they called me last night. I start on Monday."

Nasarra's eyes widened. "You got a job?"

He smiled. "Yeah."

"But what about your painting? That means everything to you—"

He held his hand up again. "Red, I can always find time to paint. Besides, I just sold three of my paintings to this really rich lady." He chuckled. "I can cover us for awhile."

Her eyes bulged. "Oh!" She put her hands over her mouth. "Rafe, that's fantastic!"

He grinned. "You enabled me to reach my goal, Red. Let me help you reach yours."

She stared at him in awe and wonder, her heart filling with tremendous affection. "Rafe, I don't even know what to say..." She shook her head. "What am I talking about? We need to go celebrate!" She clapped her hands. "We'll go to that bar up the street. The one with the fireplace." She started toward her bedroom to change. "I'll call Amanda." She poked her head back around the corner. "I really hope you don't mind buying the drinks."

He laughed. "It's fine."

She grinned and ran back into her room to find something suitable to wear. Joy was raging through her like a tidal wave. To think that she could actually go to the theatre camp... She stopped for a minute and digested the information. If she was good enough, if she proved herself, she actually had a shot at a New York audition. Her stomach flopped. Apprehension replaced her happiness. She hadn't done any of the performing arts in so long.

"Hey, yeah, this is Rafe."

Nasarra frowned as she pulled her shirt on over her head and she listened to her roommate. Who was he talking to?

"Yeah, Red and I are going out to celebrate. I just sold three of my paintings to—" He chuckled. "Yeah, thanks. Anyway, and she actually decided to go to that theatre camp so—" He laughed again. "Yeah, I know."

Her frown deepened.

"Anyway, we're going out to celebrate at that bar with the fireplace here on Geary. I forget the name off the top of my head... You know it? You want to meet us there...? Cool! See you soon."

Nasarra finished changing and put her hair up in a clip, then went back out into the living room. "Who were you talking to?" she asked, popping a piece of gum into her mouth.

"Caleb."

She inhaled sharply and sucked her gum down her throat. She started to cough violently.

Rafe raised his eyebrows. "You all right?"

"You called... Caleb?" she wheezed.

"Well, yeah. I figured you'd want to invite him, right?"

She got her coughing fit under control and scowled at him.

He folded his arms. "You like the guy, Nasarra. It's more than obvious. Besides, you left his number on the fridge, plain as day. I had to do it."

She did her best to darken her glower and snatched her purse. "Thanks a lot," she grumbled.

"Happy to help."

She rolled her eyes. "Come on, let's go."

* * *

Amanda heaved a sigh. "I still can't believe you're leaving me all alone," she grumbled. "Now I'll be stuck with Penny, who never shuts up and doesn't have a sensor. She just blurts whatever she's thinking right on out there."

Nasarra laughed and Caleb watched her, loving how she threw her head back. She looked so carefree. There was such a wild spirit about her. He could see it even though it had been tamed and restricted by the trials of life. It came out whenever she was happy, or doing something she enjoyed. If she applied that to her craft, she would be unstoppable.

He took a sip of his drink and slipped his arm around her, wanting to sample part of that unbridled enthusiasm.

She leaned into his body and shook her head. "I'm sorry, Amanda."

Amanda snorted. "No, you're not. You're going to be off acting and dancing while I pick up your slack and listen to Penny tell me about her latest male conquest in full detail."

Nasarra laughed again. "Okay, you're right. I'm not sorry. I do feel bad, though."

Amanda sighed. "Whatever, girlie, but when you become a famous Broadway star, you'd better remember the little people."

"Anybody want anything else to drink?" Rafe asked suddenly. "I'm going to go get me another."

"Ooh me!" Amanda exclaimed with a bright grin.

Rafe smiled down at her, let his eyes linger for a moment, and headed to the bar.

Amanda whirled in her seat to face Nasarra. "Oh my gosh, Nasarra! How come you never told me that your roommate was a total hunk?"

Nasarra looked bewildered and glanced over at Rafe. "He is?"

"He's gorgeous!" She sat back in her chair with an elaborate sigh. "How do you get blessed?"

"Blessed?"

"With the Hottie Patrol! Look at your guy!" She indicated Caleb. "He's like a god! Have you even looked at his butt?"

Caleb felt his face flame and he closed his eyes with a sigh.

Nasarra let out a startled squeal. "Amanda!" she exclaimed. "He's sitting right here!"

Caleb rested his chin in his hand and gave a small, stretched smile.

Amanda shrugged. "So? He probably knows he's hot. What does it matter if *I* say it?"

Nasarra groaned. "Amanda, I don't think you have a sensor either."

She laughed. "Not after three gin and tonics."

"So you're gonna have *another* one?"

Caleb chuckled.

"Here you go, Amanda," Rafe said, handing the drink to her.

Amanda grinned up at him. "Thanks, sexy." She winked and Rafe blushed.

Nasarra rolled her eyes and met Caleb's gaze. He grinned. "Friends are great, aren't they?" he asked.

"Are they? Sometimes I'm not so sure."

He laughed softly and ran a finger along her jaw line. "Tell me something?" he whispered.

She bit her bottom lip and looked up at him from underneath her eyelashes. It was a classically coy feminine move and it set his insides on fire. "What?"

He pulled her closer and leaned in like he had a secret to tell. "*Were* you? Staring at my ass?"

She gasped and he knew his wide grin reflected how devilish he felt in that moment. He chuckled at her shocked expression and couldn't help himself. She was irresistible. He moved in and kissed her without warning.

She made a small squeak of surprise and he pulled her even closer. He'd been having the worst kind of turmoil in his brain lately concerning Nasarra. He thought about her constantly and grew more attached to her every second he was with her. It went against his better judgment, but he was starting to not care. He could deal with the demons from his past on his own. There was no good reason he could think of to not be with her. She was amazing. She made him laugh. She made him feel free and...relaxed.

He hadn't realized it when Craig had said it, but it was true. He had been uptight. It was like he'd forgotten what life felt like to live it. Nasarra made him remember that. She made him remember the love he had for the theatre, his craft, and life in general.

He took her face in his hands and deepened the kiss, giving himself over to the passion she made him feel. Lust. Desire. How long had it been since he'd felt those things?

"Wooo! *Okay!* Rafe, why don't we go over...there?"

Caleb gave a sly grin and opened one eye to look at Rafe and Amanda. Nasarra pulled away, her face a bright shade of crimson, and she smoothed her hair. "Wow...um."

"Look at that fire over there!" Amanda exclaimed, pointing to the fireplace diagonally across from them. "Isn't is pretty, Rafe?"

Rafe smiled shyly. "There are a lot of pretty things in here." He gave her a purposeful glance.

Amanda stared at him for a second, then looked over at Nasarra. "Right, Rafe and I are going over to..." She shot a glance at Rafe. "Explore the fire." She grinned. "You guys have fun." She took her drink and she and Rafe exited.

Nasarra turned shocked eyes up at Caleb. "Caleb!" she exclaimed. "I can't believe you—"

He cut her off by kissing her again. Anything she would have said died on her lips and she surrendered with a sigh, wrapping her arms around his neck. He monopolized her mouth for a few minutes, taking his time, learning what she liked, and absolutely indulging himself. When he pulled back, he grinned and nuzzled his nose against hers.

"Oh man..." she whispered. She shook her head and leaned her forehead against his shoulder.

He chuckled. "What? You've never made out in a bar before?"

She raised her head and gave him a halfhearted scowl. "I haven't made out *period* in who knows how long." She frowned thoughtfully. "Unless my pillow counts."

He frowned in surprise over her confession, as well as the image it created. He squeezed his eyes shut and laughed.

She giggled and her cheeks turned pink. "Man." She brought her hand to her head. "Maybe I should stop drinking too."

He grinned and pulled her close against him in a tight embrace. He closed his eyes and held her, sighing. "You do strange things to me, little girl," he murmured.

She raised her head to look up at him. "It was the crack on the melon." She pointed to her head. "Jostled your brain."

He touched her cheek softly. "No, that wasn't it," he whispered.

She arched an eyebrow. "No?"

"No, it was the first time I ever looked into your eyes. It was hopeless... I was lost."

Her playful smile faded and her eyes filled with warmth. She ducked her head and nestled back into his arms. He smiled and reached up to unclasp her hair clip, sending her red curls spiraling out like a blanket of fire. He grinned and delved his fingers into it. He gave a satisfied sigh. For the first time in far too long, he didn't feel restless. Even the thought of teaching at the theatre camp didn't give him anxiety at the moment. He was completely and totally content.

* * *

San Francisco, present day

Maxim noticed Nasarra's enormous yawn and, as if it was done for the night also, the tape recorder shut off. He frowned and looked at it, disgruntled and annoyed that he hadn't thought to bring another tape. Then again, he hadn't planned on Nasarra's story being so detailed either. It was fantastic. She was even giving him insight into Caleb's thoughts and feelings, which would make writing the script a hundred times easier.

"Oh man, what time is it?" Nasarra looked down at her watch and her eyes bulged. "It's after midnight! I had no idea I could flap my jaws for that long!"

Maxim chuckled. "Well, my tape's done for the night, so do you want to pick up where we left off some time tomorrow?"

"Yeah, I'm sorry. I didn't mean to keep you up so late. I thought sure I'd get through the whole story tonight and I just about talked your head off." She shook her head. "Get me started on reminiscing and look what happens. I must be getting old. Just get me a rocking chair and stick me out on a porch. I'll tell children all my stories about 'the good ol' days'." She waved her hand airily.

Maxim laughed and stood, tucking his tape recorder into his pocket. "It's fine, Nasarra. I like the way you're telling the story. It will make writing it so much easier. Otherwise, I'd have to make up things that might not be true just to make the story flow right and that wouldn't be good. I love the fact that you're giving me Caleb's point of view."

"I figured it would be helpful. Besides, I know everything about him. Telling his perspective is easy."

He pulled his coat on and started to button it up. "Want me to come by at the same time tomorrow night, or...?"

"You know what? I think I'll take the day off tomorrow. My staff can handle the restaurant. Why don't you meet me at Lazy Little Theatre? I can finish telling you the story there."

"Sounds good. See you tomorrow. What time?"

"Come in the morning. I'll bring donuts and coffee or something." She flashed a warm smile.

He nodded, waved, and ducked out of the restaurant. He took the bus back to Torrey's house, pondering over Nasarra's story as he went. At the risk of feeling like a complete girly boy, he adored love stories. They made him feel warm and fuzzy and left him wanting to make love to his wife and shower her with romance. Too bad she was all the way in Oregon and all he had to go to sleep with was a pillow and a fat, orange cat named Mr. Whiskers who had decided to take a liking to him.

Too bad, also, that his wife had decided to be permanently pissed off at him for reasons he couldn't figure out.

He sighed and tried to plot out a rough outline for how the script would go. It should be fairly easy to write.

His mind wandered and he re-hashed what Nasarra had told him. He hated that she'd just left him hanging. He wanted to know about the theatre camp, and whether or not Nasarra had actually made it to the New York audition. He knew that she had done a lot of theatre, but he didn't know what and where. All he knew was what Torrey had told him, which in the grand scheme of things, wasn't that much.

Maxim got off the bus and walked the remaining few blocks to Torrey's house, his hands stuffed in his pockets to ward off the chill of the evening. When he entered, Torrey and Taegen were cuddled on the couch, watching a movie and laughing about something. Maxim sighed, feeling lonelier than ever.

He'd thought the trip to San Francisco would do him some good and get him over his writer's block, but he hadn't realized how much he actually depended on Alyx's company for his sanity, even when she was irritated at him. They never really spent much time apart. He wasn't used to not having her at his side. And, he knew it was stupid, but even though he'd only been there for about a day and a half, he missed her so much his heart hurt. He hadn't felt his heart ache that way in ages.

"Hey, Maxim!" Taegen called as she saw him walk in. "You're getting in late!"

He hung up his coat with a sigh. "Yeah, we lost track of time."

"Did you get everything down?" Torrey asked as he absently played with his wife's blonde hair.

Maxim watched as his friend did the simple gesture, and his heart twinged even more. "No, we have to finish tomorrow. I ran out of tape. You guys are up late."

"Yeah, we're just trying to finish this movie. It's almost over. We'll turn it down so it doesn't bother you," Taegen said as she reached for the remote.

Maxim frowned and held up his hand. "No, don't worry about it. I'm not going to sleep right away anyway. I'll see you guys in the morning."

"'Night, Max," Torrey called.

Maxim headed up the staircase and ran his fingers

through his hair wearily. He flopped down on his bed and kicked off his shoes, his eyes falling on a picture sitting on the entertainment center across from the bed.

It was one of him, Alyx, Javan, Torrey and Taegen before a rock concert they had seen together several years ago. It was during the trip that had inspired his first novel, had changed his entire life, and had won him the heart of the woman he worshipped. It made him smile, and at the same time, made him miss his wife even more.

With a groan, he lay back and covered his eyes with his arm. "Maxim, get a grip," he grumbled. "How lame can you be? You've been here for one freaking day. It's not like you're out of the country." Trying to rationalize his feelings away didn't work and he just ended up making himself feel worse.

He got up, changed his clothes, and checked his cell phone as he got ready for bed. His heart leaped in excitement as he saw that he had a text message from Alyx. *Guess you're still partying it up in the middle of the night. Call me if you can find the time.*

He blinked and the elation he'd felt dissipated. Partying it up? Oh yeah, right, that was *exactly* what he was doing. He rolled his eyes and flung his phone aside before flopping down onto the bed. What was the matter with her? Why all the hostility? It didn't make any sense. He hadn't changed. He still did the same things and acted the same way as when he'd met her. It baffled him, and made him severely uneasy.

He thought about Nasarra's story and remembered back to how it had felt when he'd fallen in love. Alyx had been the most amazing thing to ever grace his life. She still was. He still loved her every bit as much as back then. Had he let the romance slide since being married to her? He didn't think he had, but he couldn't be sure. Had he started taking his precious gift for granted?

He frowned and sat up, setting up his laptop and finding the yellow pages for florists in Ashland. He didn't know why Alyx was upset, but it really didn't matter. Obviously, he had done something wrong so all he could do at this point was make it up to her. He found a number and wrote it down, then vowed to call in the morning and have some roses sent to his beautiful wife.

Chapter Eight

San Francisco, 1997

Nasarra couldn't remember the last time she had been so nervous. She actually wasn't sure if she had *ever* been so nervous. She guided her vehicle slowly around the treacherous curves on the road up to Point Bonita, and was thankful that Amanda had let her borrow her car until she could find a reliable ride. Otherwise, she would have had to take a bus to the Golden Gate and then bike all the way up an incline that would have probably killed her.

She had absolutely no idea what to expect from this theatre camp thing. Caleb had told her it would be fine, that she was just supposed to go to the Bothin Room, which was where the dance class was to be held, and she would be directed from there. Well, that was just great. First of all, she had no idea what or where the Bothin Room was and her stomach was up in her throat at the knowledge that she would be competing against really polished people when she hadn't done any sort of performing in years.

She blew out a breath as she rounded the last corner and pulled into the YMCA parking lot. She'd never even been up to Point Bonita before, and for a brief moment, she forgot about her nerves. Wisps of fog drifted by and everything seemed quiet and undisturbed. Good lord, it was beautiful. Lush and green and...mystical somehow. She could see the Golden Gate and the outline of the city in the distance. It looked like a postcard.

The mist touched her skin as she opened up the car door. She shivered, reached inside to grab her sweater and pulled it on then tugged her backpack out. The wind off the ocean tossed her hair and she looked around to try and decipher where she was supposed to be. Her eyes fell on a group of girls making their way across the parking lot. One of them was blonde and so skinny it was scary. The other two had dark hair and one of them caught Nasarra's attention right away. She was slender and regal-looking with that straight-backed, dancer posture. She had luxurious black hair and walked like she already had the audition in the bag, even though it wasn't for another month.

She shook her head, dismissing the girl, and waved her arm. "Hey!" she called.

The group turned toward her.

Nasarra shut the car door and slung her backpack over her shoulder, jaunting over to the girls. "Sorry, do you guys know where you're going? 'Cause I really don't."

The black-haired girl rolled her eyes. "Of course we know where we're going. Weren't you given directions in your information packet?"

Nasarra chewed on her lip and looked sideways. No, her information packet didn't come with directions. Just really nice lips...

"Well, whatever, just follow us."

The blonde girl hurried after her, but the other brunette hung back and rolled her eyes. "Don't mind her. She's suffering from a seriously bad case of diva syndrome."

Nasarra giggled.

"I'm Laura," she said, extending her hand.

"Nasarra."

"Are you from here?"

She nodded. "Yeah. You?"

Laura shook her head. "I'm from Oregon. I flew here yesterday and caught one of the busses that was transporting people."

"Oh, cool. So you're staying here for the camp?"

She nodded, then laughed. "It's kind of weird, staying in a dorm when you're an adult." She shrugged. "Should be fun, though."

"I'm really nervous. I haven't done this in a long time."

Laura cocked her head and gave an inquisitive frown. "No?"

She shook her head. "I just recently was able to make time in my schedule. I was working myself into the ground."

"Well, all that matters is that you're here. I'm sure every-thing will come back to you."

Nasarra felt a little bit of her apprehension dissipate. She felt an instant sort of camaraderie with Laura and was grate-ful to have a friend. She hated feeling isolated and clueless.

Together, they made their way into one of the two YMCA dorms and Nasarra followed Laura down a long, tiled corridor to a large, green-carpeted room that was next to bursting with people. Most of them were all huddled into selective groups and Nasarra's eyes immediately found the black-haired woman again.

"Oh, there's Danielle," Laura remarked. "I know she's a pain, but at least she's a familiar one. Come on, let's go over there."

Nasarra couldn't really argue with that one. She'd rather stand with someone than no one. It didn't really matter who at this point. She felt like a freshman on her first day of school.

"All right, everybody! Quiet!"

Nasarra jumped as a tall, Amazonian-looking woman clapped her hands to get their attention. Geez... She was taller than Nasarra by a good head and looked like she could be a Roman warrior if she really wanted to. Talk about in-timidating. The buzzing room silenced almost instantly.

"Thank you," the woman continued with a genial smile. "My name is Carolyn Kelly. I'm the owner of Lazy Little Thea-tre and the director of this theatre camp. It's so good to see so many eager faces here. As you know, you will be attend-ing a number of master classes over the course of the next month or so. These classes will be on the subjects of Begin-ning Acting, Advanced Acting, Dance, Voice, and Musical Theatre. You are, of course, required to attend all." A few people tried to voice protest about them being too advanced for beginning acting, but Carolyn silenced them with a wave of her hand. "I don't care how seasoned you are, that's the way the curriculum is set up and that's what you'll be doing. An actor is always learning.

"Now, for those of you who are staying here at the dorms, breakfast and dinner will be provided for you, as well as a sack lunch. Breakfast will be at six a.m. Dinner will be at seven p.m. During the weekends, the bus will make trips into the city for those of you who would like to go.

"I have divided you all up into three different schedules, which you'll see in piles up here on the table next to me. When I am finished, please come select a schedule and make your way to your first class. The morning classes are Advanced Acting, to be held in the outdoor amphitheatre, Musical Theatre, which will be held in here—"

Nasarra noted, for the first time since she'd come in, that a dance floor had been erected in the middle of the room, and mirrors were set up behind her.

"—And Beginning Acting, which will be held in the meeting room listed on your schedule. Each class will run approximately an hour and a half and we will break for lunch. You'll have a half hour for lunch and then we will do our afternoon classes, Voice and Dance. Dance will be held in here and Voice will also be held in a meeting room listed on your schedules. Are we all clear so far?"

Everyone seemed to concur. Nasarra's head started to spin.

"All right. Now, at the end of the month there are going to be auditions for the play *Seven Brides for Seven Brothers*. This play requires skills in all forms of musical theatre. The people cast in that play will move on to the accommodations we have provided for you in the city and you will be working at Lazy Little Theatre from that point on. The play will open two months after that. It will run every night for two weeks. At the end of the run, several people will be selected to travel to New York to participate in an open call audition for a play entitled *Broadway Dreams*."

Murmurs followed and Carolyn held up her hands. "Now before some of you think to yourselves, 'if it's an open call, why do we have to do this? Why can't we just go ourselves?' I'll tell you that a notation will be made on your resume that you are the best out of the theatre camp. Nathan Price himself has set up this camp with the hopes that he will find some actors out of you all."

Nathan Price's name was whispered among the crowd and a shiver went down Nasarra's spine. Nathan Price was one of the best producers and directors in the theatre world. He'd won more Tony Awards than she could count. The play they would be sent to audition for was one of *his*? She shivered again as goose bumps broke out all over her arms.

"All right! Now that business is settled, come get a

schedule and we'll get started!" Carolyn gave a bright smile and the crowd started to swarm the table.

Nasarra meandered forward with Laura and the others.

"Nathan Price!" Laura whispered, grasping Nasarra's arm. "Can you believe it?"

Danielle snorted. "With the amount of money I'm shelling out to be here, it had *better* be Nathan Price," she grumbled. "If I traveled all the way to New York to get cast in some low budget production, I'd be pissed."

Nasarra frowned. Okay, so the girl had herself cast already. Lovely. She rolled her eyes and grabbed a random schedule off the table. "Looks like I have Beginning Acting first. Then Advanced." She shrugged. "That's convenient."

"I have the same as you," Laura supplied.

"I have Musical Theatre first," Danielle replied. "And Advanced Acting with you guys."

Laura shrugged and looked at Danielle over her shoulder. "Well, we have to go, but we'll see you in Advanced!" She waved and didn't give Danielle time to respond before she took Nasarra's arm and hauled her out of the room with her.

Nasarra suppressed the urge to laugh out loud.

"Sorry, but if I had to listen to her talk about how fantastic she was one more second I was going to barf," Laura said. "I had to listen to her all morning."

Nasarra giggled and they headed off to their first class.

* * *

In all honesty, Nasarra was happy that she'd been given Beginning Acting first. It had given her the chance to brush up on some things before making a fool out of herself in Advanced. Connor had been the teacher, much to her pleasant surprise, and she now was making her way with Laura over to the outdoor amphitheatre for Advanced. She shivered and shoved her hands into the pockets of her sweater, wishing she had brought something warmer. The air off the ocean was icy and, coupled with the fog, she thought for sure she might freeze to death.

"So, how was Beginning?" Danielle's voice drawled as she came out of nowhere and fell into stride with them. "As dull as I imagine?"

Nasarra almost groaned aloud. No doubt Danielle was

one of the people who had thought it was stupid to take Beginning if you were more seasoned.

"It was fine," Laura replied. "The teacher is cool."

"The Musical Theatre teacher is a dream," Danielle gushed. She flipped her hair and gave a smug smile. "I think he liked me best."

Nasarra rolled her eyes and sighed as she entered the outdoor amphitheatre, which actually had a fire pit. Too bad there wasn't a fire in it.

She let her eyes scan over the seats and her heart faltered as her gaze landed on a tall man with a black leather jacket and a familiar, sunset-colored ponytail. "Oh my gosh," she murmured.

Laura looked at her and frowned. "What?"

She blinked in bewilderment. "I know that man."

"Who? You know wh—" Danielle searched the crowd until her eyes found Caleb. She drew her breath in sharply. "No way."

Nasarra frowned at her. "Yeah way. He's kinda the guy I'm seeing. Why? You know him too?"

Danielle's clear, blue eyes turned to Nasarra and gave her a dangerous glower. "What did you just say?"

Nasarra raised an eyebrow. "I said I know that man." She pointed at Caleb. "I'm sort of dating him."

"Oh, well that figures." Her voice was a nasty hiss and she pushed past Nasarra, storming away.

"Whoa, what was that all about?" Laura asked.

Nasarra rubbed at her shoulder where Danielle had rammed into it and scowled. "Like I know. That girl strikes me as very unbalanced."

Laura laughed. "So, that's really your boyfriend down there?"

Nasarra headed down to the fire pit area. "Yeah. What he's doing here is beyond me." She shook her head. "Caleb!"

He turned at her voice and his face lit up. She held her arms out to the sides as if to question what he was doing there. He stuffed his hands into his jacket pockets and grinned. "Hello, gorgeous," he greeted as she approached. "Enjoying your first day of school?" His trademark devilish smile played around his lips.

She snorted and put her hands on her hips. "*What* are you doing here? You're always just popping out of nowhere!"

He chuckled. "You should take your seat, Nasarra. Class is going to begin soon." He winked at her.

She stared in uncomprehending silence for a second and then remembered that Connor had taught Beginning Acting, and put two and two together. Her eyes widened. "Oh my gosh! You're teaching our class?"

He nodded and grinned.

Her look of shock morphed into feigned annoyance. "Nice of you to tell me," she grumbled. "And it would have been nice of you to offer me a *ride*! I had to borrow Amanda's car!"

He looked bashful and it melted her heart. "I wanted to surprise you."

"Congratulations, Caleb. Again, mission accomplished."

He laughed. "Well, I can give you a ride from now on, sweetheart. How's that sound?"

"Sweetheart, is it? Well, isn't that adorable."

Caleb and Nasarra both turned to see Danielle standing with her arms folded, trying to slay Caleb with her eyes by the look of it.

Caleb's eyes widened and he sucked in his breath. "Danielle," he whispered.

Nasarra glanced between the two. By the way Danielle was glowering, and the way Caleb's face had gone ashen, she came to the conclusion that they knew one another.

"So, going for redheads now, are we?" Danielle sneered. "You used to like dark hair."

Caleb seemed to recover slightly from his shock and his eyes narrowed. "I usually just tend to go for women who aren't insane," he muttered.

Danielle looked taken aback.

Caleb-1, Danielle-0

"Nice, Caleb. That was low, even for you," she spat. She turned her eyes to Nasarra. "Watch out for him. He seems gentlemanly now, but one day he'll turn on you and drive a knife right through your heart and your dreams." She looked back to Caleb and raised her chin a notch. "You plan on trying to kill her too?"

Nasarra's eyes widened. "Kill?" she screeched. "What?" Caleb flinched as if he'd been slapped. *Caleb-1, Danielle-1*

Nasarra turned to look at him in alarm. "What is she talking about? Who'd you kill?"

Caleb rolled his eyes and opened his mouth to speak, but Danielle took the opportunity. "Me," she said. "In so many ways." She fixed her death glare on him for a few more seconds, then whirled on her heel and stalked away.

Nasarra blinked rapidly and looked up at Caleb. "What the—"

He let out a sigh that resembled a growl. "Don't listen to her, Nasarra. She's... Well, she has problems."

"And apparently hates your guts."

His smirk was sardonic. "You think?" He shook his head. "I had no idea she was going to be here."

"And in the grand scheme of your past, she would be...?"

"My ex-girlfriend."

She gave a curt nod. "Yeah. I figured. Just wanted to clear it up... Great."

His chuckle was soft, but not as forced as his smile had been. "Don't worry about it, Nasarra. Let me handle Danielle. Go sit down." He touched the small of her back lightly, but it was enough to send warm shockwaves through her body. "I'll talk to you after the day is done, okay?"

She nodded and threw him a smile that she hoped was encouraging as she went to find a seat. She didn't miss the way Danielle scowled at her as she walked by.

Chapter Nine

"I can't believe the way she dogged you all day," Laura said as she and Nasarra made their way out of dance class.

Nasarra rolled her eyes. "Yeah, and, yay for me, I have all but two classes with her. It's just my luck, I swear."

"That scene she caused in Voice class was ridiculous!"

Nasarra sighed wearily. Yes, her first day had definitely been anything but normal and a little far away from "smooth." Advanced Acting had been full of shivering on her part. She'd barely even paid attention to what Caleb had to say because she'd been so preoccupied with trying to feel her toes. They'd done a few exercises, which had been full of backhanded, snide remarks from Danielle that Caleb tried to ignore and just made everyone else confused. Musical Theatre had been a nice reprieve, but Danielle and her blonde watch dog had spent the entirety of lunch scowling at Nasarra. It was stupid. Nasarra felt like she'd fallen into a time warp and had somehow come back out in high school.

Voice had been a nightmare. The teacher had tested all of them to see what their ranges were and Danielle, convinced that she was a soprano when she was anything but, had tried to force herself to sing the high keys. The result had been a nails on the chalkboard screech that probably would have broken glass if any had been around. Nasarra wasn't the only one who'd chuckled, but of course, she was the only one Danielle had noticed.

She'd proceeded to ream her in front of the entire class, saying that the only reason she was there was because she was screwing one of the teachers, and that she had no talent whatsoever to speak of except for what she could do in the bedroom. Obviously.

The teacher, who actually happened to be Carolyn, had come unglued, which was a good thing because, if she hadn't given Danielle what-for, Nasarra would have, and there was no doubt in her mind that Carolyn had done the job with much less violence than she would have used.

The class had remained relatively out of the confrontation, afraid for their lives, no doubt. Carolyn looked like she could bench press a decent-sized human being. Still, the stares and curious looks Nasarra received for the rest of the day was not her idea of a good time. Not exactly how she wanted to reach celebrity status.

Dance had been almost as much of a nightmare, but for completely different reasons. After a warm up and some simple steps, they'd practiced lifts, and Nasarra had been paired with the skinniest man she'd ever seen in her life. He dropped her three times before she refused to let him lift her anymore. If she kept at it, she knew she'd go home with a broken neck or a concussion. The whole thing had, of course, been a riot for Danielle, who made a point of laughing very loud whenever Nasarra ate dirt.

"Well, I'm gonna head to my dorm and try to take a nap before dinner," Laura announced with a yawn. "I'm exhausted."

Nasarra nodded. "Okay, I'm gonna head out. See you tomorrow."

Laura smiled and waved. "You too!"

Nasarra heaved a sigh and meandered down the corridor. She stepped outside and was blasted by the icy ocean air. She sucked her breath in and stuffed her hands in her pockets, vowing to dress much warmer the next day. A few people waved at her as she made her way back to the amphitheatre to see if Caleb was there, and she smiled. Well, at least not everyone hated her.

Caleb wasn't there, but she spotted Connor, so she waved.

"Hey, Nasarra," he greeted with a warm smile. "How do you like the camp so far?"

"Camp is good. Some of the people suck, but what can you do?"

He chuckled. "Yeah, that's true."

"You know where Caleb is?"

"I think he was heading over to the Bothin Room."

She sighed. "I just came from there... All right, fine. See ya!" She waved and made her way back the way she'd just come. Sure enough, she poked her head into the Bothin Room to see a deserted dance room with Caleb lying on his back at the far end. She smiled. He had earphones in and didn't hear the door open. She unzipped her backpack and pulled out an apple she'd saved from lunch, then discarded her bag and quietly approached.

His eyes were closed, which made her plan of attack even better. Deftly, she straddled his hips and sat down, causing his eyes to fly open in shock and alarm. She grinned and held the apple up tauntingly.

His surprise melted away and a heated kind of desire came to life in his gaze. He gave her a sexy smile and pulled his earphones out.

"I brought an apple for the teacher," she all but purred. "Does that mean I can be your favorite?"

He placed his hands on her waist and gently squeezed her hips. "You look entirely too much like the depictions of Eve tempting Adam right now." He reached up and pulled the apple from her hand, then propped himself up on his elbows. "Besides, you know you were teacher's pet the moment you walked into my classroom."

She giggled and lowered herself to kiss his lips. "Wait, we won't get in trouble for that, will we?" she asked, pulling back with a worried frown.

He shook his head. "No, it's fine. People will talk, but it's not like I'm actually getting paid to be here." He rolled his eyes. "I'm doing it as a favor so they can't fire me. It's not like..." He grimaced and a dark shadow passed over his face. "College."

She gave a thoughtful frown, but didn't push the subject. Had something happened when Caleb had taught at that community college? Is that why he'd stopped teaching? The questions buzzed in her mind, but she forced herself not to ask them.

"So, how was your first day?" he asked, reaching up to tangle his fingers in her hair.

She rolled her eyes. "Well, let's see, first off, I found out that the guy I'm seeing totally neglected to tell me that he's my teacher; I have all but two classes with his heinous ex, who incidentally, hates the very sight of me. I froze my butt off in Advanced Acting, got verbally attacked by Danielle in Voice, had my eardrums assaulted by her horrendous attempt to be a soprano, and I got dropped in dance."

He raised an eyebrow. "Dropped?"

She nodded. "Three times." A slow smile spread across her lips and she met his eyes. "It was marvelous." She couldn't deny it. She would rather have a horrendous day performing her craft than have a day where she wasn't performing at all. Despite the craziness of the day, getting back into the swing of things had been awesome.

His chuckle warmed her. "Spoken like a true performing artist." He sat up and situated them so that she was sitting on his lap and his arms were wrapped around her. He ran his fingers through her red curls and smiled, pressing kisses along the length of her jaw. "I couldn't concentrate in class today," he said. "There was this gorgeous redhead distracting me."

She grinned and closed her eyes, her skin burning where his lips touched. She reached up to frame his face with her hands and brought her lips to his. She'd been dying to kiss him all day. His kisses were her worst addiction. Even worse than chocolate. And that was a pretty bad addiction. She sighed and melted against him, wrapping her arms around his shoulders and holding on.

"Oh, good lord, gag me with every utensil in the drawer."

Nasarra pulled her lips off of Caleb's and snapped her attention to... Oh, fantastic. Danielle had come in the room just as they were making out. The day just kept getting better and better. She swore she heard Caleb whimper.

Danielle rolled her eyes and swaggered over to the corner, where she had apparently forgotten something. "You know, it is nice to know that some things never change," she said airily, waving a ballet toe shoe. "I mean, how many years has it been, Caleb, and you're still making out with your students? At least you're not hiding in the janitor closet anymore. Way to go."

Her voice dripped with dark sarcasm and Nasarra slid her gaze to Caleb, who had averted his eyes to the carpet.

"You know, I am disappointed in your choice, though," Danielle continued, coming to stand in front of them with her arms folded. "You used to have higher standards."

Nasarra rolled her eyes. "Get over yourself," she grumbled.

Danielle blinked. "Excuse me? You mean *it* actually talks? And an insult no less." She shrugged her shoulders and gave a haughty laugh. "And here I just thought it just made idiotic comments."

"Danielle," Caleb warned.

Her eyes burned into his. "What is she doing here, Caleb?"

He snorted. "She's here for the same reason you are, and what does it matter to you?"

"I paid good money to be here. I *will not* surrender my dream just because someone else is pulling strings to get preferential treatment."

"Oh, you mean like you used to do."

Caleb-2, Danielle-1. Or, well... Maybe that janitor closet comment could be considered a point.

If Danielle scowled any harder, Nasarra was pretty sure her face would crack in half. "What I asked for and what was offered to me are two different things. What was cruelly *yanked* from me is all on you."

How he managed it, Nasarra wasn't sure, but Caleb somehow was able to gently push her off of his lap and stand toe to toe with Danielle in about 2.5 seconds. "Let it go, Danielle," he snarled. "I didn't deliberately do anything to you. It was all a—"

"Mistake? Riiight." She folded her arms. "Don't play innocent with me, Caleb. We both know exactly what you did."

"In case you've forgotten, you messed up my life pretty brilliantly too."

She gave a loud laugh. "Oh, poor baby. You lost your job. I almost lost my *life!*" She spun on her heel, not offering him the option to defend himself. She banged out the door and disappeared back down the hall.

Nasarra watched her go, then slid her gaze to Caleb, who looked like someone had slapped him. He let out a heavy sigh and put his hands on his hips, averting his eyes to the carpet once again. She stood and went to him, placing one hand on his shoulder. "Hey," she murmured. "You okay?"

He raised his head and turned his gaze to hers. His normally sparkling eyes held a deep kind of pain and it tugged at her heart. "Why doesn't the past ever just stay buried?" he practically whispered.

She couldn't even think of anything to say. She dropped her forehead onto his shoulder and slipped her arm around his waist. She was dying to know what had happened, but didn't dare ask. She hadn't known him long enough to think she had a right to know all his secrets. If he wanted to tell her, he would. "You want to get out of here?" she offered.

He looked down at her and a small smile touched his lips. "Yeah."

* * *

"Look, I snagged us some dinner," Nasarra said with a grin. "Don't tell anybody."

Caleb smiled as she sat next to where he was on top of one of the old, battered, stone WWII forts that bedecked the coastal countryside around the YMCA. Nasarra had managed to get the night off, which was only possible because of Rafe stepping up to the plate, and it was one of Caleb's regularly scheduled nights off, so the two of them had spent several quiet, but comfortable hours strolling around the winding paths of Point Bonita, exploring and holding hands.

His mind was in turmoil and Nasarra seemed to have sensed that so she'd been letting him initiate most of the contact and conversation. He appreciated her giving him space more than she knew. It was difficult for him to be teaching again. Even if this was a much more casual setting, he was still responsible for around 150 people and that was daunting.

He used to love teaching. It had made him feel good to know that he was making a difference in people's lives. After Danielle and the disaster his relationship with her had created, he'd vowed to never put himself in the position to compromise him or another person again. He'd sworn off teaching. It was too much responsibility. Having an influence over people and what they did with their lives was a terrifying power that he couldn't handle.

Teaching anything after making that promise to himself was difficult enough. Having to teach Danielle... It was like his worst nightmare come to life. And with his current girlfriend in the same class. Yeah, that just made everything so much better. Danielle would spread rumors that Nasarra was getting special treatment. Her talent would be overlooked because people would be skeptical. If Nasarra ended up getting cast in the play, Caleb would have to have someone else scout for the winners of the audition opportunity. He would make his suggestions to whoever was chosen for the job, that way Nathan would be appeased, but he couldn't scout himself. It would seem rigged, biased, and unfair if Nasarra was one of the performers picked by his own hand.

"What are you thinking about?" Nasarra's voice came, soft and melodic, slightly concerned, spreading warmth throughout his entire being.

He glanced at her. "Lots of boring stuff that would only hurt your head," he half-teased.

She wrinkled her nose and looked anything but convinced. "Mmmhmm...whatever. Here, have some of this." She handed him a piece of fried chicken.

"How did you pilfer this anyway?"

She shrugged. "It's dinner time down at the dorms. When I went back to go to the bathroom, I snuck in and stole some off of Laura's plate."

He grinned and turned his attention back out to the sea, his smile disappearing. The sun was setting and it cast its golden hue across the ocean waves, making everything seem to sparkle and glitter. The wind whipped and tugged at both of them with cold fingers, but Caleb didn't mind. He adored the ocean. It was peace, serenity and power all rolled into one... Much like the fiery woman at his side.

He stole a sidelong glance at her and the smile returned. He didn't know what it was about her, but she had wrapped him up in her spell and he was next to helpless. He was wary about relationships. He didn't like getting too close to women. Nasarra was an interesting development. He gave a soft sigh and looked down at the chicken leg she had shoved in his hand. "You know I haven't had a serious relationship since Danielle?" he blurted.

Her eyes shot up to meet his and she looked surprised. Probably because he'd been so tight-lipped about the whole thing. "Really?"

He nodded.

She raised an eyebrow. "Wow, must have been some blowout you two had."

He snorted. "You have no idea." He knew she was curious, but he couldn't bring himself to relay the story to her. It gave him chills just to think about that dark time in his past. He didn't have the courage to tell her yet.

"So, that must make me kind of special."

He looked over at her and smiled.

She gasped and her face turned a bright shade of red. "Not...not that I'm saying we're serious or anything. I didn't mean—" She shook her head. "I was just saying that, you know we're kind of dating, and—" She groaned. "Never mind."

He laughed, loving how cute she looked whenever she was flustered. "Nasarra, I wouldn't be here with you right now if I didn't think we had something together. I wouldn't waste either of our time." She looked up at him in a shy gesture and his heart skipped a beat.

"Meeting you was like a dream come true for me," she murmured. "I would have been happy with that. I never in my wildest dreams would have thought I'd be dating you." She shook her head and cast a thoughtful gaze out to the sea. "It's strange."

He reached out to push back her flying strands of hair. "What is?"

She shrugged. "The day you ran into me in the rain..." She giggled. "Well, I had been feeling *really* sorry for myself."

He chuckled.

"Then, three days later, you changed my whole life. In a short amount of time, you turned all of the bad things in my life into good. You even managed to bring my dreams, which I'd all but discarded, back to life."

"They were always there, Nasarra. You'd just buried them under being a responsible adult."

"Tell me about it." She looked down as if contemplating something, then glanced back up at him. "You really think I have a shot? I mean, am I just fooling myself?"

"I wouldn't have wanted you to come here so badly if I didn't think you had a pretty decent shot."

She scowled playfully. "Yeah, you seduced me into agreeing to think about it. That was pretty low."

He grinned and some of the darkness that had been shadowing him all day lifted. He loved how playful she was. He tended to fall into patches of brooding, moody silence. Having someone around him to contradict that was refreshing. He sighed and shrugged one shoulder in a lazy gesture. "Sometimes you have to resort to dirty tactics to get what you want."

She cocked her head to the side, obviously debating something. "Well, if that's your outlook..." She set their food aside and positioned herself on his lap again, wrapping her legs around his waist in a way that made his entire body ignite and his breath disappear. "Look, Caleb." She met his eyes with purpose. "I'm no idiot and I'm not going to pretend to be so let me just say this."

He raised an eyebrow and waited, snaking his arms around her back to hold her closer.

"I haven't pushed the Danielle subject because, obviously, it's painful for you, and I have no right to demand that you unbury all your memories just because I'm curious. However, if you want to keep me around for any length of time, you need to know that I'm all about honesty and open communication. You said, in so many words, that you're wary of relationships because of whatever happened. I get that. I really do, and I'm not going to pressure you. I have no right. All I want is for you to know that I'm here for you. I'll listen if you ever want to talk."

He blinked up at her, unsure of what to say. He was in awe, to say the least. Because he liked to help people, Danielle, and some of the other girls he'd been with, had usually lacked a sufficient amount of confidence, or hadn't really known who they were or where they stood. He tended to go for women like that against his better judgment because he felt like he could make a difference in their lives. He had no idea what kind of problem that meant *he* had. That was just the way he'd always been. He liked to help. He liked to matter.

How he had managed to stumble over a beautiful, talented woman who made him feel needed, but was confident enough in herself to straddle his waist and tell him how it was going to be, he would never know. He was just grateful that he'd gotten so fortunate.

He smiled and reached his hands up to frame her face. "Nasarra," he murmured, "you are an exceptional woman." He shook his head. "At times, I don't think I deserve you."

She frowned. "Caleb," she stated, "don't be an idiot."

"Well...all right then," he chuckled. Her giggle warmed his heart and he brought her mouth to his, parting her lips and tasting her sweetness. He felt his heart open for her, open in a way he hadn't allowed it to in a long time. He swore she had stepped right out of his fantasies.

"Geez," she whispered as she pulled away. She rested her head against his shoulder.

He stroked her hair in a loving caress. "What, baby?"

"Your kisses should be outlawed."

His laughter felt good and he wrapped his arms around her, holding her tight. He let his gaze drift off across the sun setting along the horizon, and he sighed in contentment. Maybe it wasn't Nasarra who needed him. Maybe he'd been the one who needed her.

Chapter Ten

Classes set into a monotonous routine for about a week or so. Actually, Nasarra's life fell into a pretty regular routine, but she wasn't going to complain about this one. Theatre camp during the day, which was relentless, more like a theatre boot camp than anything else. Work at night, which was a lot more fun now that Rafe worked with her half the time, and time with Caleb whenever she could squeeze it in. Most nights she went to bed absolutely exhausted, but she felt more satisfied with her life than she had in years. It used to be that she would go to bed exhausted because she had worked herself into the ground for next to no purpose other than to survive. She felt like the work she did now might actually get her somewhere... Might get her to the pot of gold at the end of the rainbow.

Danielle continued to be as pleasant as ever, always giving a snarky remark whenever she could fit one in. Lucky for Nasarra, Danielle only had a small group of followers who actually tolerated her. Everyone else didn't really care about the fact that Nasarra was dating one of the teachers. They just went about their business like the adults they were all supposed to be. She had actually made quite a few friends and enjoyed her time at camp, as grueling as it was.

It was colder than usual today and Nasarra had spent the whole morning shivering. Even during her inside classes, she'd been freezing. A storm was moving over the bay and thick fog covered everything like an icy blanket. She was relieved to find out that Advanced Acting had been temporarily moved to a meeting room. At least then they wouldn't all die of hypothermia.

Nasarra really wasn't in the best of moods. She was cold

and cranky and just wanted the day to be over so she could go home. What she didn't want, or need, was the way Danielle suddenly latched onto her arm as she entered the Advanced Acting room and practically slammed her up against the wall. She blinked in bewilderment and scowled, snatching her arm out of Danielle's talonlike grip. "What is the matter with you?" she spat. "Did you decide to go *completely* mental today instead of just halfway?" She rubbed at her arm to try and take away the sting.

"Look, I've sat by and tolerated this long enough." Danielle's usual voice had been replaced by that nasty, animalistic snarl she liked to use when addressing Caleb or Nasarra. "You don't belong here."

"Too freaking bad!" Nasarra snapped. "Because, in case you haven't noticed, I *am* here and I'm not going anywhere!" She shoved Danielle out of the way and continued into the room. "Go back to the second grade," she grumbled. "Maybe, if you try *really* hard, you can move onto third next year."

Nasarra swore she heard Danielle actually growl. "You don't even get it, you stupid cow! He's never going to get you anywhere!"

She was loud enough that everyone else in the room, including Caleb, turned and stared at her. Nasarra sighed, stopped, and made a slow turn toward Danielle. "Did someone forget to take their anti-psychotics this morning?" She'd meant the jibe just to irritate her, but something in her words seemed to set something else off in Danielle because the woman's eyes suddenly blazed like blue fire.

"That's enough," Caleb's voice came in warning. "Sit down, both of you. We have work to do."

Danielle directed her heated gaze to Caleb. "What's wrong? Afraid she'll find out the truth about you?"

Nasarra raised an eyebrow and looked over at Caleb. She sighed and folded her arms. "I knew it," she said flatly. "Caleb's a CIA agent in disguise, isn't he?" She flung her hands up in the air. "How could you keep such a thing from me?" Snickers followed and even Caleb cracked a smile, which only pissed Danielle off even further.

"Sure, laugh it up, all of you," she sneered, "but I would bet that half of you would walk right out of this room if you knew what your teacher really was." She fixed her evil glare back on Caleb.

Caleb scowled and stabbed his finger at a random, empty seat. "Sit down, Danielle. You can try to ruin my reputation later."

She gave a haughty laugh and put her hands on her hips, adopting a smug smile. "You know something? I am really starting to get tired of taking orders from you."

Caleb shrugged. "Then don't. You're free to leave any time you like."

Nasarra rolled her eyes and headed toward a seat, just wanting to get things started, but Danielle's claws on her arm halted her yet again and she spun to glare at the other woman. "Get your hands off me, you spaz!"

The room silenced in an ominous fashion as the two of them glowered at one another. It would have been an awesome time for the theme from *The Good, The Bad, and The Ugly* to start playing.

Danielle snorted and folded her arms. "You really need to get a clue, Nasarra."

"Give it a rest already! I don't want to hear anything you have to say." She turned her back on Danielle again.

"You don't want to hear how he told me I could have been one of the greats? How he told me I had so much talent and the best voice he'd ever heard?"

Nasarra stopped and looked at her over her shoulder only because the words she'd said had been almost *exactly* what Caleb had said to *her.*

"Danielle!" Caleb interrupted. "That's enough!"

"Oh get off it, Caleb!" Danielle exclaimed. "You're not my teacher! You're not anyone's teacher! You don't have a right to be! All you are is a big, useless fraud!"

"I'm warning you, if you don't stop this childishness, I'll have you removed from my classroom and from the camp." Caleb meant business. His eyes were deadly serious.

He and Danielle faced off for a few seconds before Danielle apparently decided that she didn't care if she ruined her chances at a New York audition. She just kept right on going. "You can't get rid of me. I *paid* to be here. Unlike your redheaded lap dog over here who just lives off the table scraps you throw her." She gave Nasarra the once-over and made a face. "It's disgusting."

"Leave Nasarra out of this," Caleb demanded. "She never

did anything to you. If you have a problem with me, fine, but don't drag her into your drama."

Danielle gave a mocking laugh. "Aww, how chivalrous. Protecting your concubine. How sweet."

Nasarra's blood began to boil, but she kept her mouth shut. She didn't want to make this already awful situation even worse. She glanced out the corner of her eye at all the staring students.

"I see you're old song and dance hasn't changed," Danielle continued. "Ever the gentleman, aren't you?" She shook her head. "I can't believe I was ever stupid enough to believe all the bull you fed me."

Caleb heaved a sigh. "Danielle—"

Danielle turned her burning eyes back to Nasarra and she stabbed her finger at her. "I don't like you," she spat, "but you deserve to know what *this*"—she pointed at Caleb—"is before you fall for him like I did and you get your life yanked out from under you too."

"Stop it!" Caleb shouted. "This is your last warning, I swear."

Danielle ignored him and spoke directly to Nasarra. "Caleb was my theatre teacher in college," she began. "I had a huge crush on him. He was dreamy and smart and talented." She shot a scowl at him. "He adored me. I was the best in his class; he told me so."

Nasarra glanced over at Caleb, who looked somewhere between infuriated and horrified.

"We got involved with one another even though it was against the rules. It was exciting, forbidden. You know how it goes. Well, of course, we got caught. It was inevitable. Caleb lost his teaching job and we ended up moving into an apartment together in New York, barely making ends meet." She shrugged. "It didn't matter. We were in love. Who cared? We were both auditioning for plays, trying our luck. Caleb always made me feel like I was so talented and capable, like I could do anything. After awhile, I started to believe him. After a lot of very hard and diligent work, I was cast as a chorus girl in an off-Broadway musical."

"Danielle..."

Caleb's protest didn't hold a lot of force behind it and Nasarra looked over at him again. He heaved a sigh and closed his eyes, looking like he just wanted it all to be over.

"Sure, it wasn't a big deal at all, but it was to me," Danielle continued. "It was a step in the right direction. I knew it was going to take a lot of work to get where I wanted to go, but I was determined. Plus, I had Caleb, who had lots of connections. I had confidence that he'd come through for me like he always promised.

"One day, Caleb came home from meeting with a director friend of his and he told me that he'd offered him a part in his new play, and that there was one for me too. On Broadway. A leading role!" She shook her head. "Lies... They were all lies."

"I never lied to you!" Caleb cried in obvious frustration.

She whirled to face him. "You left me! You were jealous! Jealous because I'd found a job and pissed off because you couldn't find one! It wasn't my fault you got caught with me, Caleb! It wasn't my fault you were careless and lost your teaching job! That stupid chorus girl part meant everything to me and you made me quit because you promised something better!"

He huffed. "I didn't *make* you do anything!"

"There was no part!" she screamed back at Nasarra, tears starting to course down her alabaster cheeks. "He lied to me! Then he ended up getting cast in *Cats* and he left me all alone!"

Nasarra slid her surprised gaze back to the other class members, who now watched the three of them with rapt attention like they were putting on their own private performance. Well...this *was* Advanced Acting. Today's lesson was apparently on how to weave a successful melodrama.

Danielle whirled back to Caleb. "You left me all alone on a subway! You walked away and I never saw you again! I got mugged that night, Caleb! A man threatened to shoot me and stole my purse! I got lost and wound up in Brooklyn in the middle of the night! Do you have any idea how *scary* it is down there? I fell asleep in an alley! An *alley*! You promised me that you would always keep me safe, that you would always be there for me. Where were you? You were gone! You got what you wanted! You got glory and prestige and your moment in the spotlight. What did I get? All I got were two slit wrists!" She pulled her sleeves up and thrust her arms toward Caleb, forcing him to look at the scars that still resided there.

He closed his eyes and turned his head.

Nasarra blinked rapidly, her mind having a difficult time keeping up with the influx of information. "You tried to kill yourself?" she cried. "Because he broke up with you?" Danielle wheeled back to her, causing Nasarra to back up. She looked crazed.

"He moved out of our apartment that night. I couldn't even get back in. All my stuff was gone. My boyfriend was gone. I had nothing. He'd ruined my only chance at success. I spent one solid week living on the streets."

"Danielle, that's not how it went and you know it," Caleb tried again.

"You abandoned me!" she wailed, her face streaked with an abundance of tears. "How was I supposed to live knowing that the one person I'd loved and trusted had stabbed me in the back, ripped my dream from me and left me?" She sniffled and looked down at her feet, starting to visibly tremble. "And then, when I woke up in the hospital, I asked my mother where you were. I thought sure you'd come to me when you found out. She said you were off performing..." She shook her head. "You didn't care about me. All you cared about was yourself. All the things you said to me were lies. You just used me to launch your own career."

Caleb opened his mouth to speak, but ended up just running his fingers through his hair and letting his shoulders droop. "I cannot believe how much you've twisted the story," he finally muttered.

Danielle's posture changed like someone had flipped a switch. In one second she went from looking sad and weary to volatile. "You're cruel and heartless!" she bellowed. "That's the real story!"

Nasarra wondered where the sudden growling roar that silenced the room came from until she realized it had broken free from her own throat. She could not and would not take any more of Danielle's verbal barrage against Caleb. It just wasn't going to happen. "It was your own cowardice that caused you to try and take your own life, Danielle," she snarled. "Caleb didn't do it to you. He didn't press the knife to your skin."

"He may as well have!" Danielle screeched.

"Enough of this! *Enough!*" Caleb's voice seemed to shake the room like thunder. Anger flashed in his green eyes.

"Danielle, shut up! *Now!* I am done with your games and your lies!"

Danielle actually shrank back at the force of his temper.

"Everyone else in this room, it would do you good to not go running off your mouth about what you've been forced to witness here today. The first rumor I hear, I swear on my life I will make sure every single one of you is thrown out of this camp. I will not defend myself against such ridiculous accusations. This is a classroom, not a friggin' court of law. If anyone has a question, or a concern, please come to me. I will be happy to allay your fears.

"Just to let you know, Nasarra is not here because I played favorites. Nasarra is here because of her own talent. That is the truth." He fixed Danielle with a dark scowl. "Whether you like it or not. For the rest of the period, I want you to practice Shakespearean scenes with one another and peer critique." He strode to the door and yanked it open.

"Caleb!" Nasarra called. "Where are you going?"

"Stay in class, Nasarra."

His voice was cold and it sent chills down her spine. Not good ones. How dare he command her—Screw that! She was *not* going to sit by and read Shakespeare when her boyfriend had just been attacked by a psychopath in front of a whole room full of people. She started toward the door. "Caleb!"

"You're going to side with him?" Danielle hollered from behind her. "You're really that stupid?" She snorted. "I should have saved my breath. I should have known a slut like you would—"

Nasarra didn't have time to think. All she knew was that one minute she was heading for the door, and the next she was spinning and sending her fist directly into Danielle's beautiful blue eye. Danielle staggered backwards, the students in the room gasped, and an intense, aching pain settled into Nasarra's knuckles. She gave the room a collective scowl and continued back out the door. She shook her hand, trying to make the pain subside, and ran down the hall. She burst out into the freezing air and shouted for Caleb, who was quickly making his way across the parking lot.

Caleb turned at the sound of her voice, but didn't look all that happy to see her. "Nasarra, I told you to stay in class."

"Right, like I'm just going to hang out in there after what just happened." She placed her hand on his arm. "Caleb, talk to me."

He shook his head and passed a dark look over her. "I don't want to talk, Nasarra. Please, just leave me alone right now. "

She frowned. "Excuse me? Leave you alone? Hello! Girlfriend over here!" She waved her arm.

He gave a dry, forced chuckle. "You mean I still have one?" His voice was full of bitterness.

"Of course you do!" she cried. "You honestly think I'm gonna believe *her*?" She jerked her thumb in the direction of the building she'd just left. "Caleb, please just tell me what really happened so we can put all of this behind us and move on."

He heaved a sigh. "I just... I don't want to deal with it right now, all right? I just got laid into in front of my entire class. I can't be here right now."

"Well, I'll come with you."

"No, I want to be by myself." He turned and started to walk away again.

She grabbed his hand. "Caleb—"

"Nasarra!"

His voice cracked like a whip and it made her jump and stare at him in mild shock.

He shoved his hands down. "Just stop pushing!"

She frowned. "Pushing?" She snorted, and annoyance replaced her concern. "You know, I have just about had enough of this. I haven't pushed you at all since the day I met you. I've never once asked you to tell me what happened with you and Danielle. I figured you would tell me in your own time. Now, you'd rather me believe what some idiot lowlife has to say than actually set the record straight because *you're* irritated?" She threw her hands up in the air. "You know what? Whatever. Take all the time for yourself that you want since I'm apparently not needed. I'm out of here. I'm friggin' sick of this crap."

She turned and stormed away, not even bothering to look back. Yeah, so men were beautiful and erotic and good kissers. They were also stupid and infuriating. Nice that no one had told her.

She skipped the rest of her classes. She couldn't deal with the stares she knew she'd be getting and the questions people would be asking. She called Amanda, who had come and picked her up after her shift.

Her anger slowly morphed into sadness and her eyes blurred with unshed tears as she walked into her room. She didn't understand why he hadn't wanted her to be there for him. She wondered what Caleb was doing, where he was. Did he know how worried she was about him? Had he even stopped to think that she might be worried at all? Probably not. It was apparent that the man's brain had taken a temporary leave of absence.

She sat down on her bed and clutched a pillow to her chest. She wished Rafe was home, but he was working. Her heart ached. It ached with sadness for Caleb and hurt that he had not trusted her enough to stay and talk to her. She briefly noticed that it had started to rain, a gentle pitter-patter on the window. *How fitting*, she thought. Rain. Rain to soothe her aching heart...

Chapter Eleven

Nasarra was jolted awake by rolling thunder and a pounding on her door. She rubbed her eyes and rolled over to look at her clock. 4:30 a.m. Geez, who could be wanting her at that hour? Lightning flared through the room, making everything momentarily bright. She swung her legs out of bed and wrapped a robe around herself. Rafe would never wake up. He slept even sounder than usual since starting work at Max's.

She walked quietly to the door. "I'm coming," she yawned.

The knocking persisted.

"Good lord, shut up," she grumbled. "I'm coming." She unlocked the door and pulled it open. Her eyes widened as they fell on Caleb, dripping wet, hands stuffed in his pockets, looking a whole lot like a drowned cat. "Caleb?" she squeaked. "What are you doing? It's the middle of the night."

"Bike broke down at the wharf," he replied through clenched teeth.

"Your bike broke down at the *wharf*?" she repeated "How did you get here?"

"Walked."

"You *walked*?" she cried.

He looked up at her. "Had to get to you." Water droplets cascaded from his hair and clothing, forming a growing puddle on her doormat.

"You couldn't call a cab?"

"The walk did me good." His teeth started to chatter. "Cleared my head. Can I come in?"

She shook her head and regained her senses. "Of course!" She swung her door wide and ushered him inside as another clap of thunder and bolt of lightning rattled the sky. She shut her door and immediately grabbed Caleb's drenched jacket. She pulled it off and flung it over the back of a kitchen chair.

"Are you insane?" she muttered. "You could have caught pneumonia." She put the tea kettle on and grabbed a towel out of her hall closet. "Come on," she said, going to him. "Take off your clothes."

He raised an eyebrow.

"You heard me," she stated. "I'm not going to have you freezing to death in my duplex. Take 'em off. You can't have anything Rafe hasn't shown me already." She handed him the towel and went to fetch a blanket.

Nasarra tried not to stare as she came back into the living room, but that was next to impossible. Having Caleb standing half naked in her house *was* different than having Rafe do the same. She cleared her throat, trying to remain calm and not stare slack-jawed at his chiseled body. He was gorgeous...and ripped. What happened to actors being scrawny, geeky, lanky guys?

"Here." She unfolded the blanket and wrapped it around his shoulders, forcing him to sit down on the couch. "Now would you mind terribly telling me what the crap you were thinking?"

His lips quirked. "I'm sorry, Nasarra." He looked up at her, his tawny hair hanging in limp strands around his face. He shook his head. "I was a real jerk earlier today."

She folded her arms and stared down at him. "Yeah. You were."

He sighed. "Sometimes, when I get overwhelmed, it's like my mind gets all fuzzy and I can't think straight. Danielle's outburst pretty much eradicated all rational thought from my brain today. All I could think about was how humiliated I was, and what everyone was going to think of me, what *you* were going to think of me..." He met her eyes. "No one wants their dirty laundry aired like that."

She nodded in agreement. "Well, no. You're right about that." She took a seat next to him.

"Still, I shouldn't have snapped at you. You were only trying to be supportive. I'm sorry."

She waved her hand and sighed. "It's all right."

He frowned. "No, it's not. You told me you wanted a relationship built on open communication and honesty. I clammed up and yelled at you." He shook his head. "Please, let me tell you the real story, okay?" He looked back up at her. "I want to let you in. I do."

She nodded, accepting his apology, and waited for him to continue.

He expelled a large sigh. "It was true that she was one of my students. I thought she was beautiful and brilliant. Back then she was so bright and full of life. It was against the rules for us to get involved. I should have known better, but I didn't care. She always looked up to me and asked for my help. Her doing so made me feel wanted and needed. That's something I've always thrived on. Plus, she had an amazing amount of potential. She had a love for the theatre, much like you do. Seeing someone brim with passion is such a turn on for me." He met her eyes and cracked a smile. "As you know."

Nasarra smirked.

"Anyway, we started to see one another and I really did fall very hard for her. For about a year we carried on our secret romance until one of the other students found out and told the dean. I, of course, was fired and Danielle was expelled from the college. She could have gone to a different school, but she didn't. She never went back. She told me she wanted to try to make it on Broadway. This had always been a dream of mine, as well, so we decided to make a go of it. You only live once, right?" He rolled his eyes.

"I was stupid and naïve and blinded by love. We were destitute, barely scraping by. Danielle had always suffered from bouts of depression and manic highs and lows, but she started to get worse. She finally had to be put on medication.

"She landed herself a part as a chorus girl in a musical after much trial and, at the same time, I was trying to get cast in a play being directed by a man I knew. I got to talking with him one day and told him about Danielle. He led me to believe that he was going to cast both of us. I was so ecstatic that I told Danielle right away and she quit her chorus girl job just like that. When we went to talk to the director, he denied ever having talked to me and told us that both of the parts had already been cast. Danielle was heartbroken. She blamed me, said I did it on purpose because I was jealous of her.

"We rode home on the subway that night and we had a messy breakup. She told me she hated me and never wanted to see me again. She demanded that I leave, so I did. I thought maybe she just needed some time to herself.

"Like I said, we had been having money problems. We hadn't been able to pay our rent. When I got back to our apartment, I was surprised to see that we had been evicted. The landlady told me that I had to be out by that night. I didn't even get to pack my things. I had a little old woman shouting at me that I needed to get out right away. I had to stay with my aunt who lived in Syracuse. I didn't even know what happened to Danielle. I had no idea she'd wound up mugged in Brooklyn. She never tried to contact me. I would have helped her if I had known..." He shook his head.

"I didn't know she had been living on the streets. I don't know why she didn't just call her parents for help. She wasn't right in the head then, I think. She didn't have her medication..." He sighed. "I got a call one night from Danielle's mother telling me that Danielle was in the hospital. I went to see her right away. I had meanwhile managed to get my part in the touring production of *Cats.* I saw Danielle in that hospital room and I stayed there all night. The doctors finally told me that she would be all right and I felt like I wasn't needed anymore. I thought that Danielle would be upset if she woke up and found me there. She hated me, after all. I didn't want to endanger her health, or cause her pain, so I told her mother I had to go to work and I left.

"I walked out of her life forever that night because I thought it was the best decision. I thought it was what she wanted. She's blamed me ever since. Said everything that happened to her was my fault." He shrugged. "I don't know. Maybe it was."

Nasarra shook her head adamantly. "*None* of that was your fault, Caleb. It was just a bunch of jacked up circumstances. Danielle's crazy!"

"I shouldn't have gotten involved with her," he stated. "That part *was* my fault. I pursued it." He looked at her. "You have to know, though... I don't go around finding actresses and telling them how fantastic they are just to win them over. Danielle had a lot of potential. She really did. I don't know when she turned into the melodramatic diva that she is now. And you, Nasarra..." His eyes filled with tenderness and he touched her cheek. "You really are extraordinary. I swear to you I'm not handing you a line."

She smiled and took his hand in hers. "I never thought you were, Caleb. Today was a disaster. Just,"—she met his eyes in warning— "never walk out on me like that again."

"I'm sorry. I just thought—" He shook his head. "Well, I wasn't thinking, obviously." He winced. "Male moment. Can you forgive me?"

She rolled her eyes. "Well, you *did* walk halfway through a city in the middle of the night...in the rain..." She tapped her chin as if she was thinking hard. "I *suppose* I can forgive you." She smiled and met his eyes.

He grinned, then whimpered. "My poor bike."

She giggled and went into the kitchen to make Caleb a cup of tea. She handed him the mug, then sat back. "What are you going to do with it?"

"Have to have it towed," he said, taking a sip of the tea. "I'll fix it at my house."

"Well, just stay here tonight," she offered. "It's too late to do anything." She arched an eyebrow. "I'll let you sleep in my bed." She knew her smile was pure evil.

Desire flashed in his eyes. "Good deal." He took another sip of tea and held his hand out to her. She took it and he pulled her up against his chest, slipping his arm around her waist. "I really am sorry, baby."

She nestled against him and closed her eyes, enjoying how it felt to rest against his strong, solid body. "I know. It's okay." She yawned. "Just don't do it again."

He squeezed her. "Never."

* * *

Nasarra awoke slowly at six a.m. She yawned and reluctantly broke away from the warmth of Caleb's arms. She rubbed her eyes and gazed down at him as he slept soundly. She smiled and let her finger trace the line of his jaw. She had slept better in the last two hours than she had in her entire life. She leaned over and pressed a soft kiss to Caleb's cheek, trailing her fingers down his sculpted chest and smiling to herself as if she was doing something naughty.

She forced herself to sit up and swung her legs out of bed. She walked out into the living room, stretched, and yawned again. She wandered over to the window and pushed the curtains aside so she could open it. She stuck her head out and gazed at her beloved city.

It had stopped raining and everything was beginning to come to life. Smells of restaurants cooking breakfast filled the air and Nasarra could see a small portion of the street below. People walked by and she could hear the incessant buzz of the city waking up, along with a few horns honking with the beginning of rush hour. She eased her chin down onto her elbow and sighed. She loved San Francisco. She turned her head sideways and could almost see the sign on The Curran advertising *Phantom*. A warm glow filled her. The best thing she had ever done was decide to see that musical.

"Hey, Red, you up already?" Rafe trudged into the kitchen, yawning and scratching his chest.

Nasarra turned to him and smiled. "Yeah, it's Saturday. No class, thank goodness." She huffed. "You don't even want to know what happened yesterday. Anyway, I have opening shift today."

He went purposefully to the coffee pot and turned it on.

She raised an eyebrow in amusement as she went to lean against the kitchen counter. Rafe looked much more scraggly than usual. His blond hair was sticking up everywhere, save one patch on the right side of his head that was mashed completely flat, and a good deal of stubble decorated his jaw. She frowned. "Man, Rafe, you look like you've been in a bat-tle. Long night?"

He stopped for a moment and slid a gaze her way, giving a noncommittal sound.

"I'm sorry, Rafe. I'll be out of here in just a second!"

Nasarra blinked in surprise at the sound of a female voice and footsteps rounding the corner. She glanced at Rafe and saw him pale considerably just as Amanda stumbled into view, struggling to put on one of her shoes. Nasarra's mouth dropped open and Amanda froze. "Oh my gosh!" Nasarra shouted.

Amanda opened her mouth, but no words came out. Her face turned bright red.

"I cannot believe this!" Nasarra shouted again. "Amanda!"

There was a sudden thud, followed by some shuffling as Caleb staggered into the kitchen, still looking half asleep.

"Wha's going on?" he slurred. "I heard somebody yell."

Amanda adopted the same expression Nasarra had moments before. "Nasarra!" she shouted, stabbing her finger at Caleb.

Nasarra shook her head. She looked at Rafe as if expecting an explanation. "Rafe!" she cried.

He frowned and indicated Caleb, who was still standing there in only his boxer shorts. "Nasarra?"

Caleb frowned and looked around at everyone in obvious confusion. He raised one finger and opened his mouth to speak, but sighed and shook his head instead. "Sleep," he grumbled. He turned and wandered back to Nasarra's room.

Nasarra shook her head and squeezed her eyes shut. "Aw, gross. I'm not here; I'm not here." She shuddered and maneuvered past Rafe and Amanda. "Do me a favor," she said to Amanda as she started for the hallway. "*Don't* give me the details on this one. I already know what Rafe looks like naked, and I know what you look like naked too now that I think about it, so I'm going to have that image emblazoned in my mind for the rest of my natural life." She shuddered again and made a face. "It's sick and wrong and I'm going to take a shower now because I feel violated and unclean." She turned and sought refuge in the bathroom. She heard Amanda and Rafe start to laugh.

Chapter Twelve

Caleb was pretty sure Nasarra was going to chew her lip right off. He smiled to himself and put his hands on her shoulders in a gesture of comfort. "You're going to do fine," he assured her.

She turned and fixed him with a look that was half *yeah right,* and half *cram it.* He chuckled.

"I think I'm going to spew," she grumbled.

"You're not going to spew."

She scowled. "How do you know?"

Thankfully, the rest of the month had gone without incident after Danielle's soap opera scene in Advanced Acting. Classes had passed, days had gone by, and it was now audition time. Nasarra had practiced more than any one person should, and he was pretty sure that if someone could be over prepared, she was exactly that. It warmed his heart to see her grip so tightly onto what she wanted. A woman with ambition was sexy.

"I really don't think I can do this," she murmured. She looked up at him. "This is stupid. I'm going to make an idiot out of myself."

He smirked. "Nasarra, you could recite these scenes in your sleep. And you can out-dance half of these people. At least that's what your dance teacher tells me. Now, stop worrying." He took her by the shoulders as they made their way to the amphitheatre. He touched her face and gave her a gentle smile. "Everything has to start somewhere, and this is where your dream begins. An audition is an audition. If you can make it through this one, you can make it through them all."

She sighed and collapsed against his chest. "This is

nerve-wracking, Caleb. I haven't done this in so long."

He leaned down so that his mouth was close to her ear. "Just show them as much fire and passion as you show me and you'll knock their socks off." She looked up at him and grinned in a way that made him chuckle. "Go on." He ushered her over to where all of the other students sat and he stood back, waiting for Carolyn to get things underway. He was not judging the auditions for obvious reasons, but it didn't really matter. Carolyn and Connor were more than capable of finding the most talented people out of the group.

He glanced over at Danielle, who sat with ramrod stiff posture and her smug nose in the air, and he rolled his eyes. What had he ever seen in her? When had she become such an arrogant witch? He sighed and tried to stifle a smile as he remembered how she'd looked sporting a black eye for about a week and a half. He'd almost had a heart attack when he'd found out that Nasarra had belted her. Needless to say, no one had messed with her since. Probably because they feared for their lives. Nasarra was pure fire in every way from her flaming hair to her scorching temper. Heaven knew how she set *him* ablaze.

"All right everyone!" Carolyn began. "It's the moment you've all been waiting for! This theatre camp has been a great success and a great joy to teach, but all good things must come to an end and, for some of you, this will be the end of your journey. However, for others, this is just the beginning! I will call you up on stage one at a time. Tell me what part you are going to be trying out for. I will pick a scene with that character in it and read opposite you. After that, you'll be asked to sing the song you have prepared."

Caleb folded his arms and waited. He knew Nasarra would get cast somewhere in the play. She practically had the script memorized she had gone over it so many times, and her voice left a lot of people in the dust. He wasn't worried, even though he knew she was.

"All right, first up is Lisa Malloy."

Lisa did well, as did the two girls after her who, of course, were trying out for the lead role of Milly. Most every woman was trying out for Milly. They moved down the list at a rapid and orderly pace and Caleb found himself enjoying the audition process. It was always interesting to see how actors performed under pressure.

One woman apparently hadn't looked over the script at all, even though they'd been given them to practice with about a week ago. She'd fled from the stage crying her eyes out. Another young man completely froze and stood there with a stupid smile on his face, eyes glazed and bulging out of his head.

When Danielle's name was called she all but strutted up to the stage, flipping her ebony hair over her shoulder like the world owed her something. She squared her shoulders and tipped her chin up in the air. "I'm Danielle Monroe," she announced. "I will be trying out for the part of Milly." Caleb didn't miss the dark glower she shot Nasarra's direction. He sighed.

Danielle did well, as always, but her flare for the melodrama seemed to have seeped into her acting abilities because she'd been much more dramatic than the character, or the scene, called for. Since the play took place in the Old West, she'd decided to give the character an accent, but Caleb thought she sounded more like a Southern belle after way too many mint juleps. He wouldn't cast her. Ever. Which was probably why he was standing on the sidelines. He couldn't have been unbiased toward Danielle even if he'd tried.

After a monotonous performance from a short, elflike man and a very good one from a man trying out for the part of Adam, Nasarra's name was called. He glanced over at her and offered an encouraging smile and a wink as she made her way up to the stage. She gave him a tremulous smile and turned to the crowd, her face ashen.

"H-Hello," she stammered. She looked down and played with her fingers.

Caleb raised his eyebrows. This was not good. His dynamic, powerful Nasarra had suddenly become a shrinking violet. He felt his heart pick up its pace. He was nervous *for* her. She couldn't freeze. Not now. Not after she'd come so far. She had so much talent. She needed this. *Come on, baby,* he thought to himself. *You can do it. Find your courage. Your sister isn't here.* He knew that whenever she started to feel less than confident about herself, her sister's voice popped into her head. Heinous woman. She'd robbed Nasarra of her future once and was threatening to do it again. *Come on. Come on. Look at me, baby.*

She did. She found his eyes and he grinned. *You're better*

than half of these people. Show them what you're made of. As if she'd read his thoughts, something seemed to fall into place inside of her and she grew taller. Her shoulders went back and her head went up. "Hello," she said again. "I am Nasarra Williams and *I* will be trying out for the part of Milly." She shot a glance at Danielle and scowled.

Caleb chuckled and shook his head. Nasarra morphed in front of his eyes and she delivered her lines clear, powerful and perfect. She stood with confidence, but not arrogance, and she made the character her own. The song she had chosen to sing was "I'm Just A Girl who Can't Say No" from *Oklahoma!* and she commanded the attention of the audience while she performed it. And she *did* perform it. A lot of the others had simply sung the songs they chose. Nasarra acted it out. He had never been more proud of anyone in his life. Broadway would never know what hit it once she got there.

He watched the rest of the auditions with a smile on his lips, and as soon as Carolyn and Connor had gone to deliberate, he made his way over to Nasarra. She was back to playing with her fingers in her seat, looking petrified. He sat down next to her with a smile and slid an arm around her shoulders. "You were amazing," he whispered.

She looked up at him and shook her head. "I almost passed out, I swear. I don't know what happened to me. I got up there, and all of a sudden, I heard Shawna in my head. 'How many starving actors actually make it in the theatre business? You're only fooling yourself, Nasarra. Get a degree in something useful. I somehow doubt you're going to have what it takes to get to Broadway when all you have is high school training.'"

Caleb rolled his eyes. Over the course of the month he had come to realize that Nasarra's sister was an absolutely delightful woman. Delightful like lockjaw.

"I really thought I was going to blow it," she continued, "but then I looked up at you and everything else dulled. I remembered what you told me about my passion. I told my inner monologue to shut up and just let it flow through me."

"Well, it was worth it. You made half of these people look like fools."

Her cheeks turned pink and she buried her face against his shoulder with a bashful smile. He chuckled and stroked her hair.

It took quite a while for Carolyn and the others to return from their conference, but when they did, Nasarra's hands started to shake so badly that Caleb took both of them and caressed them.

"All right," Carolyn began, "the results are in. These were very difficult decisions to make. You all did very well today and, if you are not cast, it is not because you didn't do well. It is just because you did not fit the parts we were looking for at this time. If this is the case, please don't be discouraged. You have all done fantastically in this camp and I am sure you will find your niche. The cast list is as follows—"

Nasarra expelled a forceful breath and Caleb looked over at her with a smile. He slipped his arm back around her shoulders and squeezed. "Even if you don't get cast," he whispered into her ear, "you're still the teacher's pet." He nipped her earlobe, causing her to jump in surprise. He chuckled and pressed a kiss to her temple.

"The part of Adam goes to Phil Jacobs," Carolyn read.

Caleb nodded. Good choice. Phil was one of the best in his Advanced Acting class.

"The part of Milly goes to..."

Nasarra bit her bottom lip and looked over at Danielle. The woman smiled like she had it in the bag. Caleb suppressed a growl

"The part of Milly goes to..." Carolyn frowned and glowered at Connor. "Connor, your handwriting is chicken scratch. All your E's look like L's and you don't dot your I's. What's the matter with you?"

Connor shrugged and Nasarra groaned. "This is agony," she muttered. "Get on with it already."

Caleb smiled and rubbed his hand up and down her arm in encouragement.

Carolyn looked back at the paper. "Anyway, the part of Milly goes to Nasarra Williams."

Nasarra's eyes bulged and she gasped. She turned to Caleb, who winked at her. Like it had been a contest. Nasarra really was one of the best actresses he'd seen in a long time. "Now it begins," he whispered.

She clenched her fists and looked like she was forcing herself to squelch the urge to squeal in glee.

"I beg your pardon?" a satiny, albeit annoyed voice interrupted.

Nasarra and Caleb directed their attention to Danielle, who had nothing but barely controlled rage on her face. Caleb heaved a sigh and suppressed a groan. Great. The banshee had returned.

"Nasarra got the part of Milly," Carolyn repeated.

"*She* got Milly?" she hissed, stabbing her finger in Nasarra's direction.

"That's what I said," Carolyn stated.

"What about *me*?" she exploded.

Carolyn frowned and looked down at her paper. "You got Dorcas."

"Dorcas?" she screeched. "But that's a minor part! You don't even see Dorcas until halfway through the play!"

Carolyn did not look amused. "Well, I am sorry to disappoint you, Your Supreme Majesty," she mocked, "but that's just the way it goes. Nasarra got the part of Milly. You got Dorcas."

Caleb smothered laughter at Carolyn's words.

Danielle stared at Carolyn for a moment, then started to laugh ridiculous, fake laughter. "Wait a minute," she said. "You mean to tell me that you picked *carrot top* over there to play Milly when you could have had me?"

Carolyn sighed in exasperation. "I believe I said that, yes." She looked at the rest of the students. "Did I just think it? Or did you actually hear me say that, as well?" Scattered snickers followed. "Would you like me to repeat it again, Danielle?" she continued. "*You* got *Dorcas*."

Danielle looked over at Nasarra, then back at Carolyn. "But I've done plays for years. I was once cast in an off–Broadway play!"

Caleb rolled his eyes skyward. Yeah, an off-Broadway play she'd never actually performed in.

"How could she have gotten it?" she continued. "She has no training!"

Carolyn turned to face Danielle with a huff. "I can't very well put a person with a terrible accent and a flair for the over dramatic in the lead role, can I? Now, shut up before I decide not to cast you at all. I'm sure that if you insist on being a prima donna, there are plenty of students here who *didn't* get cast who would like to take your place."

Danielle stared at Carolyn, then looked over at Nasarra. Blind hatred contorted her face. "Fine," she spat. "Give the part to Caleb's little pet, his redheaded lap dog. He's the only reason she was cast anyway."

"Danielle!" Caleb found himself shouting. "I swear on everything that I am, if you don't shut it right this second, you *will* regret it!"

Danielle snorted. "What are you going to do, Caleb? Sabotage me again?"

"Punch her, Nasarra!" someone called.

Nasarra blinked in bewilderment.

"Yeah, deck her again!" another voice cheered.

Nasarra's cheeks turned pink and she tried to retreat into her jacket.

"Oh for goodness sake!" Carolyn cried. "Enough of this! I have had *enough* of this! Danielle, that's it. You just had your last strike. The part of Dorcas goes to Allison Linney."

Allison Linney let out an elated shriek; Danielle looked like she had been slapped. "But—"she stammered.

"But what?" Carolyn snapped. "I warned you. Caleb warned you, or did you think I wasn't aware of the great spectacle you made of yourself in his acting class?"

She blinked and visible tears filled her eyes. "But, I—" She shook her head and stood, stabbing her finger at Caleb. "He's the one who—"

"Did his job? Was mature about the situation? Yes, you're right. Now, shut up and sit your butt down before I throw you out of here altogether."

She opened her mouth again, but thought better of it and hunched her shoulders, remaining quiet and sitting down.

Nasarra looked up at Caleb in surprise, but he just shook his head in disgust. They listened as Carolyn went on with reading the cast list, and when she had finished, she told the cast members to report to Lazy Little Theatre for rehearsals starting on Monday. Nasarra's friend Laura had been cast, which Nasarra was excited about, and Caleb was happy for her. Seeing her joy and enthusiasm made him feel warm inside.

As she and Laura talked excitedly about the upcoming rehearsals, Caleb stood and shoved his hands in his pockets, letting his eyes take in the beauty of the scenery around him. He was both happy and sad that the theatre camp was over. He was happy that he didn't have to deal with Danielle anymore, but he really did love teaching. Doing it again hadn't been nearly as horrible as he had imagined. Once he'd confronted his inner demons, he'd remembered why he loved it in the first place.

"You evil snake!"

Caleb turned with a confused frown just in time to have Danielle plant both of her hands against his chest and shove him as hard as she possibly could. It was enough to actually make him stumble backwards.

"You are lower than low!" she shouted. "I can't even believe people like you are allowed to be alive!"

Caleb held his hands out in front of him, warning signals going off at the complete, insane fury etched into her facial features. "Danielle, I didn't do anything to you." He tried to keep his voice level and calm. It was obvious that she was furious and he had no desire to make an unbalanced person even more unbalanced by screaming at her.

"Did nothing to me!" She yelled it at the top of her lungs, exerting so much energy that her face turned bright red and a vein in her forehead bulged. "You sabotaged me again!" She shook her head, angry tears coursing down her cheeks. "Why are you doing this to me?"

Caleb met Nasarra's eyes and noticed the concern mirrored in them. "Danielle." He looked back to her again. "I would never do something like that to you. It was your own anger that got you thrown out of the play."

"*No!*" She stomped her foot. "You've ruined me again! Just like before! This is all your fault!" She lashed out and delivered a vicious slap across his face that stung like a thousand needles.

Caleb blinked, taken aback, but forced himself to remain clam. He brought his hand to his cheek and slowly turned his head back to look at Danielle. "You can't blame everything that happens on everyone else for the rest of your life," he said in a neutral tone. "One day, you're going to have to start taking responsibility for your own actions."

She stabbed her finger at him and snarled. "You *will* pay for this." She spun and stormed away.

A chill went down Caleb's spine at the way she had delivered her last line. It sounded almost like a...threat.

"Caleb, oh my gosh!" Nasarra was at his side immediately, tenderly touching his burning cheek. "Are you all right?"

He trapped her hand to his cheek and forced a smile. "I'm fine, sweetheart."

"I can't believe that she just did that!"

He let out a dry chuckle. "Yeah, neither can I, actually. That woman needs help." He shook his head, slung his arm around her shoulders and sighed. "Let's get out of here. I refuse to let Danielle rain on any more parades. You were just cast in the play, which means you are one step closer to your dream. We should celebrate." He waved Laura over with a smile. "Come on, let's all go out somewhere; what do you think?"

Nasarra grinned and snuggled closer to him, creating warmth where Danielle's bizarre outburst had made his body grow cold. "That sounds wonderful, Caleb. I'll call Rafe and Amanda."

He nodded and forced himself to concentrate on the good that had happened that day. He tried to ignore the peculiar sensation around his heart as he recalled Danielle's words. Something in her tone made him concerned, but he tried to put it out of his mind. This was Nasarra's victory and her night. He didn't need to worry her with unnecessary things.

* * *

The moon was full and yellow as Nasarra stood out on Caleb's balcony, watching the lights from the city twinkle like glitter. The breeze tossed her hair and she sighed. It had been a long and stressful day. She still couldn't believe she'd been cast. And she *really* couldn't believe the psychotic way Danielle had flown off the handle. She was glad she wouldn't have to work with her, or see her, anymore.

"Do you like it?" Caleb asked as he came to stand next to her. He leaned against the railing and handed her a glass of white wine.

She took the glass and looked up at him with a smile. "Yes, you have a gorgeous view." After a nice dinner out with Rafe, Laura and Amanda, Nasarra had gone with Caleb back to his beautiful home in Sausalito for a night cap.

His green-eyed gaze swept over her in a heated caress. "I do," he said, "but I'm not talking about the ocean and the city." He lifted his eyes to hers and a mischievous glint sparkled in them.

Nasarra let out a nervous giggle much like the ones she'd hated herself for giving him when she'd first been getting to know him. She didn't know why she reacted that way. She'd been dating him for a little over a month now. He shouldn't make her blush. He shouldn't make her shy. But he did. Still. And he still made her heart race like it was competing in a marathon.

She sucked her breath in as he sidled up close to her and slipped his arm around her waist. Her body came in full contact with his and she closed her eyes as her head swam. "Caleb." His name left her lips in a soft breath before she was able to stop herself.

His eyes smoldered and he made a purring sound deep within his throat. "You'd better be careful," he murmured. "You say my name like that and I'm bound to ravage you."

Her fingers bunched his shirt beneath them and she let out a shaky breath. Heat radiated off of his strong body and caused equal waves of heat to course through hers. She shook her head and instinctively pressed closer to him. "I have no idea where you came from," she whispered.

He chuckled and took her glass of wine from her, setting it aside and wrapping his arms around her. "The sidewalk, remember? In the rain."

She held up her fingers. "Two times."

"I was delivered a blazing comet during a downpour." He tangled his fingers in her hair and brought his mouth to hover over hers. "How did I end up so lucky?"

She smiled and turned her lips up to meet his, losing herself in his gentle sensuality. His arm tightened around her and she brought her hand up to tug at the tie holding back his hair. She freed the sunset-colored strands from their bondage and twined her fingers in them. He tilted her face upwards and monopolized her mouth until she was breathless and her head was spinning. Oh, how the man could kiss. When he was kissing her, she wanted it to go on forever.

Unfortunately, Caleb's pants started to beep and he pulled away from her with a frown. "Well, now, that's bad timing," he muttered.

She giggled and stepped back to let him look down at his pager, smoothing her hair and trying to bring her heartbeat back to a normal rate.

His frown deepened. "It's Carolyn" he said. "That's weird. Hold on. Let me go give her a call."

She nodded and turned back to the spectacular view of

the city. She leaned against the rail of the deck and rested her chin on her hands with a sigh. It was only a few seconds before Caleb came running back out onto the deck and grabbed her by the elbow.

"We have to go to the theatre," he stated.

Nasarra frowned as she followed him back inside. "Why? What's going on?"

He tied his hair back into a ponytail and pulled his jacket on. "I'm not sure. She just sounded frantic and said it was an emergency."

Her eyebrows rose in alarm and she jaunted after him, throwing her jacket on as she followed him out the door.

* * *

Nasarra couldn't believe what she was staring at. The whole front of Lazy Little Theatre was charred and blackened. Parts of it were still smoking. Police, fire trucks and an ambulance were still at the scene, lights flashing blue and red in all directions. Thank goodness no one had been at the theatre so no one had been hurt, and the building hadn't been burnt to the ground, but there was a sufficient amount of damage. The whole lobby area would have to be re-done, not to mention whatever damage the smoke and water had done to the rest of the structure.

Caleb heaved a sigh as he approached Nasarra from where he had been speaking with Carolyn. "It was definitely arson," he remarked. "At least that's what the police say."

She shook her head in disbelief. "Why would someone do something like that?"

He shrugged helplessly.

"I don't know what I'm going to do," Carolyn said, approaching them with a tear-streaked face. "What am I supposed to tell the students?" She put her face in her hands.

Caleb placed his arm around her in consolation. "Don't worry about it, Carolyn. You have fire insurance, right?"

"Well, yes, but—" She held her arms out. "It'll take at least a month to repair and rehearsals are supposed to start on Monday!"

"You can use my place for rehearsal until things get taken care of," Caleb volunteered. "I'll have Connor help me move everything out of my living room. It's big enough to do in a bind. It won't be a stage, but it'll be a rehearsal space until we can get the theatre fixed. Whatever you need my help with, you know I'll be there."

She looked up at him with something close to adoration in her eyes. "Thank you, Caleb. I don't even know what to say."

He pressed a friendly kiss to her forehead. "Don't worry about it. The show must go on, right?" He offered her a comforting smile. "We'll figure something out."

She nodded and went back over to talk to the police again.

Nasarra wrapped her arms around herself and stared in horror back at the desolation in front of her. "Caleb, who would do this?" she repeated.

"I told the police my suspicions," he replied.

She frowned and turned to meet his eyes. "You mean?" She blinked. "You think Danielle could have done this?"

He shrugged. "She threatened me right there in front of you. You tell me."

"You honestly think she would be capable of doing this?"

He shook his head sadly. "I don't put anything past her anymore. She had motive. What better way to get back at the people who ruined her shot at Broadway? Burn the theatre down. If there's no theatre, there can't be a play. No play, no one gets to go."

Nasarra's mind refused to compute that kind of twisted logic. She shook her head. "Well, at least no one was hurt."

"Not physically." He shot a glance back over at Carolyn. "This theatre is her home, her life. It was like a direct personal attack."

She ran her hands through her hair. "Well, I just hope they catch whoever did it..." She chewed on her bottom lip. "If it was Danielle, I hope they can get her the help she obviously needs." She met his eyes. "Are you sure you won't have a problem having rehearsal at your house for awhile?"

"It'll be a little frantic, but it should be fine. I'll have to give you the key, though. I won't be able to be there because I'll be working."

She raised an eyebrow and couldn't help but tease. "Giving me a key to your place now, are you?"

He grinned slyly. "Only if you promise not to come over while I'm sleeping and sneak into bed with me." He raised an eyebrow and devilment filled his eyes, as well as a deep, burning desire.

"Better give the key to someone else then." She gave him a look that mimicked his and smirked.

"My life was very dull before you, beautiful." He chuckled and pulled her close to him.

She snuggled against him. "Likewise." She yawned. "I'll be happy to host the cast at your house," she said. "Anything you need help with, just let me know. I'll do whatever I can."

He kissed the top of her head and gave her a little squeeze. "That means a lot. To me and to Carolyn."

She pulled back with a sigh and looked over at the distraught woman. Her heart twinged as she watched Carolyn turn to look at her theatre and start to cry again. She hoped that the police caught whoever had done this soon. The sooner the perpetrator was caught, the sooner repairs could be started and everything could be put behind them.

Nasarra wondered if it really had been Danielle. She was stupid if it had been. She, of all people, claiming to be such a diva, should know that the show always went on. One way or another. It was the way of the theatre. Somehow, some way, nothing stopped the rise of the curtain.

Now would be no different.

Chapter Thirteen

Present day

"She tried to burn the theatre down?" Maxim exclaimed in an outburst of complete surprise.

Nasarra smirked and nodded as she took a drink of coffee.

"I can't even wrap my mind around that." He shook his head and leaned back. They were sitting on the empty stage with the remnants of their breakfast. He took a good look around the theatre for the first time since they'd gotten there that morning, and tried to imagine what it had looked like charred and half-eradicated. "Was she actually convicted?"

"The police arrested her several days later." Nasarra met his eyes. "Danielle was insane, but far from a criminal mastermind. They found two cans of lighter fluid in her car, and three eye witnesses pinned her at the scene of the crime."

"I just can't believe anyone would stoop to that... Over a part in a play?"

Nasarra shrugged. "It was more to her than that. In Danielle's world, it was her whole life. We never heard anything from or about her after that. She was, thankfully, removed from our lives. Now we only have an interesting story left behind. An honest-to-goodness villainess. Who needs theatre when you have that kind of thing going on in your real life?"

"So, the play went on, though?" he prodded. She had him hopelessly intrigued.

"It sure did. We had some insane rehearsals at Caleb's house for awhile and Carolyn repaired the theatre in time for the curtain to go up. The play basically went off without a hitch, and at the end of Opening Night, Carolyn and Connor deliberated and posted a list of everyone who would be going to the New York audition."

Maxim smiled. "I take it you were on it?"

She grinned mischievously and gave a nod. "Caleb purposely stayed out of the judging in order to not cause conflict, or have people say he was playing favorites. He did, however, set me up with some accommodations with some friends of his in the city so I didn't have to stay with all of the theatre camp people."

"Were you surprised you were among the ones chosen?"

"Are you kidding me?" She snorted. "I was dumbfounded. I'd given up all hope of ever even seeing New York, much less audition for a Broadway play. A Nathan Price play, no less!" She wagged her finger. "There were only two things that were going through my head that were negative."

He frowned. "What?"

"Well, it sucked that I had an actual shot at being in a Broadway play at the exact same time that I had stumbled across the man of my dreams. I knew that, if by some divine miracle, I was cast in the play, I would be staying in New York and Caleb would be all the way across the country. I had absolutely no idea what to do about that."

"And the second thing?"

"Well, when I got home from the play on Opening Night, I had a message on my machine. With splendid timing, as always, my sister had decided she was going to drop in for a visit. Suddenly, my parade wasn't only rained on. It was flooded..."

1997

Shawna Williams-Davis. The most successful defense attorney in California. From what Nasarra had heard, criminals were practically on a waiting list wanting to be represented by her, and prosecution prayed before they had to go against her in court. Nasarra wasn't really that surprised. Shawna had always been a barracuda.

She'd practically killed herself trying to get ready for her sister's visit. She'd spent one whole day making sure that the duplex was clean and orderly and had all but been standing on her head waiting for her on the day she was supposed to arrive. Of course, she didn't show up when she said she would so Nasarra had been forced to leave her place and go to the theatre for her show. The play still had several more performances left and she wasn't going to put her life on hold just because her sister ran on Shawna time.

Caleb had come to pick her up after both of their shows were over and she'd almost completely forgotten about her sister until Caleb pulled up in front of her duplex and she spotted a black Escalade with plates that read "DADAVIS." Nasarra whimpered. DA Davis... Very humble.

Caleb removed his helmet and frowned at her over his shoulder. "You whimpering back there? What's going on?"

She pointed to the Escalade. "My sister," she groaned.

He winced.

"Yeah, she was supposed to show up earlier, but never did." She sighed. "I was hoping maybe she would have for-gotten me." She looked up at Caleb, trying to portray a pleading note in her eyes. "Please come in with me," she begged. "Don't send me to the sharks all by myself."

He chuckled and turned his engine off. "Of course, baby. I wouldn't dream of it." He shot her a wink and a playful smile.

Nasarra expelled a breath of relief and tried to straighten her hair while they climbed the steps. She prepared herself and opened the door, only to have Rafe shout her name with a great amount of enthusiasm and blow past her as he men-tioned something about how he had somewhere he needed to go to do that "one thing he was supposed to do."

Nasarra suppressed a grimace. Great, Shawna had al-ready driven her roommate out. She wondered if Rafe had been naked when she'd arrived. If he had, no doubt Shawna had spent a good amount of the conversation criticizing his package. It was just something she would do.

Caleb stumbled as Rafe bullied past him down the stairs and Nasarra steeled her resolve, turning her gaze to her im-maculate sister, who was standing in the middle of the room, commanding attention.

She was in a crisp, blue suit and her golden hair waved around her shoulders in perfection. Behind her, her husband David sat in a chair, relaxed, looking gnomelike, as always. Nasarra had never really understood what Shawna had seen in him. She supposed it was because he was rich. Shawna was always able to overlook everything else when she had dollar signs in her eyes.

"Nasarra!" Shawna exclaimed, holding her arms out. A warm smile dimpled her face. "It's so wonderful to see you again!"

Nasarra stared at her sister, dumbfounded. "Shawna...hello." She blinked a few times, then tried to smooth her hair again. Caleb cleared his throat behind her, reminding her that he was still standing outside on the steps. She quickly moved out of the way, but still avoided going farther into the room.

Shawna's gaze fell on Caleb and her smile disappeared as her eyes narrowed. "And who is this?" she almost sneered.

Caleb raised an eyebrow.

Nasarra huffed and closed the door. "Caleb," she stated. "My boyfriend."

Shawna raised her eyebrows in amusement. "Boyfriend?" She giggled. "You mean you actually decided to give dating a try? It's about time. I was beginning to think you were a lesbian with the way you avoided men."

Nasarra rolled her eyes as she flung her purse into a chair. "I didn't avoid men. I just didn't actively pursue them." She folded her arms. "Nice of you to show up on time, Shawna."

Shawna waved her hand airily. "Well, you know how it goes. It took forever to check into the hotel and then I had to take a nap because the trip took so much out of me."

Nasarra blinked. *Yeah, L.A to San Francisco. That's a long, arduous journey...*

"Where were you anyway?" Shawna prodded. "Not like you to be out of your hovel this late at night."

Her words were always in good humor, thinly veiling the rudeness beneath. "There's a play I've been performing in. I couldn't wait around for you forever so I went to do my show. I see you met Rafe."

"Yes, I did." She didn't sound impressed. "I don't know why you keep company with such weirdoes. They're only going to drag you down." She stabbed her finger over at one of Rafe's paintings. "And what is *that*?" She turned back to Nasarra, amusement sparkling in her blue eyes. "Trying your hand at painting now?"

Nasarra sighed. "No, those are Rafe's." Shawna made a disapproving face and opened her mouth, but Nasarra cut her off. "*Anyway*, how have you been?"

"Oh, we're just wonderful!" She switched gears as Nasarra knew she would. There was nothing Shawna liked better than talking about herself. "We're staying here for a few days. San Francisco is such a quaint, cute little city." She flipped her hair.

Nasarra arched an eyebrow.

"We're staying at The Hyatt Regency. Lovely place."

Nasarra's eyes widened. "The Hyatt—Geez, Shawna! How can you just throw your money around like that?"

Shawna gave Nasarra an incredulous look and sighed. "Well, David and I are both very *successful* at our jobs. I have never lost a case, you know."

"That's great, Shawna," she muttered flatly. Nasarra suppressed the urge to scream and she shot a glance at Caleb, who still hadn't taken his jacket off. He looked like he wanted to bolt out like Rafe had done.

Shawna glanced at Nasarra's couch as if she wanted to sit down, but made a face and remained standing. "What are *you* doing now? Still working as a waitress?"

"I'm going to Broadway in a few weeks," she hissed.

Shawna frowned. "Really, Nasarra. You don't have much money as it is. Shouldn't you be thinking about finding yourself a decent place to live instead of going on a very expensive vacation?"

"I'm not going on vacation. I'm going to an audition." She brushed aside the nagging part of her psyche that told her Shawna might be right. She would *not* go back there again. If it hadn't been for Shawna, she would have already been on Broadway. Besides, she had mostly managed to keep Shawna's meddlesome voice out of her head for the past few months and she wanted to keep it that way. It was so typical Shawna to march in and start criticizing her within minutes of her visit.

"An audition? For a play?" she asked.

"No, for a traveling circus. What do you think?"

Shawna's eyes narrowed. "Very funny."

Nasarra heaved a sigh. "Look, do you want some tea or something? Or do you want to go out somewhere and get—"

"No, we aren't staying that long. We have to be in bed by a respectable hour."

Nasarra's teeth gnashed together. *Right, of course. You*

only came to see me long enough to criticize every aspect of my life.

Shawna wheeled around to Caleb. "What do *you* do?"

Caleb looked horrified. Nasarra's eyes widened. Oh no, she'd decided to go in for the kill. "He's a performer in *The Phantom of the Opera*," she jumped in. "Do you remember when Mom took us to see *Oliver* when we were little?"

"Vaguely."

"Remember that boy I was totally obsessed with?"

"Who could forget? You talked nonstop about him for weeks. It was ridiculous."

Nasarra slid her gaze to Caleb, who was smiling at her. "Well, that was Caleb."

She stared at Nasarra, glanced to Caleb, then stared some more. "Oh give me a break," she spat. "You don't mean to tell me that you actually *believe* that croc of bull!"

Nasarra blinked, taken aback. She wanted to growl. Her sister's ability to find something horrible in every sentence that came out of her mouth really amazed her. She could say something obscure and unimportant such as, "the cheese is moldy" and Shawna would somehow come up with a reason as to why it was Nasarra's fault.

Shawna threw her hands up in the air. "Oh! I cannot believe you! You should really come and live with us, Nasarra. You need someone to take care of you and help you make an actual life for yourself."

Nasarra's annoyance level rose. What did her sister think she was? Mentally handicapped? Now she needed live-in home care? "I do have a life," she muttered.

Shawna ignored her. "You will believe anything anyone tells you! You are so naïve."

"Why don't you ease up, dear?" David broke in. "We just got here." Shawna shot him a deadly look and he shut up.

Nasarra stabbed her finger at Caleb. "Look, his name is Caleb Makepeace. How many Caleb Makepeaces are there in the world?"

Shawna heaved a sigh and flopped down on Nasarra's couch in defeat. "Nasarra, dear," she said in a condescending voice, "let me tell you something about the world. Romantic things like what you're trying to make me believe do not happen. This guy is just some bum who wants you to fall madly in love with him so he can get in your pants. I wouldn't be surprised if he already has. He's going to leave you with a kid and run out on you." She snorted. "That is so like you."

Caleb, thus far, had been quietly standing by, looking like he wished he could retreat into a corner. Now he stood tall, scowled, and took a step toward Shawna. "Now, wait a second," he protested. "I *am* standing right here."

Shawna glanced at him, then dismissed him with a wave of her hand like she was a queen holding court.

Nasarra felt her blood start to boil. She had been dealing with her sister's arrogance and condescension her entire life and she found that she was beginning to have no tolerance for it any longer. She'd had to deal with Danielle for the entire duration of the theatre camp and she found that she really didn't have many nerves left for people to grate on. "Would you like to see the programs, Shawna?" she snarled. "Would you like proof that they are the same person, or do you think that he doctored those too? Maybe you want his social security number so you can do a background check on him. Fingerprints, maybe? Hey, why don't we take some DNA samples and make him do a breathalyzer while we're at it!"

Shawna glanced up at her, but did not respond. "And why are you with him anyway?" she continued on. "Because you are entertaining some foolish fantasy you had as a small girl? You can't just go plowing into a relationship, Nasarra. It takes time to get to know someone and—"

"Yes!" Nasarra interrupted. "And you need to know whether or not the person is right for you, or is all they pretend to be."

"Exactly," Shawna replied smugly. "Now you're starting to talk sensible."

Nasarra gave her sister a petulant smile. "I'm sure David has kicked himself every day for not heeding that advice."

Shawna glowered at Nasarra with acid in her eyes, but David snorted a chuckle that he couldn't suppress and Caleb bit his bottom lip to keep from grinning.

"And about this Broadway nonsense," Shawna went on, her voice irritable and snippy. "What would *you* know about Broadway, Nasarra? Broadway requires talent. It requires you to know how to act, sing, dance. What makes you think you even have a chance? You never went to college. If you ask me—"

Nasarra felt something explode inside of her like a small grenade that ignited a very large and overdue fire. "No one *is* asking you!" she shouted.

Shawna looked up at her in bewilderment and Caleb actually retreated a step.

"Hello, Shawna, it's nice to see you too. I'm so glad you came to visit me to tell me about how successful *you* are. You've always been ready and willing to share your successes!"

Shawna folded her arms. "Yes, well, that's because I've made something of my life—"

"Because of *me!*" she bellowed. "You made something of your life because you were able to go to college because of *me!* I worked my butt off all through my senior year so you could make your million dollar dreams come true! At the cost of my own! You robbed me of my dreams!"

Shawna huffed. "Mother and Father just knew that *my* dreams were actually feasible where yours were—"

"Shut *up!*" she cried in frustration and anger. "It is *my* turn now! I am so sick and tired of listening to your voice! I'm talking now! What makes me think I can get to Broadway? I was in every play in high school with either major or supporting parts. I just finished up a theatre camp where I was hand selected to be in a play and then hand selected again to go to a New York audition! I sing every nightshift at Max's and get huge tips because of it. I danced in ballet and jazz and tap for years before you went to college! Where were you? Oh, wait, I remember. You had your head shoved so far up your arrogant butt that you never noticed it was me paying for your schooling!"

Shawna stood, her eyes blazing. Caleb put his hand over his mouth, no doubt in an effort to quell laughter.

"Why are you here, Shawna?" she asked. "You don't care about me. Why don't you go back home? Go back to your fabulous mansion in Beverly Hills where you can sit all day and admire yourself and tell yourself what a fabulous person you are. At least you'll have someone thinking so. Go and win your cases because I will not listen to you bash my dreams and my ambitions anymore. I have lived all my life with your meddling voice in my head telling me that I was worthless and what I was doing wrong. I finally got you out and you're not invited back! Ever!

"I have talent, Shawna, and I'm going to make it on Broadway! Someday you're going to realize that I am just as successful as you are and when I'm up on stage accepting my Tony Award, I'll remember not to thank you, but you'd better thank me every friggin' time you're interrogating a witness because you wouldn't be there if not for me. Maybe you'd be working in retail, or worse, as a waitress.

"*Go home.*" She put heavy emphasis on both words. "Go back to your mansion and live there all alone while I'm living the life I've always dreamed of. I'm hoping one of these days David wakes up, sees what a heinous banshee he's married to, and runs out on you before you devour him alive! Then you'll only have your money, and that can't keep you warm at night."

She took a deep breath as her monologue raged on. "I am just as capable and competent as you are, my dear sister, and you will see that one day. Until then, don't come and see me anymore. You're not welcome here." The last part, she practically growled, and she found herself feeling very tall.

Shawna scowled indignantly for several heartbeats. "Fine," she spat out, "if you want to destroy your pathetic life, I can't stop you. David!" She swaggered out of the room and motioned for her husband to follow.

David stood and squeezed Nasarra's hand on his way out. He grinned at her. "I think I may have picked the wrong sister," he whispered. "You are a fiery thing!"

Nasarra grinned. "Take care, David. Let me know if you need me to hire an assassin."

He chuckled.

"David! *Now!*" Shawna roared from outside.

David kissed Nasarra on the cheek, then waved at Caleb. "Nice meeting you."

Caleb held his hand up, looking bewildered.

Nasarra watched David go, then went to the door and shut it quietly. She heaved an enormous sigh, feeling confused and shocked. What had just happened? She could swear someone had possessed her body. It was the same someone who had possessed her when she'd decked Danielle. She had just pretty much told her sister where to go. She had never foreseen that coming. Shawna had always intimidated her so badly. She turned to look at Caleb with a pained expression.

"That was...interesting," he stated.

She scratched at the back of her head as she crossed the room. She stopped in front of him and frowned. "You know, I—" She was cut off by him pulling her into his arms and devouring her mouth in an all-consuming kiss. All of her tension melted away and she wrapped her arms around his neck, giving herself over to his passion and dominance.

"You were brilliant," he murmured as he pulled away and smoothed her hair. "Fire and passion. Everything you are on stage. Everything you are in life." He took her face in his hands. "Don't feel guilty about telling your sister off. She deserved it." He frowned. "Especially after the things she said about me." He gave an arrogant sniff and Nasarra giggled. He smiled. "You're an amazing, talented, and beautiful woman. Don't ever let anyone tell you otherwise."

Her heart melted and, as he lowered his lips to hers again, a split second of indecision flashed through her mind. It was a moment that was insignificant in the span of time, but it was long enough that she understood it.

For that tiny second, she wanted a life with Caleb by her side ten times more than she'd ever wanted Broadway, but the doubt was chased away by sheer determination. She would not surrender her dream this time. It was all she'd ever wanted. She had to prove she could do it, that she was good enough. She *would* prove it. Period.

Chapter Fourteen

Nasarra heaved an enormous sigh as she stepped off the plane. There was so much she had to do. She took a few steps forward, but just ended up collapsing into the nearest hard, plastic chair. She put her head in her hands and closed her eyes, feeling the cool metal of the silver necklace she wore against her skin.

A pang of grief twisted her heart and she moved her hand to clutch it. It was the comedy/tragedy masks symbol. Caleb had given it to her right before she'd left San Francisco to embark on the most anticipated and terrifying path of her life. New York City.

All of the others who'd been picked from the theatre camp had gone on the same flight, and Nathan Price was putting them up in a hotel for the duration of the audition, but Nasarra had flown solo since she was staying with Caleb's friends instead of at the hotel with the others.

Saying goodbye to her friends at the airport had been difficult, but saying goodbye to Caleb had nearly killed her.

"I have something for you," he'd said while placing the box in her hand. "Don't open it until you are in the air. Remember when you wear what's inside, that you can do this. You can get up on stage and make people cheer. You possess that ability. You always have. You remember that you are every bit as good as your sister. In fact, you are better because she only ever takes from people, where you give so much to everyone you touch. You gave Shawna her success at the sacrifice of your own. It's time to give yourself something. Also, remember that you have people back at home rooting for you. A crazy, naked artist, and your very best friend. And..." He'd swallowed hard as if choking on his own emotion. "And a person who is looking up at the stars at night and wondering if you're looking at them too. Someone who never wanted to love you, but whose heart decided to against his better judgment. Someone who never regrets that decision. And, even though he lives at the other end of the country, he has enough love in his heart for you to fill the universe."

He'd kissed her with longing, as if he never wanted to let her go. She almost hadn't gone. As she'd been walking toward the gate, there had been one moment where she'd actually stopped. It was pure stubbornness that had enabled her to keep going. At that moment, Broadway hadn't mattered. New York was nothing to her. The theatre was a hobby and nothing more. At that moment, the only thing in her world was Caleb.

Getting on the plane was the hardest thing she'd ever done.

She heaved another sigh and forced herself out of the chair, shoving her sorrowful emotions down and trying to focus on what lay ahead. She was being handed an opportunity to accomplish her greatest dream. Caleb had given her so much. It wouldn't be right to turn away from all of it now. It would be a slap in his face and she'd regret it for the rest of her life. She had to finish this. She had to see it through, no matter what the outcome.

She retrieved her luggage from the baggage claim and caught a cab to Times Square. She was supposed to meet up with Caleb's friends Colin and Jenna at the theatre where they worked. They were both in the new play, *Jekyll and Hyde,* and Caleb had told her to give her name to the guard at the door and tell him she was a friend of Jenna and Colin Daniels.

She thought it was awfully nice of Caleb's friends to let her stay with them, considering she was a stranger. She'd told Caleb that she didn't mind staying at the hotel with the others, but he had insisted, saying that she would get more out of her New York experience living with natives.

Nasarra's first impression of the city as she rode along in the cab was that it wasn't that impressive. All she saw were dilapidated brick buildings with black fire escapes snaking down the sides like veins. There was nothing spectacular about anything, but as they reached the inner city, her opinion began to change. Buildings reached high into the sky, plucking at the clouds. There were cars everywhere, backed up and making their own traffic laws while swarms of people walked the streets at a brisk and hurried place. Everyone looked like they had an agenda.

A group of young women sauntered down the street in club attire. Homeless people wandered, or performed some kind of talent for money. It wasn't that different from what she saw in San Francisco, but it all seemed so much more exciting because it was New York.

Times Square took her breath away. All of the marquees on the theatres, as well as the tower in the middle of the square with advertisements, were lit up and blinking like fireworks as dusk descended on the city.

Giddy delight bubbled up inside of her and she rolled down her window to get the full experience. Horns echoed through the chaos and yellow cabs sped in every direction. She heard sirens of an ambulance in the distance, and a constant, droning hum that marked the pulse of the city. Smells of every kind of food imaginable mixed together in a heady, intoxicating blend that was quickly destroyed as the cab took a turn and she was blasted by the nauseating stench of sewage. She made a face and quickly rolled her window back up. Okay, nix the full experience idea.

The cab driver dropped her off on a random corner and Nasarra got out and unloaded her luggage. He sped off as soon as she paid him and she stared in bewilderment down at her bags. She had two suitcases, a backpack, and a purse. That was just going to be fun to lug up the crowded New York street. Was she out of her mind?

With a heavy sigh, she hoisted her backpack onto her back and picked up one suitcase in each hand after slinging her purse over her shoulder. She turned up the street, wondering why she hadn't grown a brain and told the cab driver to drop her off at the theatre.

A strange sensation filled her as she craned her neck, looking for the *Jekyll and Hyde* marquee. She didn't know if it was excitement, jubilation or horror. Maybe all three mixed together. She was amazed to be there, but terrified to be out of her comfort zone. What if she bombed? What if everyone laughed at her?

She shook her head. "Shut up, Nasarra," she told herself. "Just find the theatre."

She refrained from jumping up and down in joy when she

finally did find it. She probably looked like a complete idiot dragging her bags along with her. She was surprised she hadn't been mugged yet.

She searched for the backstage door of the theatre and kicked at it until a huge, burly, balding man who looked like he should be in the WWF opened the door and glared at her.

"What do you want?" he growled. "The homeless shelter ain't here, lady."

"I-I'm Caleb's friend," she puffed.

He frowned. "That's nice." He started to close the door.

"No, wait!" she exclaimed. She shook her head. She had Caleb on the brain. "I mean, Jenna and Colin Daniels. They're in the play. I'm a friend of theirs." Her purse fell off her shoulder and she scowled. She grabbed it, stuck the strap in her mouth, and fished around in her pocket for the backstage laminate Caleb had given her just in case she was given any trouble. Apparently, Colin had mailed it to him. She held it out. "Eee?" she mumbled, her purse still in her mouth.

The guard gave her a skeptical once-over, then took the pass and inspected it. Recognition seemed to dawn on him after a few minutes. "Oh, right!" he exclaimed. "You're that Nessar chick, aren't you?"

Nasarra sighed as she situated her purse once again. "Nasarra," she corrected. "Yeah, that's me."

"Come on in. Go find a place for yourself in the dressing rooms. Intermission should be soon. Just try and stay out of everyone's way."

"Thanks." She waddled down the steps into a long, sterile corridor. She could hear Dr. Jekyll screaming when she went past the stage door, and she figured she knew where they were in the storyline. The actor sounded very convincing as he transformed into Hyde. That was who she was supposed to meet. Colin Daniels. He had been Caleb's understudy in *Joseph*.

Nasarra made her way toward what she assumed was the dressing room. There was no label on the door saying whose was whose so she just went in the first door she saw and hoped it was the right one. She needed to set her things down before her arms fell off.

She let her suitcases flop to the ground with a thump, and only afterwards did she bother to look up. Her eyes widened. The room was full of guys from the ensemble. Great.

That was just her luck.

She stood straight and plastered a smile on her face, then brushed back a lock of her rebellious hair. "Hey guys," she greeted. "Sorry to barge in on you like this. Wasn't really looking for the guys' dressing room, but I just flew all the way from San Francisco and wandered halfway down Broadway toting these stupid bags. If I don't put them down and rest for a second, I'm gonna drop dead."

All of the guys exchanged surprised looks. One of them stepped forward. He was tall with dark brown hair and amazingly blue eyes. His smile was absolutely breathtaking and it made Nasarra's heart falter for a split second. "You're welcome to stay as long as you like," he said suavely, holding out his hand. "Not like we're going to complain if a gorgeous woman decides to hang out with us."

"I'd rather it be a gorgeous man," one of the others said, causing laughter to sound throughout the room.

Nasarra grinned and looked up at the handsome actor. She smiled and placed her hand in his.

His smile was roguish, as was the twinkle in his eye. "I'm Jason," he said softly.

"Nasarra."

"And what are you doing here, lovely Nasarra?" he questioned.

She felt her cheeks turn pink and she averted her eyes. "Um...I'm trying out for a play in a few days and I'm supposed to be staying with Jenna and Colin Daniels. Because of the time of my flight, they couldn't pick me up so I'm supposed to meet them here."

"Coincidence," he stated. "Or fate." He winked. "I haven't decided yet."

She arched her eyebrows. "Excuse me?"

He folded his arms, his smile ever-present. "I'm auditioning for a play in a few days, as well. Think it could be the same one?"

"Um...Nathan Price's new play? Called *Broadway Dreams.*"

His grin was went from roguish to wolfish. "Fate."

Her face flamed again and she gave a self-conscious laugh. "I don't believe in fate, but at least I'll see a familiar face at the audition." She turned toward the door, suddenly wanting out of the room. Was it hot, or was it just her?

"Look, do you mind if I leave my stuff in here? I'll be back in just a second. I want to see if there's a vending machine somewhere."

"Down the hall and to the right," he replied. "And we'll watch your things for you." He jabbed his thumb in the direction of the actor who had made the comment about wanting to see a gorgeous man. "I can't promise that Jack won't go through your undies though."

She laughed. "Well, have at them. Just be sure you put them back when you're done." She waved her hand and darted out of the room, needing to be back in the cool hallway and away from the scorch of that man's beautiful eyes. A vision of Caleb flashed before her and she placed her hand over her necklace. A pang of guilt washed over her, even though she hadn't done anything to be guilty for. She felt guilty for simply thinking that Jason was good-looking.

With a sigh, Nasarra wandered and watched as the actors buzzed around getting ready for the next act. No one seemed to care that she was there and she was grateful for that. She just wanted to blend in right now.

She suddenly spotted the stage door and bit her bottom lip, feeling mischievous. She glanced around, saw no one was looking, and opened it, disappearing into the backstage darkness. She just wanted a peek. A little glimpse into the life she might actually get to have.

Nasarra peered around the curtains and gazed out across the stage. She sighed in bliss. It was grand, magnificent... She could hear the hum of the audience talking amongst themselves as they waited. The house sounded full. She smiled to herself, then backed up as she heard a group of actors filter through the door to get in their places for the start of the next act. She didn't want to be in anyone's way.

She felt her back come in contact with something and she turned, only to find herself staring up at an ominous figure with dark eyes and scraggly black hair. He wore an enormous fur coat and was shrouded in shadow. He looked positively demonic and she jumped back, opening her mouth to scream.

A heavy hand clamped down over her mouth as his other hand came to grasp her arm. "Shhh!" the demon hissed. "What are you doing back here? Who are you?"

"Nesawaa," she tried to say through his hand. She rolled

her eyes as her heart started to return to a normal rate. She felt completely stupid. Demon. Right. Since when did demons lurk in stage corners? She swatted at his hand and let her breath out in a huff. "Colin Daniels," she assumed.

He arched an eyebrow.

"I'm Nasarra, Caleb's girlfriend."

A slow, warm smile of recognition spread across his face, transforming his otherwise frightening appearance. "Oh, hello! You made it all right, then! Yeah, I'm Colin!"

"You scared the crap out of me," she grumbled.

He chuckled. "Sorry about that. This is kind of an intimidating get up. How was your trip?"

"Tiring." She ran a hand through her hair, feeling the weight of the fatigue for the first time. "Overwhelming."

"Well, I have to start Act Two here pretty soon. Just go relax for the rest of the show. Jenna and I will find you after and get you all settled in. It's good to meet you."

She managed to give him a friendly smile. "You too. Thanks. Break a leg!" She left the backstage area and returned to the men's dressing room, where she proceeded to shoot the breeze with Gay Jack for most of the second act. When a techie announced it was time for curtain call, she decided to lug her stuff out and wait in the hall. That way, all of the guys could change without her in there pretending she was invisible, and it would be easier for Colin to see her.

It took both of them awhile to get out of makeup, but Nasarra spotted them easy enough when they were striding down the corridor, and she stood with a smile. Colin looked completely different out of his costume. He had light, short-cropped hair and his features were much kinder than when she'd seen him looming in the shadows. Jenna was short with a happy smile and kind hazel eyes.

"Hi, I'm Nasarra," she introduced, shaking Jenna's hand. "I already met your husband backstage."

Colin chuckled and picked up her bags. "Yeah, I scared the wits out of her."

Jenna grinned and the two women followed Colin down the hall. "Caleb spoke so much about you," Jenna said. "He's very proud of you."

Nasarra felt her cheeks turn pink and she smiled. "I really appreciate you guys letting me stay with you. I know it must be weird letting a stranger crash at your place."

Colin shook his head. "Don't be stupid. It is more than obvious that Caleb is head over heels in love with you. He is a very good friend of ours. You are no stranger."

She bit her bottom lip and let her mind fill with thoughts of Caleb. Had it only been that morning she had said good-bye to him in the airport? What an agonizingly long day it had been.

The Daniels' apartment was a lovely two bedroom that reminded her of her own place. It was comfortable, not stuffy, and just cluttered enough to make her feel at home.

"The guest room is yours," Jenna said. "Make yourself right at home."

"Thanks again so much. I can't even express my appreciation."

Colin waved his hand and grinned. "We're always more than happy to help out a fellow actor."

Nasarra stretched her back out with a sigh and spotted a sliding glass door that led out onto a small balcony. "I think I'm gonna make some calls and then go to sleep," she said. "I'm really tired."

"No doubt," Jenna said. "You had kind of a hectic day. If you hear a monstrous noise coming from the bedroom, it's just Colin snoring. He sounds like a hibernating bear."

Nasarra giggled as Colin grabbed his wife and began to tickle her toward the bedroom. They shouted a goodnight at her, then closed the door in laughter.

Silence filled the apartment save the constant, droning hum of the city. She grabbed the cordless phone from an end table by the sofa, slipped out onto the terrace and made the necessary calls to her parents, Rafe, and Amanda. When she got to Caleb, she felt a strange mixture of elation and pain as she listened to his voice.

When she hung up, she stared up at the glowing Chrysler Building for the longest time, trying to figure out if the tumult she felt within herself was normal, and if it had a name. She didn't feel as excited as she should, and that was strange to her. She tried to tell herself that it was just nerves and feeling out of her element, but something deep inside of her told her it was much more than that. She missed the foggy city and her little duplex far more than she should. What she'd seen so far of New York was beautiful, but...lacking, somehow.

With a weary sigh, she pushed herself out of the deck chair and went back inside. She hauled her things into the guest room and flopped down on the bed. In the morning, things wouldn't seem so completely muddled. She'd get a good night's rest and explore some of the city the next day. Once she got familiar with her surroundings, she was sure that the uneasiness would go away. This was her greatest dream, after all. All of her crazy emotions had to just be cold feet and fear of failure.

"You'll be fine," she murmured to herself with a yawn. "You'll see."

Chapter Fifteen

Jason placed his hands on Nasarra's shoulders and began to rub them gently. She tensed, at first, from the unexpected contact, but knew he was only trying to be encouraging...in his own flirtatious way. She let out a long, slow breath, trying to get her nerves under control. All of the applicants had been waiting in line for three hours, and the line just kept getting longer. It snaked all the way out of the theatre and down the street for about a block. She was somewhere toward the middle with Jason and Laura.

Jason had actually shown up at Jenna and Colin's door on Nasarra's second day in the city with an invitation to take her to breakfast and show her around. His charming smile and sparkling eyes had made her feel uneasy so she'd called up Laura over at the hotel where the others were staying and invited her along. The three of them had gotten along amazingly well and had spent two days running around the Big Apple. Jason, despite his playboy disposition, was actually a very genuine and decent person. They had all decided to go to the audition together. Strength in numbers.

But Nasarra wasn't feeling very strong at the moment. She felt like she was going to vomit. All of these people were trying out for the same play. It was intimidating and nerve-wracking and made her audition at the drama camp seem like a walk in the park. The line was moving like molasses and Nasarra took turns twiddling with the necklace Caleb had given her and the bracelet her friend in high school had given her. She wasn't superstitious by any means, but they made her feel better, and she needed all the help she could get.

"Number one forty-nine!" a petite woman shouted, sticking her flaxen head out the door. They had all been handed numbers, but had to remain in line as there was no room in the lobby. Nasarra looked down at the slip of paper in her hand and her stomach dropped. Her number was one fifty-two.

"Hey, it's almost your turn," Laura observed.

Nasarra stared at her blankly, unable to speak or move. It was difficult enough just to breathe. A taxi laid on its horn and came to a screeching halt right beside the patch of side-walk they were standing on and Nasarra just about jumped out of her skin. She heard Jason chuckle and she looked up at him.

He placed his arm around her in reassurance. "I remember my first audition. I thought I was going to spew all over the director."

She smiled tremulously.

"You'll do fine," he said with a wink.

She turned back around and chewed on her lip until she thought she just might pull it straight off. She started to run through the monologue she had chosen for her audition piece like it was a mantra. It was just a bit from one of her scenes from *Seven Brides For Seven Brothers.* She knew it inside, outside and backwards, but she found it comforting to say. It took her mind off of how terrified she was.

"Number one fifty-two!"

She took a deep breath and her heart started to hammer. She gripped her headshot and resume in her hand and all but flew to the entrance of the theatre, not even saying anything to Jason and Laura.

The petite woman's eyes fixed on Nasarra. "You number one fifty-two?"

She nodded mechanically.

"Come on inside."

"Where is our next performer?" a menacing baritone voice bellowed from over the headset the woman wore. "Do we have a next performer, or did she throw up and leave like number one thirteen?"

The woman rolled her eyes. "Nathan, cool your jets. She had to come all the way from the back of the line."

"We need to keep things rolling here, Denise! What do I pay you for?"

Nasarra was horrified. Was that Nathan Price? He was actually reaming his assistant? She felt herself blanch. She didn't stand a chance. Caleb was friends with this man?

But Denise didn't seem phased. "Cram it up your butt, Nate!" she shouted back into the headset.

To Nasarra's surprise, she heard laughter coming from the other end. Denise shoved a clipboard in her hand and made her sign in, then told her to go on into the house of the theatre.

Nasarra felt like she was marching in front of the firing squad. If she survived this, it would be a miracle. She walked stiffly through the main doors leading to the house and thought that a walk up the aisle to the stage had never seemed so long.

She came to stand before a panel of people in the front row. One man was tall and muscular with red hair and eyes that looked like they were mocking everything. He lounged in his chair as if he had all the time in the world, and he twirled a pen absently in his long, slender fingers. He reminded Nasarra of a slightly more attractive Conan O'Brien.

Two men and one woman flanked him. One man was short and bearded with thick, black glasses and the other was shaggy-looking with a chin that could have cut glass. The woman was very tall and thin, thinner than Nasarra thought was healthy.

"So, who are you?" Conan O'Brien asked bluntly.

She took a deep breath and collected herself, then stuck her hand out in greeting. "Nasarra Williams."

His eyebrows went up in vague surprise. "Hey, you're the first person so far to not look at me like you're either going to die or take over my theatre." He stood and gave her a firm handshake. "Nathan Price. I run this shindig. Can I have your headshot and resume, please?"

She obeyed and handed him the required documentation.

"Thanks. Go ahead and go up on stage. Start your piece whenever you're ready, but try to get a move on. We don't have all day."

She ignored his brashness and climbed the steps to the stage. She stood and faced all of them, squaring her shoulders. *Best to just get this over with.* "I will be performing a monologue from the play *Seven Brides For Seven Brothers.* I will be playing the part of Milly." She opened her mouth to start, but he cut her off.

"Hey, you're one of the girls from Caleb's drama camp,"

he stated. A grin blossomed across his face as he continued to glance over her resume. "Cool... Proceed."

She cleared her throat and launched into the monologue, morphing into her character and feeling like she'd gone straight back to the Little Theatre. It wasn't as scary as she'd thought it would be. Caleb wasn't there to cheer her on, but she knew he was in spirit.

"Thanks," Nathan said when she had finished. "How do you think you did?"

She blinked. "I beg your pardon?" What kind of crazy director even cared?

"It was a simple question. How do you think you did?" He assessed her as if looking for something in particular.

She bit her bottom lip and shrugged self-consciously. "Well, I did my best."

"What if your best isn't good enough?"

She frowned and her heart skipped a beat or two. Was this some sort of game? She huffed and raised her chin in defiance of the mockery in his eyes. "Well, then I would apologize for wasting your time and go on to some other director who *did* think it was good enough." It came out with much more attitude than she had intended and she figured she'd probably blown any chance she'd had right out of the water.

Nathan grinned and chewed on the end of his pen. "'Kay, come here. Take this number." He handed a slip of paper out to her. "Go and wait in the backstage dressing room. Someone will come and get you when it's time for the next part of the audition."

She obeyed and disappeared into the blackness of backstage. It was easy to find the room he was talking about. It was stuffed and overflowing with people. She sighed and found an empty space in the hall, sitting down and pulling a book she had brought out of her purse. She tried not to dwell on the strange audition she'd just had. Caleb had told her he was friends with Nathan Price, and he'd mentioned that the man was a bit unorthodox, but he'd never said anything about him grilling the applicants like a psychiatrist.

"Who are you?" a girl with way too much makeup on asked with a slight snobby air.

Nasarra introduced herself and inquired about the next part of the audition. The more prepared she was, the better.

"It's the singing portion. Have you ever been to a Nathan

Price audition before?"

She shook her head.

"Well," she sniffed, "he narrows it down as he goes. He sifts through to find the ones who can act, then sends them through the singing stage. After that, the ones who are left go through the dance portion. At the end of the day, he decides who he wants to call back."

"Oh, okay," she said with a nod. "So all of us back here made it through."

The girl nodded.

Well, that was encouraging. At least she hadn't been sacked on the first go-round.

"Nasarra!"

She turned her attention to the sound of her name and saw Laura heading her direction. Her eyes widened and she stood, catching her in an embrace. "You made it!"

"Yeah, thank goodness." She frowned. "That guy was weird."

Nasarra nodded and went on to relate her own experience. After about ten minutes, Jason sauntered backstage also. He still seemed relatively relaxed, which grated on Nasarra's nerves. The man always seemed relaxed. Sure, he was a professional and all, but she would have felt much better about her own nerves if his confidence had waned just a little.

"Are you even fazed by any of this?" she muttered up at him when a peppy brunette came backstage and started hollering numbers again. "I'm having a small heart attack and you're just standing there."

Jason turned his gorgeous blue eyes down at her and grinned. "Nasarra, I have been doing this forever," he stated. He casually placed one hand in the pocket of his black slacks. "You win a few, you lose a few, but they're basically all the same. Besides, the more unabashed you look, the less likely you are to get sent home right away. Confidence is key." After a few seconds, he bent his head down to her and whispered in her ear, "Just don't go anywhere near my underarms."

She laughed in spite of herself and eased a bit at his admission. A gentle smile softened his handsome features and, against her will, her heart made a funny flip in her chest. She frowned and stomped on the feeling as Caleb's visage chased out the picture of Jason's.

The vocal audition went a little differently than the acting one. Because they were all backstage, she could hear all of the applicants sing, or at least attempt to. Her new number was forty-five, which meant quite a few people had been eliminated in the first round.

"Number forty-five!"

She almost screamed. Laura patted her on the shoulder and said she'd do fine. Jason offered warm words of encouragement also, but she barely registered his voice as she all but ran toward the stage entrance.

She walked out and saw the same group of people in the audience as before. The only difference was the piano on the stage

"Hey, it's you again!" Nathan Price exclaimed at her entrance. "Didn't I tell you to go home?"

She blinked and swallowed painfully. "No..." Had there been some kind of mistake? "You gave me a number and told me to go backstage."

He frowned. "Aren't you that real obnoxious one with the *Macbeth* audition? The one that kept popping gum the entire time?"

She arched an eyebrow. "No."

"Oh, wait!" He waved his hand and shook his head as he shifted in his seat. "You're *Seven Brides*. My bad. You all start to look the same after awhile. Go ahead and sing whatever you have prepared when you're ready."

She had chosen "Memory" from *Cats*. It had always been one of her favorites and she thought she sang it particularly well. When she finished, everyone was silent. It was unnerving.

"Miss...Williams, was it?" Nathan finally said.

She nodded, her spirits lifting just a bit at the thought that he'd remembered her name.

"Marlice has a piece of music from the show. I'd like to hear how you sing it. Can you do that for me?"

Nasarra nodded and grabbed the sheet music from the woman at the piano. She wasn't the greatest at sight-reading, but she gave it her best shot. Luckily, she got to listen to it once before she butchered it, and it wasn't that difficult. She lost her place once, but thought she did all right for not knowing it.

When she had finished, she gave the music back and turned to face the panel once again.

He gave curt nod and told her to go back and wait some more.

Eternity passed. By the time everyone had finished their vocal audition, it was well passed four o'clock in the afternoon and they had begun at six that morning. It was hot backstage and everyone was hungry, tired and cranky. Jason and Laura were still hanging in there with her, as were a couple people from the drama camp, but the group had thinned out considerably since that morning.

They were informed that there was going to be a short break and then the dance audition so Nasarra stretched to the best of her ability, annoyed that she was going to have to dance in her black, pinstripe slacks. "You know, the least he could have done was let us know that we were supposed to bring dance clothes," she grumbled.

"Nathan likes to take people by surprise," Jason said. "He likes to take them out of their element and see how well they adapt." He shrugged as he took a long drink from a soda he'd snagged from the vending machine. "He must do something right. He's won a ton of Tonys."

"Have you ever been to the Tonys?" she asked, hopelessly intrigued at the fact that he'd been a Broadway actor for so long.

"Once," he said with a smile.

"Ever been nominated?"

He chuckled and set his bottle down, then split his legs in front of him in a straddle stretch. He made a pained face. "These pants are gonna tear straight down my crotch, I just know it," he muttered.

Nasarra laughed and he held his hands out to her, indicating that they could help one another with the stretch. She moved across from him and matched her feet up with his, splitting her legs in the same position. She linked her fingers with his and he pulled her forward slowly. She grimaced, still not as flexible as she could have been.

"In answer to your question, no," Jason said. "Never been nominated." He glanced up at her. "What about your boyfriend? Has he ever been?"

"Nominated?" She sat up and leaned back, pulling him forward in the same way he had done to her. "No, I don't think so." She grinned as she thought about Caleb and how enamored she'd been with him, well, for her entire life. "He should have been though. He's fantastic."

Jason glanced up at her with a flat expression. "Wish some hot girl would say that about me."

She giggled, but wasn't sure how much he was actually teasing. "Jason, I'm sure you're wonderful."

"I'm sure you'll find out one day."

Both of her eyebrows arched upwards as his statement was heavy with double meaning and laced with arrogance.

He feigned innocence. "What? We might get cast together. Then you'll get to see me act." He frowned as if her reaction had been improper. "Come on, get your mind outta the gutter," he chided.

She laughed, as she always seemed to do around him, and felt the tension ease out of her once again.

"Everyone out onto the stage, please!" the peppy brunette shouted suddenly.

Nasarra sighed and pushed herself into a standing position. She wandered out onto the stage with the rest of the bedraggled group and looked back out at the audience. Everyone looked a little worse for the wear. Nathan Price almost looked like he was going to fall out of his chair. The short man with the glasses had his head propped up in his hand and the shaggy man looked even shaggier. The thin woman was up on stage next to the piano.

"I am so sick of looking at all of you!" Nathan wailed.

Nasarra couldn't help but giggle. He was a little obnoxious, but humorous nonetheless. He was more human than she had imagined. She'd pictured some kind of stuffed shirt with no personality.

"What are you laughing at, Williams?" he barked.

Nasarra started and looked over at him. She bit her bottom lip, then shrugged. "Well, I agree with you. I'm sick of looking at everyone too. Especially when it's close to a sauna backstage and some people didn't wear deodorant." Laughter erupted and Jason crossed his arms over his chest as if she'd meant him, which just made everyone laugh harder.

Nathan couldn't suppress his chuckle and he shook his head. "You're killing me, Williams. All right, let's get this show on the road. I'm hungry and if I don't get some steak in me soon I'm gonna open fire. Take it away, Nancy."

The thin woman stepped forward with all the grace and elegance of a seasoned ballerina. She broke them into groups of ten and gave them all a set of dance steps. Marlice accompanied on piano and all of them had to hoof it right there. One girl froze, looking like she wanted to cry. One man tripped over his own feet and fell over. Laura did well; so did the last remaining few from the drama camp. Nasarra was grateful for the drama camp as she went out with her group. She never would have remembered the dance steps otherwise.

"All right, lemmings," Nathan said at the end of the audition. "That's finally it. Callbacks will be announced in two days. Don't call me. I'll call you. If I don't call you, don't come back. Capiche?"

Everyone made their way out of the theatre and Nasarra heaved a sigh once she and her companions were outside. She was exhausted.

"That was terrible," Laura stated. "Do you think you guys will make callbacks?"

Nasarra shrugged. "Who knows? That guy was impossible to read."

"Nasarra, you did amazing," Jason said. "Both of you did. I'm sure you'll be fine."

"I honestly don't care right now," Nasarra grumbled. "I just want some food and a place to sit."

"I know a place right up the street. You guys game?"

"Absolutely!" Laura exclaimed.

They started down the New York street as dusk bathed the city in a tranquil glow. Nasarra mulled over the audition, wondering if she'd been adequate enough to make callbacks. She hoped so, but if not, it didn't matter. She could just go back home and be with Caleb.

Her reaction surprised her because it was out of character. She expected herself to be devastated if she didn't make callbacks. Having a cavalier attitude toward it was not like her at all. She frowned and tried not to dwell on it, but it was strange at the very least. Deep down, she wondered what it really meant.

Chapter Sixteen

And then there were two.

Nasarra hadn't been able to eat breakfast, and she'd barely been able to find something to wear to callbacks as she had thoroughly convinced herself that she had failed and had packed all of her belongings. Nathan Price had literally called her at the last minute and, after phone treeing everyone she knew, found out that Jason had also made the list, but Laura had not.

It felt wrong to not have Laura there. She'd been with Nasarra since the beginning. At least she still had Jason, but it was a small comfort. She felt worse than she had at the actual audition because she knew this was the defining moment. She had been hand picked to come back. There was no room for mistakes now. It was all or nothing.

Nathan told everyone that they would be doing cold readings of the play, and he gave a little bit of back story on the remarkable girl who had inspired it.

She'd been a renaissance girl, heavily involved in the arts, and an inspiration to everyone with her unbridled enthusiasm and zest for life. The play itself followed the lives of several of her closest friends, now adults, and how they had been affected by the extraordinary teen who had been taken too soon in life.

"Her mother once said that her greatest fear was that her daughter would be forgotten," Nathan said. "The main purpose of this play is to show how she never will be. She will be immortalized in the hearts of those she touched, and her great dream of being on Broadway will be realized with this production. She will go on touching people for years to come because her story is being told through this play. Every person who comes to see this show will get to know her and what she represented. Courage. Life. Individuality. Everything we all want to be, but half of us are afraid to be. It is vital that every part be played flawlessly and with the utmost grace. Does everyone understand?"

Nasarra felt tears sting her eyes and she joined everyone else in nodding her head.

"All right, I've already cast two of the parts. You'll be reading opposite those parts today."

Nasarra was asked to read for one of the larger roles, which surprised her, but flattered her at the same time. At the end of the day, she had read with many different people. She'd even read opposite Jason once. After everyone had gone through the gauntlet, Nathan said that the cast list would be posted the next day. Nasarra walked out of the theatre in a trance. Jason was jabbering on about something, but she wasn't paying attention. Her stomach felt like it had a hole in it and she knew there was no way she was going to get any sleep that night.

Present day

"And I *didn't* get any sleep that night. It was the most agonizing night of my life."

"So...did you get cast?"

A sly smile crossed Nasarra's attractive features and she shrugged.

"I'm going to take that as a yes."

She giggled. "I was really surprised to see my name on the cast list the next day. As you've probably figured out by now, I'm kind of a pessimist."

Maxim chuckled. "Expect the worst, and if the worst doesn't happen, it's a pleasant surprise."

"Exactly!" she laughed. "But, yes, I got a decent-sized part. Jason was cast too...and my entire life exploded after that. We had three months to throw the show together and it was chaos. We had two weeks to memorize lines, and blocking the play was more like an episode of *The Three Stooges*." She held her hand up and rolled her eyes. "It is amazing how quickly professional actors forget their right from their left when they're put on stage and told to walk around."

"Did Nathan throw a fit?" Maxim asked with a grin.

"No, actually, he just laughed...a lot. Dance choreography was even worse, and my days were suddenly filled with costume changes and rehearsals and running. I ran *a lot*. And, also, I didn't just have the play to worry about. I had to break the news to everyone back home that I wasn't coming back. That meant Rafe was saddled with all of the rent and Caleb suddenly found himself in a long distance relationship, which stressed him out. He tried not to show it, but I know it did. Especially when my best friend in New York just so happened to be my very attractive and flirtatious co-actor. Jenna and Colin told me I could stay as long as I liked, but I knew I couldn't leech off of them forever. I had to find my own place and start settling into a routine for my new life."

She heaved a sigh. "It all happened so quickly. I was so excited I didn't really see what was happening to my relationship in the process. I became so preoccupied. But I started to call Caleb less and less. I was so tired from rehearsing and the time difference made it so that every night when I had a free moment, he would be working. Time was against us, life was against us, and even though I had my dream firmly in my grasp, finally, I think I just lost sight of who I was somewhere along the line.

"It was like there became two different Nasarras. One lived in San Francisco and watched TV with her naked, French roommate, and had a gorgeous boyfriend who worshipped the ground she walked on. The other one lived in New York and spent all of her time running to play rehearsals. She lived off bagels and deli sandwiches and spent all of her time flirting with her friend and going out on the weekends with the people in the cast. Both lives were what I wanted, but I think I turned my back on who the real me was. I was so caught up in 'finally having my greatest dream' that I forgot all about what was really important to me."

Maxim frowned in contemplation. "When did you figure it out?"

She smirked. "Well, there were several events that happened in succession. The first thing was that Caleb called me up and told me that he wasn't going to be able to make it for Opening Night."

Maxim raised his eyebrows.

She nodded. "Yeah, it totally wasn't his fault, but I was a real jerk about it. I was disappointed, but I took it out on him much more than I should have..."

New York, 1998

He kept apologizing profusely, pleading with her almost, but she was too angry to care. She was so stressed and frazzled from all of the preparations for the show, and now Caleb was dumping this on her at the last minute! "Caleb, this is Opening Night!" she all but shouted. "The Opening Night performance of my first Broadway play! We discussed this a month ago and you said you'd already cleared it with the director."

"Yes, I know, baby, but things happen that are not always in my control. Chad has *pneumonia*, Nasarra. We can't wheel him out on stage in a stretcher. I have to stay here."

She snorted and ignored the hot tears that trailed down her cheeks. "I cannot believe this," she muttered. "This sucks! How many times is this going to happen? Only once, Caleb! I'm only ever going to have my first Opening Night once! You've always been there to stand by me and support me and now the *one* person I was counting on seeing isn't even going to be there... On the biggest night of my life!" She knew she sounded like she was throwing a tantrum, but she didn't care. She was angry and hurt. Even if it wasn't his fault, it still hurt the same. "Caleb, none of this matters without you!" She flung it out there just to make him feel guilty, which immediately made her feel like the lowest life form on the planet. It was sheer stubbornness that kept her from retracting the statement.

Caleb heaved a great sigh. "Don't be stupid, Nasarra. This was your dream long before you met me. I've said I'm sorry. I don't know how many times you want me to say it. I promise you I'll come see you as soon as he comes back to work, baby. That's all I can do. You have to know how awful I feel."

Nasarra squeezed her eyes shut and forced herself to not scream and yell like she wanted to. "I know...I understand." She was not going to tell him it was okay, because it wasn't. He said nothing for a long moment, and neither did she. She had nothing she wanted to say. Suddenly, the most exciting moment of her life looked black and dismal. "I have to go, Caleb," she finally said, her voice sounding colder than she'd really meant for it to.

"Wait, sweetheart, don't go yet," he almost begged. "Tell me more about your day. Tell me about dress rehearsals."

"I really have to go," she practically snapped. "I have a lot I need to do before the show. I'm going to be really busy. Besides, I have plans to go to dinner with Jason." She knew it was completely moronic and infantile to fling Jason at him. She knew very well that Caleb was already slightly jealous of the man. It was not in her nature to be purposefully spiteful. Her temper was coming from the severe amount of stress she was under, but that was really no excuse. Caleb didn't deserve that amount of venom.

"Oh..." he murmured. "All right, baby. Well, you have a good time. Call me when you can. I love you."

"Yeah, bye." She hung up the phone, seethed for half a second, and then was barraged by a wracking wave of guilt. She sighed and rolled her eyes. "Real mature, Nasarra," she mumbled to herself. Caleb was the best thing that had ever happened to her. He had stood by her and supported her through everything. He had single-handedly given her everything she now had. He absolutely did not deserve to be treated that way. How old was she? Fifteen?

She shook her head and picked up the phone again, dialing his number. She suppressed a smile when his voice sounded wary as he answered. "Caleb, that was juvenile," she stated. "I'm acting like an idiot. I'm sorry. I'm just really stressed out."

"I know you are, sweetheart." His tone softened, but he still sounded hurt.

"I just..." She fiddled with the necklace he had given her and fought more tears. "I really miss you, Caleb. I want you to be here. I want you to take me in your arms and hold me until I don't feel so petrified anymore. I'm so afraid I'm going to blow it."

He sighed. "Nasarra, you're not going to blow it. You're going to be amazing. You'll dazzle them like you always do. I wish I was there also, baby. You have no idea how much. Maybe I can make it out for the Tonys. You're going, right?"

She bit her bottom lip and her eyes stung as her anger abated and turned into sorrow. "Yeah, I think so."

"Well, that's only a couple months away. I'm sure everything will be back to normal by then and I can come escort you."

There was a note of hope in his voice that made her smile, but it didn't really make her feel any better. "Sure...okay."

"All right, honey. Get some rest. You have a lot on your plate. I love you."

His sweetness killed her inside, twisted her heart in the most agonizing way. The threatening tears spilled over. "I love you too, baby." When she hung up, she wasn't angry anymore, only sad. Caleb had been at her side through all of this. Opening Night was like the grand finale and it seemed hollow without him there to celebrate with her. He was the one person she'd counted on seeing, the one person who had always believed in her. He meant everything to her, and she wouldn't even get to see him smile in the audience during curtain call. She wouldn't get to rush into his arms after the show and feel like she could finally rest. She just had to go it alone.

It sucked.

Period.

Deciding that if she stayed there and thought about it any longer, her heart would shatter into a thousand pieces, Nasarra snatched her purse and headed out of the apartment.

Nightfall found her in Times Square, taking in the sights absently as she wondered when the amazing fulfillment of accomplishing her dream had dissipated to a dull, throbbing emptiness. It didn't seem right at all. Broadway was supposed to solve all of her problems, be the solution to everything in her life that had ever gone wrong. It wasn't supposed to solve several select problems and then crop up a bunch of new ones in replacement.

She strode blindly down the street with her arms folded, watching the traffic, people and lights. She wandered past a coffee shop called The Amazing Psychotic and stopped outside of it with a curious frown. What a bizarre name. She took a step closer to the front door and peered through the glass window, but couldn't see anything other than her own reflection. Her curiosity piqued, she decided to go ahead and go in. If it was some scary place where only people with multiple body piercings could eat, she'd just go about her merry way.

As she stepped in, she realized it was just an artsy place with an offbeat atmosphere. The lights were dim and works of art from local artists lined the walls. New age music played in the background and calmed her somewhat. There was a bar at the far end of the room and she went to it, debating on whether or not she wanted a drink. Drowning her sorrows in alcohol was not her style, but the idea didn't sound half bad to her at the moment.

"Nasarra?"

She frowned and looked over her shoulder to a table nearby. She blinked upon seeing it was Nathan Price. She arched an eyebrow. "What are you doing here?" she questioned.

"This is my restaurant," he stated. "What are *you* doing here?" He motioned her over to the table. "Pull up a chair."

"You own this place?" she asked in surprise.

He nodded with a smirk. "What can I say? Jack of all trades and all that."

She attempted to smile, but knew it came off looking pathetic.

Nathan noticed it too. "What's the matter with you, Williams?" he muttered. "You look like your dog just died." He heaved a sigh and kicked the chair across from him out. "Sit down, hun. Spill."

She flopped into the chair with the grace of a disgruntled teenager. "I'm fine," she lied. "Just stressed. You know, with the show and all."

His eyes narrowed and she knew he didn't buy it for a second. "You're a terrible liar, Williams." He threw back the amber-colored drink he had in front of him, then gave her a level stare. "Caleb isn't coming, is he?"

She stared at him in shock. "What, is psychic on your list of many talents?"

He chuckled and the lines around his eyes crinkled with amusement. "Not much can usually upset an actor the week before their Opening Night."

She heaved a defeated sigh and stared out the window. "Yeah, I guess his stupid understudy has pneumonia," she grumbled.

Nathan gasped in an exaggerated fashion and put his hand over his chest. "How dare he?"

She rolled her eyes. All right, she knew she was acting ridiculous. She didn't need him to rub it in.

He laughed softly. "Performer's lives are not easy, Nasarra. You know this. We work odd hours, don't make the money we deserve, and have to sacrifice a lot for our craft. But Caleb understands that because he lives the same life you do." He sighed and reached out to pat her hands across the table. "Listen, I've known him a long time. I didn't think he would ever let anyone close to him after that harpy Danielle got through with him. Do you think this is easy for him? Standing by, being left behind while you gallivant off across the country? Think about his position for a minute. The woman he loves is unreachable to him now. Don't you think that bothers him?"

The guilt started to become overwhelming to her, making it impossible to continue feeling sorry for herself. She played with her fingers and looked down at the table. Tears burned her eyes, once again. "I'm not mad at him," she all but whispered. "I just..." She sniffled. "I'm here because of him. I wanted him to see...to be proud of me." The tears slipped out and she wiped at them hastily, feeling stupid for blubbering in front of her producer.

"Nasarra," he said, his voice oddly comforting even in its chastisement, "if I know Caleb at all, he's already proud of you."

"But I wanted to see him." She sounded feeble. And pathetic. And she could have cared less.

He chuckled again. "I know, but this is still your Opening Night. Don't let any of this ruin that for you. Opening Night can make or break the running time of a show. Leave your problems at the door, remember?"

She nodded, knowing, and hating, that he was right.

"Why don't you stay and eat something?" he encouraged. "It's on the house."

She shook her head. "Nah, that's okay. I should probably head back."

He let out a frustrated huff. "Shut up and stay, Williams."

She glanced up to see him grinning at her with that mischievous look. She smiled in spite of herself and felt some of her dark mood lighten just a bit. "Aye aye, Captain."

Chapter Seventeen

Nasarra paced nervously back and forth in the wings of the stage. Back and forth... Back and forth...

"Five minutes to curtain!" a techie shouted. "Places!"

She jumped and started to gnaw on a fingernail. The mix of exhilaration and terror she felt was odd. Strange combination.

"Nasarra!" Jason's voice came. "Stop pacing! You're gonna make me crazy!"

She obeyed, but continued to chew on her fingernail and bounce in place.

He put his hands on her shoulders. "That's not any better! Calm down." He ran his hands up and down her arms in a soothing gesture. It reminded her of something Caleb would do, which comforted her and made her feel sad all at the same time.

"You're going to be amazing," Jason assured her. "Stop freaking out. Just remember not to screw up the first number or Nathan will murder us all."

Nasarra gave him a wry smile. The opening number was the only one they had still been having some difficulty with. Almost everyone in the cast was on stage at once and there was a lot of dancing. The choreography had been sloppy in the dress rehearsal and Nathan had threatened them all with dismemberment if they messed it up during the show.

With some effort, Nasarra managed to force some air into her lungs right as the lights dimmed in the house. Her heart somersaulted and she shot a petrified look up at Jason.

He was disconcertingly calm, as always, and it irritated her. As if he could tell, he lifted one of his arms and pointed to his armpit. She giggled, remembering his words at the audition after she had confronted him about his nonchalant front.

He grinned and slipped one arm around her shoulders, pulling her in for a hug. "You're going to be incredible," he whispered against her ear. "I know you are."

She tried not to shiver as his warm breath tickled her, but she really couldn't help it. Luckily, she couldn't dwell on the reaction because the curtain went up and the orchestra struck the first few notes of the opening song. She sucked in her breath and her heart flopped around in her chest like a fish out of water. This was it! Her dreams came true in three, two, one...

She took a deep breath and strode out onto the stage, followed by Jason and several other actors.

Amazingly, the opening number did not give them any problems. It was beautifully flawless and it instilled hope in Nasarra that the rest of the show would go just as smoothly. She fell into her character with ease and didn't stop to think about how many people were watching her. She didn't dwell on the fact that Caleb wasn't there, either. She just enjoyed everything about being on the stage. The echo of her voice in the microphone, the slippery stage floor, the heat of the lights. Most of all, she loved the applause, the laughter, the smallest reaction from the audience. To think that maybe someone watched her as she had once watched others... It was a heady rush.

The end of the play was emotional, and Nasarra always barely got through it without crying. Throughout the story, the main characters' lives were followed one at a time, all showing how their chosen paths had been affected by their young friend. At the end of the show, all of the characters reunited after fifteen years of not seeing one another. They each shared memories of their friend, and the play went out with a recitation of a fitting Shakespearean sonnet, followed by a beautiful dance that highlighted many of the memories the main characters had spoken of. It was a wonderful tribute, but both happy and sad. It tugged at Nasarra's heartstrings and, judging by the thunderous applause that followed the close of the curtain, the audience felt the same way.

Nasarra went out with Jason for the curtain call, and holding his hand as they took their bow was a breathtaking experience. It should have been the highlight of her life, but it felt somewhat hollow. Her eyes scanned the crowd, but all of the faces were unfamiliar. Rafe and Amanda hadn't been able to come. They didn't make enough money to afford a cross-country plane ticket. And Caleb wasn't there... Somehow, not being able to share her victory with her friends caused deep sorrow to take root in her heart.

It didn't help that, when she got home, Jenna and Colin were gone and she was left all alone. With a sigh, she set her bag down and went to check the messages. She was exhausted, and to her surprise, just wanted to go to sleep. Jason had offered to take her out for drinks to celebrate with some of the other cast members, but she just couldn't shake herself out of her doldrums. She couldn't get her mind around the fact that it should have been Amanda taking her out to celebrate.

The first message was one from Caleb, which made her smile even as it made her heart twinge. He expressed how proud he was of her and how he wanted to hear all about the show. The second message was from her mother, saying basically the same thing. There was also a pointed little addendum attached to the message relating how Shawna had just lost the biggest case of her life. That brought a grin to Nasarra's lips. Justice was sweet.

The third message was from Amanda, who talked so fast Nasarra could barely understand her. What she did hear made her eyes pop almost clear out of her skull.

"Rafe asked me to marry him, and I said yes!"

The second half of the message hit her like an arrow straight to her chest.

"I, of course, want you to be my maid of honor, but I don't know if you'll be able to get away from the play. Find out and let me know. I completely understand if you can't make it. You are, after all, a Broadway diva now."

Amanda didn't sound upset, but that wasn't surprising. Amanda was never upset. She took things in stride and made the best of every situation. Nasarra, on the other hand, felt a little sick to her stomach.

She went to the sliding glass door and looked out at the city lights. They seemed brighter than the ones in San Francisco. More obnoxious and less magical. Her two best friends were getting married. They were going to have a happily ever after and Nasarra might not even be able to make it to the wedding.

And her own relationship was a shambles because she lived at the other end of the freaking continent. She was all alone after the biggest night of her life and it hurt. Her best friends were going on without her, and strangely, that hurt too.

She heaved a sigh and glanced up a the Chrysler Building. For some reason, it didn't seem to shine the way it had when she had first come to the city.

-Several Months Later

"Nasarra, you look amazing!" Jenna gushed as she gave Nasarra the once-over with an excited grin.

Nasarra smiled and turned slowly, enjoying the feel of the teal fabric as it slid over her skin. She loved the dress, she had to admit. It made her red hair stand out like a blaze of fire and it complemented her skin tone nicely. Her silver shoes were a nice touch, also, if you asked her. "So, am I Tony worthy?" she asked.

Jenna laughed. "Nasarra, you're not only Tony worthy, you're Oscar worthy."

Her cheeks burned with a blush at Jenna's praise and she fluffed her curls a bit as she waited for Jason to come pick her up. She had a strange and brief feeling of de ja vu. It seemed like so long ago when she had been in her duplex, fantasizing about a handsome man coming to escort her to the Tony Awards. Now, she actually *was* waiting for a handsome man to come escort her to the Tony Awards. She should have felt beyond jubilant, but like so many other things in her life over the past several months, she found the entire experience rather lacking.

She was excited, most definitely, but not the way she should have been. Not the way she would have been if she'd been going with Caleb.

She was supposed to be going with Caleb, but he'd cancelled on her—again. Apparently, they were closing the running of *Phantom* at The Curran and he couldn't get away. This piece of information upset her for two reasons. The first one was obvious; she missed Caleb desperately and wanted to see him probably more than anything in the world. The second reason was because the thought of *Phantom* ending its run was depressing. It was like a symbolic ending to a chapter of her life and she didn't want it to conclude that way. That play had brought her Caleb, and ultimately, her dreams. Because she'd decided on a whim to go see it, her entire existence had been altered. It seemed like, with the play closing, Life was saying, *This is it. Time to move on.* She wasn't ready to move on. Not in the least.

So, needless to say, she was going to the Tonys with Jason.

A knock sounded on the door and Jenna opened it, revealing her friend, looking dashing in his tux. Nasarra stared at him for a moment, and her heart warmed at the way he raised his eyebrows when he caught sight of her.

"Nasarra, my gosh," he breathed. "You look absolutely ravishing."

Affection for him filled her, but she still would have rather heard Caleb say those words to her than any other person. She took a deep breath and tried to banish her negative thoughts. "You look wonderful too!" she exclaimed, stepping forward to take his arm. "Very debonair."

He grinned and leaned down to press a kiss to her jaw, lingering a second longer than usual. "You smell really nice," he whispered against her skin. He seemed to debate with himself for a moment before one of his arms snaked around her back and pulled her up close to him.

Nasarra blinked in bewilderment as she suddenly found herself pressed to his unyielding chest. She'd been hugged by him many times before, but this felt different. There was something more intense in his touch that made her heart trip over itself.

He buried his free hand in her hair and held her gently, but firmly, against him for several long seconds. She placed one hand tentatively against his chest. "Jason...?" she questioned with a frown.

He pulled back enough to look down at her, but not enough to relinquish his hold. "You have to know the way I feel about you by now." He smiled as he said it, and stated the words very matter-of-fact. "Don't make me pretend any longer. At least let us have it out there in the open."

She stared at him, then sucked her breath in and bit her bottom lip in concern. "Jason, you know..." She cleared her throat and averted her gaze so that she wouldn't have to see the hurt in his blue eyes. "Caleb..." For some reason, she couldn't form a coherent sentence.

He tipped her chin up and gazed down at her with nothing but warmth in his eyes. "Yes, I know about Caleb," he said. "I know you love him, but that does not change the fact that he isn't here. I am."

She opened her mouth to defend Caleb and go off about how it wasn't his fault, but Jason's fingers against her lips stopped her.

"I'm not trying to oust the guy," he said with a chuckle. "I'm just trying to be honest with you. You deserve to know how I feel, one way or the other. I'm not going to make it weird. I just wanted you to know. Simple as that." He released her almost as quickly as he'd grabbed hold of her, and within seconds, his easy smile was back on his lips. He offered his arm again. "Let's go."

She took his arm almost mechanically, shooting a furtive look back over her shoulder into the apartment, grateful that Jenna had removed herself somewhere during the conversation. Her face was hot from the things Jason had said to her, even though he really hadn't said all that much. The message was implied. She wasn't an idiot. Truth was, she'd known for a while now how Jason felt about her, but she'd ignored it because it frightened her so much. Jason had grown to be her closest friend in New York and she didn't want to warp their friendship because he cared for her more than she could care for him.

The other disturbing part was that some small part of her knew she *could* care more for him if she let herself. She felt like she had two lives and two paths, two choices that both offered her splendid things, but ripped away others. One path offered her old life with her old friends, and Caleb. The other offered the excitement of Broadway and New York, and Jason. The two paths could not converge and it was painful to think that, either way, she would lose something that meant a great deal to her.

But she knew she couldn't put the choice off forever. She'd been avoiding it long enough already. Sooner or later, she would have to decide which path she wanted to walk down.

* * *

Nasarra clapped as the award for best revival of a musical was announced. She sighed, feeling like it was taking an awful amount of effort to do that simple gesture.

"Nasarra?" Jason leaned over and whispered in her ear. "Are you okay?"

She made a face and shrugged. "I don't know. I'm not feeling all that great." And it was true. She wasn't. Her heart was twisting and her stomach was turning. Everything felt like it was in knots. About halfway through the ceremony, she realized that the Tonys were nothing if she couldn't share them with Caleb. Broadway was nothing if she couldn't share it with him. He'd been her inspiration long ago, and he had revived the love within her. He had started it all. Without him, it all just felt like empty glitter.

"Do you want to go?" Jason queried.

She glanced at him and nodded, not wanting to have to sit there and pretend any longer. She wanted to mope. And after she'd moped, she had some things she needed to figure out.

Jason led her out of the theatre and they drove in silence back to Jenna and Colin's. She watched the city zip by out the window and sighed. New York. The city she had longed to live in for so long. It had seemed like the Promised Land to her. Now it just seemed like a gilded cage.

At the door to the apartment, Nasarra turned to face Jason and glanced up at him. "I'm sorry we had to leave early. I just..." She shrugged. "I don't know what's wrong with me."

His eyes narrowed as if trying to figure something out. "I didn't...freak you out earlier, did I?"

Her eyes widened. "Oh, no!" she cried. "No, you didn't." She shook her head adamantly.

"Okay, because regardless of what I feel for you, I'm your friend, first and foremost. I don't want to ruin that."

"No, no, of course not. No, Jason, I...I don't know what my deal is." She bit her bottom lip and stared at the apartment door.

He watched her for a long moment, then heaved a sigh. "Nasarra," he said. "I'm beginning to wonder if this dream of yours, this dream of being on Broadway, is really everything you think it is."

She met his eyes with a frown.

"I'm wondering when it went from being your greatest

dream to being something you were determined to accomplish out of sheer pride."

She opened her mouth to deny what he was saying, but couldn't. Something in his words rang true.

He seemed to see her hesitation and smirked. "Listen to me. I know you love acting. That is more than apparent. You have a true passion for the craft, but you can do that anywhere. You don't need to be on Broadway to do what you love. All I've heard from you since I met you is how much you want this, how this has always been your greatest dream. You keep saying it like you're trying to convince yourself, and yet, you don't seem any happier to have attained it. The only time I ever see you happy is when you're telling me about your roommate painting naked, or how your friend Amanda has no verbal sensor, or about how the fog rolls in over the Golden Gate Bridge, or how free you feel while riding on the back of Caleb's Harley."

Her heart made a dismal thud in her chest at the memories his words invoked.

"When you talk about those things, your eyes light up. The way you talk about those things is the way you should talk about being here, if it is, in fact, your greatest dream come to life." He gave her a chastising look for a second, as if she should get a clue.

"But—" She frowned. "But being here has always been my greatest dream."

"Yes, and you attained it. Nasarra, somewhere along the line, the dream of being on Broadway became more than just a dream to you. It became the one thing that you could rub in every person's face who never believed in you. You graduated high school with the intent of one day being a Broadway actress. Your sister, and the trials of life, convinced you along the line that you just weren't good enough, that you'd never make it. The dream became more than just a dream. It was personal. It was a rite of passage. And guess what? You did it. You did everything you didn't think you'd be able to do. But just because you attained one dream, doesn't mean you can't have more, different dreams for a different person. You're not a high school drama kid anymore with stars in her eyes. You're a grown woman who's extremely talented and can take that talent anywhere." He took her gently by the shoulders. "Don't sacrifice every other dream you have just for the one you *think* should matter the most."

His words shot straight to her heart and she felt the truth of them. All this time, she *had* been viewing Broadway as the one thing that would finally prove she was worth something. She just hadn't realized it. She hadn't realized that, while she was thinking that she'd never be good enough to attain her goal, she had formulated different goals that were just as important.

She met Jason's eyes and frowned. "But what am I going to do?" she murmured. "I feel so helpless. I can't just ditch out on the play. Nathan'll put a hit out on me."

His eyes twinkled and he grinned. "You can do anything you want to do. I think you've proven that to yourself."

She sighed and the apartment door suddenly opened, revealing Jenna, who looked completely bewildered to see the two of them standing there. "Oh!" she exclaimed. "What-what are you doing back so early?"

"Nasarra wasn't feeling very well," Jason supplied.

Nasarra waved her hand. "Sorry, Jen. Didn't mean you startle you." Her brow creased because Jenna's face still looked mortified. "What's wrong?"

Jenna blinked and shook her head. "Oh...well...Caleb was just here."

Nasarra's heart plummeted like she was on a roller coaster, then promptly flew up into her throat. "Caleb?" she squeaked. "He was *here?*"

Jenna nodded and bit her lip. "I guess he just bailed on the play to come take you to the Tonys like he promised. Said he couldn't stand to be away from you any longer."

Nasarra's eyes bulged and dread crept over her. "You totally told him I went with Jason, didn't you?"

"Well, I kind of had to! You weren't here!"

"Why did he leave?"

"I tried to stop him, but he said he needed some time to think about some things. He went downtown."

"Downtown? Like Times Square, downtown?"

Jenna looked about as frantic as Nasarra felt. "Yeah, he said he wanted to talk to Nathan. Was going to go to that restaurant he owns. The Psycho Lunatic or whatever."

"The Amazing Psychotic? He went there?"

"Yeah! That's it!"

Nasarra spun and met Jason's gaze.

He smiled and stepped aside. "Go, gorgeous. Go make your dreams come true."

She flung her arms around him and held on. "You'll always be my friend, right?" she whispered.

He squeezed her tight. "Forever, baby. Go find your man." He pulled away and gave her a playful shove.

She grinned, hiked up her skirt, and fled to the elevators.

Chapter Eighteen

It seemed like it took an unnaturally long time for the cab driver to reach Times Square, and once he got there, Nasarra couldn't wait while he loped along in traffic to get the restaurant. She could get out and run faster so she told him to pull over and let her out so she could do just that.

Her mind spun as she raced down the street, still reeling from Jason's very astute observations, and the fact that Caleb had bailed on his own play to come and see her at the last minute. She hoped he wasn't upset that she had decided to go to the Tonys with Jason. It's not like it had been a date or anything. She'd just wanted to go. And it's not like she'd suspected he was going to show up out of the blue.

She rounded a corner and continued to run, her feet protesting the movement in her silver heels. She wondered if he would look the same, or feel the same. Would his lips taste the same? Shivers worked along her spine at the thought.

She spotted the lights of the restaurant's sign and she picked up her pace, her chest laboring with her breath. She bolted across the last intersection and had just reached the door when a customer emerged from inside. She gasped and tried to slow down, but she had too much momentum going. She crashed right into the unsuspecting person with a force probably close to a freight train. The air was driven from her lungs and she staggered backwards, almost falling when one of her heels busted off. She stumbled and fought to keep her balance, then held her hands out in front of her, immediately launching into apologies.

"I'm so sorry! I didn't even—" The man she'd run into started to say the exact same thing and she glanced up at him, her breath catching in her throat as her heart did gymnastics. "Caleb?" she whispered.

He blinked, obviously just as stunned as she was, and he straightened slowly. "Nasarra?" His look of shock melted away and he chuckled as he shook his head. "Still crashing into people, I see." His green-gold eyes raked over her and he sucked his breath in. "You look like a goddess."

She let her eyes take him in for a moment, every inch of glorious perfection. He had his jacket on, even though it was warm outside. Time ceased to move. She swore she even saw the speeding cars slow. He was the picture of complete confidence, even in his bewilderment. He owned the piece of sidewalk he stood on, just as he had owned the stage thirteen years ago. Just like he had owned her heart from the minute she had mowed him down in the rain. He stood directly in front of the door, the neon lights of the restaurant sign reflecting off of his sunset-colored ponytail. Her heart fluttered like butterfly wings. Everything seemed startlingly clear all of a sudden. Forget the play. Forget New York. All she wanted was him, his hands on her body and his lips on hers.

Possessed by a ravenous hunger that she was unable to control, she all but launched herself at him, flinging her arms around him and knocking him backwards. He stumbled over the small step leading into the restaurant and fell back into the door. It flew open and he tumbled through it, landing on the hardwood floor inside with her on top of him.

He grunted as the air left him, but he chuckled and his hands came up to tangle in her hair. She attacked his mouth with hers, kissing him deep and erotic. She pulled back and trailed kisses all across his face and neck as tears of joy cascaded down her cheeks. "I missed you so much!" she cried in between kisses. "I don't want to be without you anymore. I'm going to quit the play and come home."

He shook his head, taking her face in his hands and pushing her away so he could look into her eyes. "You don't have to do that. I'm pretty sure I'm fired. It's okay. I'll come here. I'll find work here. That's what I wanted to talk to Nathan about. I was just heading back to Jenna's to tell you."

"But you love San Francisco." She couldn't believe he had just left the play. She couldn't wrap her mind around someone wanting to sacrifice so much for her.

His grin was slow and beautiful as he reached up to touch

her cheek. "I love you more."

More tears stung her eyes, but she shook her head. "No, I don't want that. I don't want to stay here. I want to go home. I want to be with Rafe and Amanda and I want to ride down to the wharf on the back of your motorcycle. I want the fishy brine on the pier and the seals and the fog and the smell of eucalyptus on the breeze. That's what's important to me. I can act there." He looked like he wanted to protest, but she stopped him from speaking with a kiss. She needed his lips like she needed the air. "I mean it," she said when she pulled back. "I want to go home, Caleb. You are my ultimate dream. None of this means anything without you... And my home is my beloved city by the bay. I was deluded about a lot of things."

"Very touching," a familiar voice drawled, "but do you think you could continue this off of my floor? This is not a dinner theatre."

Nasarra glanced up to see Nathan standing, arms folded, staring disapprovingly down at them. Her cheeks grew hot and she sat up, realizing she had just put on a nice little show for all of the customers.

Caleb chuckled and sat up also, but pulled her back into his arms, nuzzling his nose against her neck. He nibbled on her earlobe, making her sigh and shiver, then pressed an unhurried line of kisses along her jaw. "So...home then?"

She pulled back and met his eyes. She nodded.

"You're sure?"

"Positive."

"And everything else?"

She grinned. "We'll figure it out."

Nathan heaved an enormous, exaggerated sigh. "Great," he grumbled. "Now I'm going to have to replace you. Thanks a lot, Williams." He shot a deadly glower Caleb's direction. "Thanks a lot, Caleb."

Caleb gave a nonchalant shrug. "Paybacks for making me teach the drama camp. We're even now." Nathan snorted and Caleb turned back to Nasarra with a smile. Ignoring all of the people who were still watching with rapt attention, he took her face in his hands and kissed her thoroughly.

Nasarra heard one of the customers mutter something about how this was the best off-Broadway play she'd ever seen. It made her grin as joy welled up within her, and she thought it just might have been the best compliment she'd ever received.

* * *

As Caleb's Harley pulled into the parking lot at Half Moon Bay, Nasarra looked down at the bracelet her friend from high school had given her. Little planets, suns, moons and stars. She sighed as she got off the motorcycle and un-hooked the clasp.

Caleb frowned as he turned off the engine and came up to her. "What are you going to do with that?"

She gave him an enigmatic smile and headed down to the sandy beach as the setting sun made the waves sparkle. Caleb followed after her and came to stand behind her on the shore. He wrapped his arms around her from behind and pressed tantalizing kisses along her neck.

She closed her eyes, relishing in the feel of him, as well as the cold fog that blew in from the magnificent ocean. She let him kiss his fill before she looked back down at the bracelet. "My friend Jane in high school gave me this when we gradu-ated," she explained. "She told me that it was a reminder to reach for the stars. She said that when I accomplished every-thing I'd ever wanted, I had to fling it into the ocean because I wouldn't need it anymore. I wouldn't need the stars she'd given me because I would have found my own."

His arms tightened around her waist and he rested his chin on her shoulder. "You sure you want to fling it so soon?"

She grinned and nodded. "I made it to Broadway. That was a big one. And I found myself through it all, found what I truly wanted. That's more than I could ever ask for." With-out a second thought, she hurled the bracelet into the waves. It created a tiny, almost insignificant splash.

She felt strange realizing the bracelet was gone. It had been with her for so long, but as Caleb's lips returned to tease her neck and jaw, she knew it wasn't important and wasn't necessary. She was completely satisfied with her choices, and she had accomplished dreams she didn't even know she'd had. Her heart was full. She had achieved every-thing she'd ever wanted and more. *This* was the way the chapter of her life was supposed to end.

She turned to face Caleb and threaded her fingers

through his hair as she studied his beautiful features. She was happy. Happier than she'd ever thought she could be, and as Caleb's lips came down to meet hers, she knew her happiness was only just beginning. He was her happiness. He was her greatest dream, and he had been unexpected. That made it better than all the rest.

He was her ultimate happy ending.

* * *

Present day

Maxim sighed as Nasarra finished up her story. He had eaten almost the entire box of donuts. Both his heart, and his stomach, were full. "That's an amazing story, Nasarra," he said.

She grinned and a small blush touched her cheeks. "I've never regretted my decision. Not once. I love him just as much now as back then. More, even."

Maxim smiled. "I understand now about you guys wanting to run The Amazing Psychotic when it opened up here."

"Oh yes, Caleb was all over Nathan for that job. It all worked out really wonderfully in the end. We run the restaurant and teach theatre. It's a fantastic life. I wouldn't trade it for the world." She giggled. "I hope the story isn't too boring to try and make a script out of."

He snorted. "Are you kidding me? This is awesome. With any luck, I can kill two birds with one stone and make it my next best seller." He chuckled as he started to collect his things. He had a lot of work ahead of him. He needed to get started right away.

She stood. "Well, I hope so! That would be a great honor!"

He shoved his tape recorder into his backpack and faced her as he zipped it up. "I'll try to get this finished up as soon as possible. I know you're not working with a lot of time."

"I appreciate that. The sooner the better. My actors are professional, but I don't want to give them panic attacks. They're already going to have to learn their lines in record time. If we pull it all together in time, it'll be a miracle."

"Well, I'll go back to Torrey's and get to work on it. I'll call you as soon as it's finished and give you a copy to go over."

"Sounds great. Thanks, Maxim. This means a lot to me."

She pulled him into a hug and he smiled. "It's not problem, Nasarra. You're probably saving my life."

She laughed and he waved as he headed out the theatre, his mind already turning with stage directions and how he was going to plot the story out on the page.

Chapter Nineteen

Maxim had basically pulled a week with very little sleep and had managed to get Nasarra's script written running on nothing but coffee and random food that Taegen brought him like a prison warden about three times a day. When he'd presented the finished product to Nasarra, she'd seemed completely shocked, but he wasn't sure if that was because of how quickly he'd written the script, or because he'd looked like a werewolf in transition when he'd handed it to her. Either way, it didn't really matter. She'd been able to start work on the play sooner than expected, which made everyone happy.

Nasarra had requested that Maxim stay for the beginning stages of the play. She wanted him to oversee stage direction and make sure everything was going according to his "vision." He didn't bother to tell her that he had no idea what his vision was. He was a lot of things, but director was probably the furthest thing on the list. Mostly he just sat there and pretended to be useful while Nasarra did the directing. He ended up doing a lot of menial things like sweeping the stage and fetching food and coffee for the cast.

Nasarra had gone off on a tangent about that, saying he shouldn't have to be treated like a lackey. He neglected to tell her that the job was self-imposed because he felt so useless. In the two weeks he sat there to watch the production take shape, he probably only said about four comments that actually had to do with the stage directions or the delivery of lines.

He was expecting to return home at the end of the month, which he was dying for because, despite her out of character moodiness, he missed his wife terribly. She'd softened after receiving her flowers, but every once in awhile, she'd still do or say something that had him scratching his head. He was anxious to get home and see what the problem was, so it didn't make him the happiest person in the world when Nasarra requested that he remain until the show was over. She wanted him to see the finished product and she'd expressed how it would mean a lot to her for him to be at the final show.

Maxim had a problem saying no to people. He always had. Alyx had *not* been happy after hearing this news and Maxim was pretty sure that any good progress he'd made with her had been obliterated at that point. He'd managed to hang around and pretend to be involved in the play rehearsals for about two and a half weeks, but then he couldn't take it anymore.

He bailed.

Just like Caleb.

He completely ditched out on the play and caught a red-eye back to Oregon. He couldn't hang out with a bunch of actors and pretend to be having a great time when something was seriously bothering his wife. Whatever the problem was needed to be solved before she tried to divorce him.

Just the thought made him sick to his stomach. He didn't know what he would do with himself if he ever lost Alyx. She was his entire world. He would be nothing without her.

He arrived at his house in the car he'd rented from the airport at an ungodly hour of the morning, so he tried his hardest not to make much noise when he unlocked the door. Any little thing that may incur her wrath was something he wanted to avoid.

He closed the door silently and set his duffle bag down. He'd left his suitcase at Torrey's because, as soon as he sorted things out with Alyx, he had to go back to San Francisco before Nasarra killed him. He knew that she could deal without him being there for the last week of the rehearsals, but it meant a lot to her for him to be at the performance. He wasn't so much of a jerk that he would bail on that too.

He crept toward the master bedroom and could see the sleeping form of his wife beneath the covers. The blanket was over her head and he smiled. He slipped off his shoes, followed by his shirt and cargo pants. He set his glasses on the night stand and climbed in with only his boxers on, happy to be next to her again and looking forward to getting some much needed rest.

He snuggled close to her and wrapped his arm around her waist, but frowned because she didn't feel as small as she usually did. Alyx was slender and lithe. He couldn't understand why she felt...bulky. And, if that wasn't enough, she let out a monstrous snore that sounded like the abominable snowman.

Maxim blinked; his exhausted brain, coupled with the fact that he was virtually blind without his glasses on, made it difficult to put his finger on what exactly was wrong with this picture.

He tried to peer closer at his wife, but didn't have time to formulate any thoughts. The slumbering person turned over, muttered something in his distinctly masculine voice, and flopped his arm across Maxim's neck in something close to a chokehold.

Maxim's eyes bulged and he tried to get away, but the guy's grip was relentless. He managed to fumble around on the nightstand and find his glasses, then shoved them on and scowled. "Javan!" he shouted. "Javan, get *off* of me!" He shoved at the man's chest and roused him enough for him to loosen his hold. Maxim took the opportunity and jerked away before he grabbed a pillow and bludgeoned his friend with it.

"Whoa!" Javan exclaimed, putting his arms up to shield his face. "What's going on? Come on, man!"

"*Why* are you sleeping in my bed?"

"Where else am I supposed to sleep?" He dodged another swing and scrambled out of the bed. "The more appropriate question is, why were *you* trying to spoon with me? I was having a nice dream! I thought some hot chick was trying to show me some love!"

Maxim made a gagging noise and flung the pillow down. He scowled at his disoriented friend, then shuddered. "I need to take a shower now."

Javan scratched at the back of his head. "What are you doing here?"

"I *live* here! What are *you* doing here? And where is my wife?" His eyes widened suddenly as a horrid puzzle piece fell into place. "Oh my gosh, that's it, isn't it? You're sleeping with my wife!" He bolted off the bed and advanced toward Javan.

Javan looked genuinely terrified as he held his hands out and skirted the bed. "What? Are you *insane?* Ew! That's sick, dude! She's like my sister! Besides, how can you even think that I would do that to you?"

Maxim stopped in his attack mode, but he kept his hands on his hips and glowered. "Then what are you doing here?"

"Alyx asked me to house sit while she was gone! I didn't dare tell her no! The woman's been a loose cannon for weeks! I thought she'd castrate me!"

Maxim blinked, then frowned. "Wait a minute, where did she go?"

"She went to see you, you idiot! She drove down to Frisco! Said she couldn't stand being away from you anymore!"

His frown deepened. "What about the play?"

"Oh, something weird happened with the play and it had to be put on hiatus for like a month. Both of us are off for a while. Seriously, what has been *with* her?"

"She's been weird to you too?"

Javan's eyes bulged and he blew his cheeks out with an exhale. He nodded. "I'm sure it's not gonna be any better when she gets to Torrey's and finds you missing."

Maxim groaned and sunk down on the foot end of the bed. "Gimme a break! What is this? I swear, I don't believe in destiny, but sometimes I think that, somewhere, someone is writing my life. And whoever that person is has a sick sense of humor."

Javan chuckled. "So, I'm guessing you skipped out on your project to come sneak a few days with her?"

"Yeah, and now I have to go all the way back. Great waste of money, flying back and forth. Not to mention, I don't think I've slept in weeks." He forced himself to stand and went to put his pants back on. "Well, I guess I'd better get a move on. Have to show up before she gets there and realizes I'm not there, then comes back up here."

"Want some company?"

Maxim rolled his eyes as he tugged his shirt on. "Absolutely. Besides, you owe me."

"Hey, come on, don't be like that. That's the most affection I've gotten in months."

"Gross." He stuffed his feet back into his shoes. "Come on, let's head out. The sooner I can find my rogue wife, figure out what's wrong, put this play behind me, and get back to my quiet, comfortable routine, the happier I'm going to be."

* * *

As if Maxim wasn't already completely worn out, when he and Javan burst into Torrey's house in the late afternoon, they found both him and Taegen surrounding Alyx, who was huddled on the couch and sobbing.

It took Maxim a second to understand what was going on—his brain was working on autopilot—but as soon as he made sense of it, he let his bags drop and all but ran to his wife, almost knocking Taegen right off the arm of the couch. "Alyx?" he questioned.

She looked up at him, her eyes red and swollen, and shock mirrored for a minute in her green depths. "Baby?" she squeaked. "What are you doing here?"

He knelt at her feet, letting out a large sigh. "Javan and I hopped the first flight we could catch after I spontaneously showed up at our house and tried to cuddle with him."

Alyx blinked, then gave a short laugh that momentarily chased the shadows away from her face.

Maxim smiled and reached up to wipe the tears off of her cheeks. "Sweetheart, what's the matter?"

She shook her head as her bottom lip trembled and fresh tears spilled from her eyes. "Oh, Maxim," she practically wailed. "I'm sorry. I've been so horrible to you." She sniffled and wiped at her eyes. "I've just been so...scared." She choked on the last word as she fought a sob.

Maxim's brow creased in concern and he came to sit up next to her on the sofa, pulling her into his arms. "About what? Baby, what's wrong?"

She looked up at him, but then burst into tears again, burying her face against his shoulder.

Maxim turned his bewildered gaze up to Torrey.

Torrey heaved a sigh. "You're going to be a father, Maxim."

He stared. The statement wouldn't process.

"I'm so sorry!" Alyx cried. "I know we talked about it and you said you weren't ready to have kids yet! I don't know how this happened! I thought we were so careful! I-I don't know! I'm so sorry!"

Maxim shook his head, trying to will his mind to work. He cleared his throat and felt a wave of dizziness, but it subsided. "Wait...I'm sorry. It's been a very long twenty-four hours. Could you please repeat that small bit of information?"

Alyx raised her head and met his gaze as tears ran rivers down her cheeks. "I didn't even realize..." She shook her head. "All I knew was that I just started hating everybody for no reason! I was so moody and I just wanted to eat...well, everything. One day, after I almost took Javan's head off for something really insignificant, I started to think maybe something was wrong. That's when I realized I hadn't had my period in over two months. I went to the doctor and..." She gave a helpless shrug, then looked away in dejection. "I didn't know how to tell you. I knew you'd be upset."

"Whoa, wait a second," Maxim interrupted. He took her gently by the shoulders. "Upset? You mean, you're just pregnant? That's all that's wrong?" He chuckled and his heart warmed at her confused expression. "Baby, I thought you were going to divorce me!"

She frowned. "What?"

"I thought the refried beans had put you straight over the edge!"

She laughed in a way that was much more characteristic of her personality and her eyes lit up. "You mean you're not upset?"

He caressed her face and gazed at her with warmth. "I told you I wasn't ready to have children because the thought of being responsible for another person in such an enormous way scares the living crap out of me. That doesn't mean that I'm not also overjoyed at the prospect." He trailed his fingers down her neck and brought his hand to hover over her stomach. A strange, foreign tremor went through his heart, both frightened and elated. "My baby," he whispered. He reached up to take his wife's face in his hands. "My baby mama." He grinned, brilliant light filling his heart at her laughter. He chuckled and brought his lips down to kiss her.

She clutched at the front of his shirt and sighed. "So...you're happy?" She looked up at him imploringly.

He smoothed her hair back and pressed a kiss to her forehead. "I'm ecstatic, sweetheart. You've been worrying for nothing. We'll figure it all out." The words from the final act of Nasarra's play echoed in his mind. Caleb and her at the Amazing Psychotic. *"And everything else?" "We'll figure it out."* He sighed. It was true. Life threw some curve balls, but everything could be sorted out if you had love backing you. "Will you guys stay for the showing of the play?" he asked, glancing up at Javan.

"Of course!" Alyx cried. "It's been killing me to be away from you and I want to see what you've been working so hard on. I know it will be amazing."

Maxim smiled down at her and pressed several little kisses across her face, making her giggle. His cell phone started to blare suddenly and he scowled, grasping around in his pocket until he located it. He flipped it open. "Hello?"

"Maxim!"

He had to pull the phone away from his ear because of the shrill, frantic pitch in her voice. He frowned. "Nasarra?"

"Oh my gosh! I need your help! You need to get to the theatre, *right now!"*

He blinked because she hung up unexpectedly. He stared at the phone. "She can be really demanding when she wants to be." He heaved a sigh. "Apparently, there is some emergency at the theater."

Javan chuckled. "This close to the show? There always is."

"I want to come with you," Alyx said. "I'm sick of being away from you."

"Yeah, I'll come too," Javan volunteered. "Maybe I can help with something."

Maxim nodded. "Sure, but I'm gonna go get in the shower first. I am operating on next to no sleep and I've spent the better part of twenty-four hours in an airport. She can wait a few extra minutes." He kissed Alyx on the forehead again. "I'll be out in a sec." He stood and started up the staircase just as he heard Taegen start to gush about the baby and how she wanted to throw a shower when it got close to the delivery. Maxim grinned as joy surged through him like electricity. He was going to be a father.

"We'll figure it out."

Of course they would. They had love on their side, and after hearing Nasarra's amazing story, he knew that anything was possible and dreams came true in strange ways. He had never had a dream of being a father, the thought had always terrified him, but now it didn't seem quite so horrible. It

made him wonder if, deep down, he'd wanted it the same
way Nasarra had wanted her life with Rafe, Amanda and
Caleb in San Francisco. Some dreams were subtle. Some laid
low, barely detectable, but ended up being the most powerful
ones of all.

Chapter Twenty

Maxim felt like he was in a permanent state of perplexed. "Your three principal actors have mono?"

Nasarra tangled her fingers in her hair and let out an anguished-sounding wail. "What am I going to do?" she cried.

He frowned. "How is that possible? I thought it was the kissing—" His eyes widened as some sort of sense returned to him. "Oh."

"Caleb is coming home in a week! What am I supposed to do? There's no one to replace them!"

"Why don't you play Nasarra?" Maxim suggested. "I mean, it's not like it would be hard."

"I can't! I have to direct and take care of all the stage duties! This thing was thrown together in a short amount of time. It's not staffed properly! I have to make sure things run the way they're supposed to!"

"Wait, hold on a second," Alyx interrupted. "You say the parts need to be learned in a week?"

Nasarra nodded.

Alyx shrugged. "Easy. I'll do it."

Maxim frowned down at his wife. "You're gonna take on the lead role in a *week*?"

"It's what I do," she replied simply. "I once learned an entire part in a night because the person I was understudy for got the stomach flu. This won't be a problem."

"Alyx has a memory like a steel trap," Javan supplied.

Nasarra clasped her hands in front of her. "Thank you so much! Here." She handed Alyx a script. Her eyes scanned over the trio for a moment before they focused on Maxim and lit up in a way he didn't like. "You have to play Caleb!" she shouted, stabbing her finger at him.

Maxim's eyes bulged. "*What?* Are you out of your mind?"

She shook her head and approached him, placing her hands on his shoulders. "Please, Maxim, you're the only one who can do it right."

"What are you talking about? I'm not an actor!" His voice had risen in pitch about two octaves.

"But you wrote the script! You know Caleb's character!"

"Make Javan do it! *He's* an actor!"

"But you *know* the character! You wrote him! Please, Maxim, you have to! This is Caleb's present! If his character is played wrong, it'll be a disaster!"

He shook his head adamantly. "No! This is insane! I don't like being in the spotlight! I am a strictly behind the scenes kind of guy! You can't do this to me! I just found out I'm gonna be a father! How much do you think one man can take in a day?" He drew in a breath that resembled a wheeze. "I think I'm gonna hyperventilate." He put his hand to his chest.

Nasarra was not deterred. "Please, you're the only one I trust to do it right."

He stared at her for an agonizingly long moment, and only snapped back to reality when Alyx reached out to take his hand. He glanced at her.

"You can do it, baby. I know you can." She gave him a warm and encouraging smile.

Seconds ticked by while he felt his resolve slowly slip away. He looked from Alyx back to Nasarra and groaned, tangling his fingers in his hair. "Damn it!" he shouted. "What the *hell*?" Both Alyx and Javan's eyes widened and they exchanged a surprised glance. Maxim never cursed, but right about now, it felt really good. He let his shoulders slump in defeat. "Gimme a freaking script."

Nasarra let out a sigh of relief and obeyed. "Thank you, Maxim. Thank you so much. I owe you for life."

He grumbled nothing intelligible and started to flip through the thing that was quickly becoming the bane of his existence.

"Wait, we need one more emergency actor," Nasarra said. "We have no one to play Danielle."

Everyone looked blankly at one another for a moment before they all simultaneously seemed to focus on Javan.

It took him a second, but that was normal. His eyes widened and he took two steps back. "No way!"

"You have to! There's no one else!" Nasarra wailed.

"Come on, Jave," Alyx said. "You're a professional. Besides, all the men played women in Shakespearean England."

"Does this look like Shakespearean England to you?" he exclaimed.

Maxim grabbed a script and shoved it at Javan with what he knew had to be a petulant look. "You said you wanted to help. Get to work," he snapped.

* * *

In the course of Maxim's life, he had never been more petrified than he was at this moment. Not when his brother had forced him into a life-altering road trip. Not when he'd gotten married. Not when he'd had to do a book tour and be in front of tons of people who wanted his autograph. This left all of those events in the dust.

He peered out the curtain at all the people who had shown up. His stomach protested and his hands started to shake. He immediately moved away and combed his fingers through his hair. "I must be out of my mind," he muttered to himself.

His eyes were bugging him because he had contacts in. Caleb never wore glasses, but Maxim hardly ever wore contacts. It would be his luck one of them would fall out and he'd spend the majority of the play bumping into the set. He didn't have a hip ponytail like Caleb had either, but he supposed that was all right considering Caleb no longer had that ponytail. Still, he was a sad representation.

Caleb's character was supposed to be the hero in the play. Maxim made a sorry leading man. Maybe he was sexy to his wife, but to the mass public he probably looked like a computer nerd, or someone who should be working in a new age coffee shop. He didn't think he was unattractive, per se, but definitely not hero material.

"Maxim, you look like you're gonna ralph," Javan's voice whispered from behind him.

Maxim glanced over his shoulder and suppressed the urge to laugh. Javan was tall and had an athletic build. Sticking him in a black wig and a dress only made him look like an Amazonian drag queen. For a second, Maxim felt like his job wasn't nearly as bad.

Javan's eyes narrowed. "Sure, laugh it up, hot shot," he

grumbled.

"Guys!" Nasarra whispered from the wings. "Get in places! Curtain in five!"

Maxim's stomach did flips again and he groaned as he made his way over to the wings. Alyx was already back there, going over her lines for good measure. She had a red wig on and looked gorgeous, but then again, she always did. Maxim took refuge somewhere in the shadows and hoped it would all be over soon.

Nasarra made an announcement over the loud speaker about how the play was a gift for her husband. This was followed by loud applause and whistling, letting Maxim know that the audience was mostly full of Nasarra's and Caleb's friends.

Before Maxim could even process what was happening, the lights went up, the curtain raised, and Alyx walked out onto the stage to deliver her first lines. His heart started to beat too fast to be healthy and he actually had to sit down and put his head between his knees for fear he was going to pass out. He took several deep breaths and tried to return to some small state of calm.

"You can do this," he whispered. "You have to. Nasarra is counting on you. Alyx is counting on you. Everyone is counting on you." That didn't help. Too much pressure. He shook his head. "Okay, try again." He drew in a long, cleansing breath. "Just suck it up and do it, Maxim. One day you'll have an awesome story to tell your son or daughter about how his or her dad saved the friggin' day." For some reason, that thought made warmth chase out most of the cold dread in his body. It was a momentary fix, but it lasted long enough to give him the courage to him stand and plunge out onto the stage right when he heard his cue.

Thankfully, because he did know the script so well, he had no issues with his lines, and he launched into a sort of business mode where he just needed to get the job done. His fright subsided, but that was greatly due to the fact that he was playing opposite his wife. It was easy to forget all the eyes watching him when he was only staring into hers.

In the moments he spent up on that stage, acting out how Caleb had fallen in love with Nasarra, he felt his own heart slipping. It was as if he was falling in love with Alyx all over again. If he got nothing else out of the experience, everything would have been worth it just to feel that rush.

Everyone was pretty cool about Javan. No one laughed or sniggered. Thank goodness everyone must have had good imaginations because he really did make a hideous woman. But, like the professional he was, he made the part his own and pulled it off exceptionally well. Despite his size and his bulk, and his five o'clock shadow, he made an excellent villainess.

As Maxim and Alyx finished the last scene and the curtain closed, thunderous applause sounded and a relieved breath wheezed out of Maxim as if he'd been holding it all night. He walked off the stage as some of the other actors started to go out in front of the curtain to bow, and he waited his turn.

He glanced over to Alyx, who was grinning and gushing at Javan about how awesome he'd done. Maxim smiled as Javan shook his head and laughed. She came over to him next, wrapping her arm around his waist and pressing a kiss to his cheek. "Baby, you did so wonderful!" she whispered. "I'm so proud of you!"

His heart melted as he gazed into her eyes and he pulled her up against him, lowering his mouth to hers in a slow, drugging kiss. He was dimly aware of the continuous applause and knew that they would need to go out to take their bows soon, but he didn't rush. He took her face in his hands and tilted her head slightly, sliding his tongue over hers in a sensual caress that caused her to grip her fingers in the material of his shirt.

When he finally pulled back, she drew in a shuddering breath and her face flushed as she looked up at him. "Maxim," she gasped, putting her hand over her heart. She shook her head and her surprise morphed into deviousness. She wrapped her arms around his waist and pressed her body close to his. "Is there a janitor's closet somewhere around here?"

He burst out laughing and slipped his arms around her, losing himself in her eyes and preparing to kiss her again, but someone shouted, "Guys! You're up!" and started to shove them toward the stage.

Alyx laughed, grasped his hand and pulled him out into the spotlight once again. The audience cheered, and he bowed. The recognition was exhilarating and he could understand why people like Nasarra and Alyx thrived on it. He basked in it for a moment, then resigned himself to never doing it again.

He stepped back into line with the rest of the cast and waited for Javan to come out. They had all decided that he would take the last bow, considering he had, by far, done the most acting.

He came out in full costume, then yanked his black wig off and flung it into the audience, taking a dramatic bow. The crowd went crazy, all giving a standing ovation and cheering.

Maxim chuckled and joined the cast in the final bow, then glanced over to Caleb in the front row, who had been joined by his wife. Nasarra looked elated as her husband grinned down at her with love in his eyes that was tangible. He bent to whisper something into her ear, then pulled her into his arms and held onto her like she was the most precious thing ever created.

Maxim glanced over at his own wife, feeling strangely electric from the show and the applause and the romance in the air. He reached out and grasped her hand, dragging her out of the spotlight and through the darkened backstage area.

"What are you doing?" she whispered as she stumbled along behind him. "I can't see! I'm gonna break my neck!"

They meandered through the backstage corridors until they came to an unmarked door. Maxim yanked it open and pulled her inside, shutting the heavy door, and stifling most of the sound. It was near pitch black inside and all of the clothing within made the standing space small.

"Where *are* we?" Alyx whispered. "What the heck are you doing?"

Maxim waited for the sliver of light coming in from under the door to help his eyes adjust, then he grinned down at his wife. "It's the costume closet," he stated.

She blinked and glanced around before she seemed to understand his implication and her jaw dropped as she stared up at him. "Maxim deBoer!" she breathed. "What has gotten into you?"

He grinned, because the whole thing was *completely* out of character for him, but he just gave a nonchalant shrug. Right now, he felt pretty much invincible and it was giving him boldness he wouldn't normally have. "Are you object-ing?" he asked, lowering his lips to run teasing nibbles along her neck.

She shivered and groped along his chest. She shook her head and gripped both sides of his black button-down, yanking so that all of the buttons popped off and scattered along the floor.

His eyes widened. "Geez, woman!" he exclaimed, pulling back.

"Shhh!" She laughed softly and ran her palms up his bare chest. "We have to be quiet. And we have to be fast. People will start to wonder where we are."

He cocked an eyebrow and took in every detail of his wife's beautiful face in the dull, shadowy light. His heart filled with magnificent warmth. He shook his head and smirked. "Screw that," he murmured, taking her face in his hands. "Let them wonder." Before she could respond, he lowered his lips to hers, and the world outside fell away.

The whole two months he'd spent with Nasarra, helping her work on her present, had revolved around dreams and what was most important to a person.

Every dream he'd ever had came true each time he looked into his wife's eyes.

Epilogue

It was an unusually warm and sunny day for San Francisco as Nasarra sat in the park and waited for her husband. They were supposed to have lunch together, their hectic lives converging for one small moment in time. A cool ocean breeze tugged on her hair, bringing with it the smell of eucalyptus and salt water. She closed her eyes and let it wash over her, relishing the smell that was so familiar, and yet, still so cherished.

When she opened her eyes again, she spotted Caleb striding toward her. She grinned.

He was carrying two hot dogs and the sun glinted off of his hair, making it look bronzed. Her heart skipped a beat or two. That small reaction to her husband made her fill with warmth. Still, after years of marriage, her heart reacted as if she was looking at him for the first time. He was still that beautiful to her.

He was at her bench in a few long-legged strides and he pressed a kiss to the top of her head before sitting down. "Hey you." He handed her one of the hot dogs.

She giggled. "Now *this* is a gourmet meal."

"It was easy."

She took a bite, then sighed and rested her head against his shoulder. "How's work?" she asked casually.

He snorted. "Please, you know how slammed that place gets at lunch hour. I'm lucky I escaped with my life."

She smirked.

"You?"

"Pretty good. The new batch of kids in the children's theatre class are adorable. I was talking to Rafe and I think he's going to teach a tap class this summer again. The kids seemed to really enjoy that. I think he did too."

Caleb slipped his arm around her shoulders and nodded. He fell into silence for a second, causing Nasarra to glance up at him. He was frowning as if deep in thought.

She raised an eyebrow. "What's wrong?"

He looked down at her and a brilliant grin lit up his face. "Nothing's wrong. I was just thinking..." His smile remained even as he let the sentence die.

She frowned. "Thinking about?"

"Well..." He shrugged. "Do you ever get tired of teaching theatre classes and only being in local productions?"

"No!" she said almost defensively. She sat up straight so she could look at him full on. "Why, do you?"

"Well, no. It's just...Nathan talked to me yesterday and he's going to be producing a new play soon. He asked me to ask you if you'd be interested in trying out."

For half a second, she actually pondered it, and her entire Broadway experience flashed through her mind at full speed. It would be different with Caleb. It wouldn't be as empty and painful. But then she saw all of the happy faces of her students, and remembered how much joy she got out of seeing them strut their stuff up on stage. Little Calebs...every single one of them. She wouldn't give that up for anything.

She met her husband's eyes and shook her head. "Nah."

He looked a little surprised. "Really?"

She rolled her eyes. "Caleb, are you happy here? Do you have any regrets in your life I don't know about?"

"No, of course not! I love my life here with you! I love the restaurant and I love teaching."

"Then why are you trying to get me to move across the country again? Didn't I spend a lot of hard work not too long ago putting together a play to show you how happy I am? To show you how I have no regrets either?"

He chuckled and hugged her tighter. "Yes, baby, and it was brilliant. I was just trying to be considerate."

She smirked and took another bite of her hot dog. "Well, thank you, but it's unnecessary. I have no desire to change anything about my life."

"Nothing?"

It sounded like a loaded question so she gave him a measured stare. "Is there something else you wanted to tell me?"

His green eyes sparkled with mirth. "Well, as you may recall, Nathan likes to have the cream of the crop to pick from at the auditions. He wants to host the theatre camp again."

She stared at him for a second. "It's like history repeating itself."

"Yeah, except for the fact that he wants *both* of us to teach classes at it."

"Me too?" She couldn't mask her surprise. Even though she had tons of experience under her belt, she still felt inadequate next to a genius like Nathan Price. And she still didn't see herself anywhere near as talented as Caleb. She guessed she never would, no matter what anybody told her. He was untouchable to her.

"Yes, you too." He chuckled softly. "Wanna do it?"

"Sure!" She shook her head as her mind replayed the theatre camp that had been the beginning of so many of her dreams. "But if Danielle is there again, I'm gonna shoot myself."

He burst out laughing. They were quiet as they finished their lunch, then they both headed back into the city, hand in hand. As Nasarra walked, she thought about the paths she had taken to bring her to this moment. Life was strangely cyclical, but that wasn't necessarily a bad thing. Not in this case, anyway.

They wandered past a bookstore and she glanced in the display window, only to screech to a halt.

"What are you looking at?" Caleb asked.

Her mouth dropped open as she stared at the cover of one of the books. *Broadway Dreams* by Maxim deBoer. "He told me he would call me when it released! I can't believe he forgot!" She yanked the door open and marched inside.

"Well, they did just have a baby," Caleb said, following after her. "I think the guy might have license to be a little distracted."

"I suppose I can let him off the hook just this once," she muttered.

Caleb smiled and waited while she paid for the book. Once she had it, she flipped through it with elation. Their story. Hers and Caleb's. Maxim had turned their love story into a beautiful work of art. She hugged the book to her chest and looked up at her husband.

Several different things seemed to flash through his eyes while he gazed at her, and he finally resulted in a decisive-sounding sigh. "Come on," he said, reaching down to take her hand. "You and me, we're going to ditch out on the rest of work today."

She blinked. "We are?" she asked as he led her out of the store.

"Yup. We're going to let everyone else deal with the monotony of everyday life, jump on my motorcycle like we used to and ride to Half Moon Bay. When we get there, we're going to have dinner, watch the sunset, and read that book. I don't know about you, but I never get tired of falling in love with you. I want to do it all over again."

She giggled, catching some of his carefree euphoria. "But I thought that was what the play was for."

He turned to face her. "I fell in love with you twice that night," he said. "Once because I was watching our story replayed on stage, and twice because you were so thoughtful in creating such an extraordinary present. But that was six months ago. I am in dire need of a fix." He pulled her up close to his body and rested his forehead against hers.

She wrapped her arms around his neck.

"Let's go make all the rest of our dreams come true," he whispered.

She reached up to tangle her fingers in his hair and nodded. "You always have been, and always will be, my ultimate happy ending," she murmured, quoting the last words of Maxim's script.

His smile could have illuminated the darkness, and as she followed after him through her beloved city, she knew no dream would ever be as sweet as the one that came true every single morning when she woke up next to the man she loved, and could live another day with him by her side.

About the Author

    If someone were to ask me what I am, it could be summed up in one, simple word: Dreamer. Ever since I was a small child my imagination has run wild. I have been telling stories for as long as I can remember, creating grand worlds in my head and going on adventures that were invisible to others around me. Am I eccentric? Yes. Am I proud of that? Absolutely.

    I write about the things that inspire me, both in this world and in realms only seen with the imagination. My heroines are sassy and strong. My heroes are sometimes shy. I have an obsession with music (and musicians) and a fascination with wings. I believe true love does exist, and sometimes it is found in the strangest, most unexpected places. I also believe that family and close friends are the glue that hold people together.

Above all things, I believe in being true to yourself and seizing the day. Life is an amazing gift. Make your experience as beautiful as you possibly can.